I0689789

Trash Panda

Shift Work #3
Alex Silver

Copyright © 2024 by Alex Silver

Cover designed by Alex Silver

ISBN: 978-1-998885-12-1

Contents

Blurb

Seb

For all that I've told my best friend, Rollie, that his past doesn't define him, it's hard to believe it about myself.

I'd give Rollie anything he needs. After all, he gave me a place to live when I needed space from my family. It doesn't seem like a big deal to share my prescription with him too. We share practically everything else these days, so why not help him out? Not like anyone else is willing to help shifters like us.

Except my condition is getting worse and I can't seem to hide it anymore. That's not the only thing I can't hide; somewhere along the line, I fell for Rollie, but how could he feel the same about me when I feel like garbage?

Trash Panda is an M/M omegaverse romance between a raven shifter omega and a raccoon shifter omega. It includes hurt/comfort, infertility, adoption, found family, mental health struggles, past trauma, and all the shiny things. A more complete CW list is on the next page.

Content Warnings

THIS BOOK IS HIGHER angst and deals with several heavy mental health issues. If any of the following could be harmful for you to read about, exercise caution and feel free to reach out to me on social media or at asilverauthor@gmail.com for further information. Trigger warnings: suicidal ideation, past suicide attempts, self harm (including through risky/self-destructive sex acts), alcohol abuse, domestic violence, infertility, past medical trauma, abusive family, past coercive medical care, self-medicating and rationing needed medication.

Prologue
Rollie (Several Years Earlier)

IT'S NOT EVERY DAY that I get royally plastered and puke on a stranger's shoes, but man, can I pick 'em. The shoes in question are gorgeous. Pointy-toed leather boots polished to a glossy shine. They've got enough pizzazz that they were probably a pain in the ass to find in a large enough size to fit the gorgeous shifter standing before me. Probably expensive. I groan as I swipe the back of my hand over my mouth.

I track my eyes up the long lanky body in front of me, take in the skintight faded jeans. The toned muscles under an aquamarine mesh shirt with silvery threads of metallic glitter that make him look almost magical. I can see his dusky nipples through the barely there fabric. I have to tear my eyes away from the shiny silver hoops threaded through those pretty nubs up to his face.

An aquiline nose set over full, kissable lips, his glossy dark hair frames his face. Dark, dancing eyes meet mine with amusement when I finally stop ogling him long enough to notice I've captured his attention. The sardonic grin he flashes me is a relief; the beautiful stranger isn't pissed off about the shoes I ruined.

"Sorry," I slur, weaving in place. "Send me the dry cleaning bill?"

The stranger laughs. "You can't dry clean knock-off Manolos, hun. They'll wash just fine. Are you here with anyone?"

"Nope. Just me. Alone. Lonely." I clap my hands over my mouth. I did not mean for that last word to slip out. Fuck, what am I even doing?

He snorts with laughter and gently puts an arm around my shoulders, guiding me away from the puddle of puke on the sidewalk outside the bar I just left. "Okay, Lonely, let's get you cleaned up, shall we? Do you have a name?"

"Thomas." My nose wrinkles at the bitter taste of my legal name. "But my friends call me Rollie."

"Ah, and do you often make friends by puking on them, Rollie? If so, I may have discovered the root of that loneliness problem for you. I'm Seb, by the way. Short for Sebastian, but only my moms call me that."

I turn my face into his chest to try to hide my embarrassment, baffled that he's being so nice to me. He smells good, so I nose in closer, chasing that whiff of vanilla and a hint of sweet lime. "Sorry, I'm wasted." I mumble into the rough mesh of his shirt.

"I couldn't tell." Seb gives a dry little chuckle as he nudges my face away from his armpit. "Lucky for you, I'm an avian shifter, so puking is sort of a way to show your love. If we squint real hard and pretend you've also got feathers."

"Sorry," I repeat, unsure whether he's mocking me.

"Don't be. I've been there. Let's get you cleaned up and into a ride home."

"I'd ride you home," I blurt.

Seb laughs. "Not when you're this drunk, Rollie. Ask me again when you're sober." He winks at me. And then he guides me back inside the dimly lit, too-loud bar. He nods to the bouncer, who must know him because the burly shifter just nods back. Seb leads me past the dancing crowd to the washroom.

The single stall is hosting multiple occupants and I'm pretty sure they're fucking. Seb pulls me to the sink and wets a paper towel to swab my face. Then he bends to take care of his boots. I feel like a total perv as I lean heavily on the wall and ogle his ass in those skintight, bedazzled jeans.

"Ask me when you're sober, Rollie," Seb repeats, with a wink when he glances over his shoulder and catches me looking.

"I'm not an alpha," I clarify, since from the whiff of scent I got from him, I'm all but certain he's an omega.

"So?" Seb arches an elegant eyebrow at me.

"You're an omega, right?" I swallow hard. Bile rises in my throat at the reminder of the roles that were drilled into my head growing up. Gorgeous omegas don't settle for betas.

A dark look flits over Seb's expressive face and I'm worried I said the wrong thing again. Or misgendered him. Trans secondary gender shifters who embrace an identity outside the one they're born with are a concept I've learned about since leaving home. I've known about static humans having transgender people, since I'm a trans primary gender shifter. Secondary gender is different.

I grew up in a raccoon shifter community—called a gaze like a group of static raccoons. My gaze made it seem like secondary gender was an immutable biological reality. To my family, primary gender is about cosmetics and blending into static human society, but secondary gender is what determines a shifter's role within the gaze and the home.

Only, in Four Corners, I've met some shifters who aren't the secondary gender they smell like. Not all shifters are traditional about what that means when it comes to sex and relationships either. Even some of the cisgender shifters in the mixed species community have vastly different roles associated with their secondary gender. Bear omegas are the heads of their households; the opposite of how my gaze taught me things should be. It's been a huge culture shock, and I've felt so disconnected and out of place, but hopeful that I could fit. More hopeful than I ever felt at home with a gaze that had no use for a beta shifter. Except I might've just fucked up by making this gorgeous shifter think I'm as set in my ways as the gaze I left behind. Ugh.

"I am," Seb says, tone unreadable. Or maybe I'm just too drunk and spiraling into guilty regret to parse the complicated emotions in that simple statement. "I'm pansexual though, so I fuck pretty much anyone who catches my fancy. Alphas, omegas, betas, and even statics." He winks at me.

"Oh." That's a bold declaration to make to a stranger. Or are we friends now? He's calling me Rollie and wiping up my sick, so maybe we're friends? The heavy weight in my gut at knowing I'm not anything he could possibly want dissolves into fizzy bubbles of hope that maybe I could fit in here, be among shifters who see me as more than my anatomical lacks. Seb just told me something personal. But then again, I asked him something personal. "Sorry."

"That I'm pan?" Seb raises that elegant eyebrow again in question. I suppress the drunken urge to rub my fingers along it. That would be weird.

"Gods, no! Sorry if I made you uncomfortable. I just meant you smell really nice."

"When you're sober, Rollie," Seb repeats in a lilting sing-song that makes me really wish I was sober.

Right, I'm still coming across as flirty. Seb's smile is so pretty. I could stare at him for ages. Seb shakes his head like my older sister does when I say something socially inept, and she's despairing of what to do with me; like he thinks I'm cute and funny, if a little awkward.

Seb loops an arm around my shoulders to steer me outside again. "Time to get you home."

He pours me into a cab, then settles into the back seat next to me. I give my address and Seb grins as he rattles off his own, not too far from mine in Four Corners. I'm thrilled with the company for the long drive out to the shifter community where I live now.

"Fellow shifter, huh?" he asks as our driver pulls into traffic. That's an easy guess; almost everyone who lives in the cozy little community of Four Corners is a shifter. Not to mention most of the patrons at the bar we just left smelled like shifters. Still, it's odd that he didn't realize sooner.

"You can't smell it on me?" I ask, taken aback since even three sheets to the wind I recognize a fellow shifter by scent. Even without his declaration earlier, I'd have guessed he's an avian shifter. They have a feathery scent that's hard to describe.

"Took scent blockers earlier. Wasn't really looking for a pushy alpha's attention tonight. Forgot to bring a second dose, hence calling it an early night."

Oh. Well, they must be wearing off, since I smelled him just fine. Only with my nose pressed practically into his scent glands though. That explains why—try as I might—I can't seem to catch another hint of his enticing scent. We chat about Four Corners and what brought me to the area. Being from away always invites questions.

I want to use the ride to chat Seb up, but the lulling vibrations of the car have me nodding off. I wake up when we pull off the highway at Four Corners. It takes me a few groggy breaths to remember Seb taking me under his wing, even though my face is pillowed on his shoulder. His scent is stronger now, and even more enticing in the enclosed space of the backseat. The mesh from his shirt pressing into my cheek is uncomfortable, so I sit up and glance over at him. Seb smiles at me. He doesn't seem to mind that I used him as a pillow for most of the drive.

"Sorry, didn't mean to drool on you," I say sheepishly.

"It's fine." Seb's lips quirk into a playful grin. "Seems like you need a keeper, Rollie. If you're going to get so wasted that you can't get yourself home, at least bring a friend next time, yeah? Safety first." He winks at me.

"Yeah. I know. I'm still new to the area, is all." I stare at my hands, embarrassed to admit that I don't have any friends here.

"That your way of saying you need a friend? Next time you want to tie one on, give me a call, okay?" Seb nudges a slip of paper with his number scrawled on it into my hand. "Text me so I have yours too."

"Oh. Sure." My skin flushes with warmth and my heart races with pure elation. He's giving me his number. I somehow got the sexiest omega I've ever met's phone number. I obediently type his digits into my phone and text him a dorky message. "Thanks."

His phone pings with a notification and Seb makes a show of checking it. He snorts when he reads what I wrote.

Rollie: Hi. It's Rollie. Sorry about your shoes.

Seb: Stop apologizing.

He sticks his tongue out at me when I check the reply, and we exchange grins. It's so ridiculous, sitting next to each other and texting, but this feels so utterly nice and normal. It's one of those little things that I watched my siblings do with their friends back in high school, and envied with a hollow ache of knowing it wasn't ever going to be for me. I didn't have a place with the other raccoon shifters we grew up among, and the static kids we attended school with weren't ever allowed around enough outside of school to get really close to them.

It's ridiculous to feel like he's someone I could text silly inside jokes to from across a room someday. We only met tonight, and I spent the bulk of our time together snoring on his shoulder. But hope and longing are a heady thing and he's so bright, the most sparkling treasure I could imagine. I want to cling to any scrap of his attention he'll allow me.

When our ride stops at my place, Seb makes sure I get inside and waves from the backseat as I blush furiously and wonder if I'll see the flirtatious omega again soon or if I blew my chance with him with the terrible first impression I just made. As the taxi pulls away with him in it, my phone buzzes in my pocket.

I pull it out and beam at the message.

Seb: Drink some water, Rollie, and don't forget me once you've sobered up ;)

Chapter 1

Rollie

"You don't have to go." I reach for Seb's hand as he brushes past me toward my dresser, currently covered in his various cosmetics. My best friend is a vain creature, but over the years I've come to suspect that's an avian thing. My theory is that since their animal forms spend so much time tending to their pretty plumage that they don't even realize they carry over that drive to primp and preen into their human forms.

Normally, I enjoy watching him apply his makeup and get dressed for a night out. Today, I know he's going to make choices that hurt him, and I'm helpless to stop it.

"Pft." Seb snorts derisively. "Sure, Rollie, let me just skip my clutchmate's baby shower and see how well that goes down with my entire baby-crazed family."

I roll my eyes. "It's not even his first clutch. The twins aren't even two yet, so it's not like they need more baby stuff."

"Clutchmates aren't the same as twins. And that is *so* not the point of a raven shifter baby shower, Rollie. I don't know if you've been, like, covering your eyes and ears when you visit the rave, but we like babies. I swear all my cousins are having clutches now too." Seb tries to keep his tone light, but the bitter ache of knowing he won't be joining them in welcoming a clutch of his own is clear to me.

"I thought you said only Bram calls it that?" I tease, trying to get him to crack a smile as he aggressively blends foundation to hide the bags under his eyes from lack of sleep.

"Yeah, well, he's right; rave sounds better than the other options." Seb sticks his tongue out at me, then pouts his pretty lips to apply a shimmery coat of gloss.

I get distracted for a second, thinking about what they'd feel like pressed against mine. I've never actually fucked Seb, but we've shared the occasional alpha and he sure can kiss.

"You know I can't skip the shower. Bram will feel bad and then he'll fuss and I don't want to take away from his happiness." Seb dips the applicator back into the gloss tube for a second coat.

"Yeah, I get that, but he has to realize it's hard for you," I say, only referencing his infertility obliquely because I know how much it hurts him. From the force with which he stabs the application wand back into the gloss and twists it closed as though he'd rather be wringing my neck, I wasn't subtle enough. He tosses the tube back among the other bright jewel-toned makeups in his collection.

"That's exactly why I *have* to go, Rollie. He knows, and he worries. I won't have him feeling bad about me when he should be excited about this new baby."

"Okay, but like, isn't it a bit soon for more babies?"

"Not really? Leighton will be two next month, and Kyrie's hatchday is a month after that."

"And wasn't Myra's birthday last month? Are they going for a birthday kid for every month of the year?" My attempt at a joke falls flat. The due dates line up though if I'm mathing right.

"That's so not a thing." Seb jabs a long, brightly lac- quered nail toward me. "Don't let Bram hear you suggest it—just to be safe. I love my niblings, but twelve is a whole heck of a lot of diapers." Seb gazes up at the ceiling as he applies mascara. "I'm going—end of discussion. You don't have to come with me if it's such an issue."

"No, I want to go with you." I sigh, shoulders slumping in defeat. Looks like we're going to the party. "I just don't want to see you hurting, Seb."

Seb shakes his head at me. "It's fine. I haven't seen the babies since Myra's birthday party. I'm overdue for a visit. Now that Cory's pretty much settled on masc pronouns, I've got actual competition for favorite uncle status. I mean, assuming Elric ever makes their pronouns official so that Cory can announce to the flock without upstaging them."

It takes me a second to connect Seb's grumbling with the raven shifter coming-of-age tradition of having an official gender reveal when kids settle on their adult names and pronouns. They call it a fledging party because it means the young shifters are growing up and getting ready to leave the nest soon. The official part of the proceedings is fairly simple, but the significance of being accepted with a more adult role within their flock makes a clear difference to the raven kids.

Most avian shifter babies gestate in their bird form and don't have obvious physical gender differences when they hatch. Their digestive tracts aren't developed enough to shift between avian and mammalian forms until they're several months old, so their custom is to use neutral pronouns until a kid picks their own. It seems strange to me, but I also kind of love it.

"Yeah, do you think Elric is any closer to having their fledging ceremony?" I ask, since it's a foregone conclusion that they will have one, and that seems safer than getting into it with him about his mental health again. At least I know his family cares about him as deeply as I do, even if they're at just as much of a loss as to how to help him with his self-destructive tendencies.

Seb shrugs expansively. "I think our moms are going to have a chat with Elric about it, cause Cory won't do his ceremony until Elric has their moment. Cory is still young for it, but he seems to be set on his adult name and pronouns. He's been antsy to make it official. Sometimes fledglings are in a rush for their first flight, and sometimes they need a little nudge to jump into the unknown."

I've always envied how easily Seb's two moms accept all their kids and treat Bram's mate—a big, bearded, genderqueer bear shifter alpha named Ty—with equal respect and kindness, no matter their current gender presentation. The entire family accepted Ty's daughter, Myra, as their own, just as much as her younger half-siblings.

It's the polar opposite of how out of place I've felt in my family home since puberty's failure to arrive revealed my status as an intersex beta. My genetics meant I was never going to fit into the gender binary constructs of shifters or static humans.

"Cool. Guess we'll have another party to look forward to soon then," I smile at him, safe in the assumption that he'll fold me into his family like he has for years.

Seb grins at me as he pulls more sparkly bangles out of his drawers. He selects several to slide onto his wrists, adding them to the two I gave him over the winter holidays. He saves one particularly gaudy bracelet to offer to me. I take it, because trinkets are his love language. And maybe mine too. I love that he always wears at least one of the things I've gotten him along with gifts from his clutchmates and other family members, literally wearing our love on his arms.

"Mhm, make an extra batch of your iced tea for that? Lydia has been asking for your recipe," Seb says. She's one of his cousins who always makes sure our glasses are full of the spiced liquor that's ubiquitous at these flock gatherings once the hatchlings are sent off to their beds.

"Of course. It's nothing fancy. Tell her it's lots of fresh brewed tea and even more sugar."

Seb shakes his head at me, looking amused. "Nope, you can't just share the recipe, Rollie, that's part of the fun. Besides, you're what makes it special; my cousins ask for your tea because they want to be sure you're there with me."

Oh. That's nice. The tacit reminder that I'm wanted and I belong here. His family has taken me in, and sure they tease us about when we're going to admit we're practically mated, but that's all in good fun. The point is that they've always welcomed me, from the first time Seb introduced me as his friend.

Sometimes I wonder if my parents would have understood me better if they had similar customs to the raven shifters who have made Four Corners into the home I needed and dreamed of finding. My folks were disappointed when I turned out to be a beta. That wasn't something they ever put into words. I just knew from the ways it changed how they treated me compared to my siblings.

They only spoke about my medical issues and my indeterminate secondary gender in hushed whispers that I wasn't meant to overhear, but I knew. They weren't quite sure what to do with a kid who wasn't alpha or omega. With our gaze, alphas are supposed to be big strong protectors and omegas are supposed to be sweet loving nurturers. And then there's me, not really fitting either of those boxes and desperate for approval.

There's not really a set stereotype for a beta shifter like me—beta is basically the default catchall term for any shifter who doesn't fit neatly into the alpha or omega labels. So everyone around me assumed I couldn't have a place among other shifters once I was grown. I saw my parents bursting with pride over Blake. My older alpha sister's achievements were always celebrated. They doted on Alan, my younger omega brother. So I tried to be like them, and I failed where my siblings succeeded.

My parents meant well. They did what they could for each of us. My siblings got support in pursuing their dreams, and I got shuttled between doctor appointments that were meant to fix me. It took moving away and years of Seb helping me to unpack all of their subtle digs to realize that I was never broken in the first place.

They made sure Blake had everything she needed to pursue her passions. She earned a basketball scholarship to a small private shifter college and then went on to law school. What a wonderful provider she'll be when she meets the right omega. And no question that when Blake settles down, it will be with an omega. Preferably a raccoon like us, but another small mammal shifter would also be acceptable to the gaze.

They helped Alan and his mate buy a house when he gave them their first grandchild. They weren't thrilled that he chose a lynx alpha for a mate—a predator, really, Alan?

But they changed their tune when he put his tiny bundle of half-lynx cub joy into their arms.

I got the cold hard reality that I wasn't the child they wanted me to be, and I never could be. I didn't have a place in our raccoon shifter gaze, but I do in Four Corners.

"You ready?" Seb asks me, interrupting my ruminations. No, I'll never be ready to watch him hurting over the dreams he'll never hold in his arms.

"Yes." I nod.

"Cool. Let's roll." He tosses me the keys to my car. We share it most of the time, but he rarely drives since the incident we don't talk about.

The worst night of my life. We were so damn lucky that the worst that happened to him was a brief stint in the hospital, a misdemeanor on his record, losing his license for a month, and paying a fine. I close my eyes and count to ten. It's less painful to think about my family than the night I almost lost Seb, so I let my mind wander to my parents as we drive toward Bram and Ty's place across town. I love that Seb's moms and siblings have folded me into their little flock, but it's hard not to compare his loving family to mine.

The entire raven flock is a stark contrast to my gaze back home, who never made me feel as included and loved as Seb's family does. Even back when I was still presenting as a beta, the flock welcomed me into their home, despite my lack of a clear-cut secondary gender. It's still hard to believe my luck in finding them sometimes.

The ostracization back home was less obvious when I was a little kid, but it was always just under the surface. In retrospect, there were signs even before I had an inkling of what was to come. The uneasy glances between my parents when other members of our gaze made the usual inane comments tying my interests to my probable future secondary gender. How they never teased me about a future mate the way they sometimes did when my siblings had playdates. How there were less than six months between my birth and Alan's and distant relatives we only saw at holidays always commented on what a blessing Alan is since my folks had planned on having two kits.

The little things that didn't really register as a child, but hit like a sack of bricks once I learned the truth they'd been hiding for my entire life. Lies on top of lies that made it so hard to believe Seb's family really could just all love each other the way they do, and wrap me up in that love along with their son. Even when I came out to them as a trans omega, their care never faltered.

My folks still don't know I'm an omega. I don't visit and only call on holidays. They handled my transition from daughter to son better than my beta status. Raising a son was something they had a script for—a pattern to follow. When you can shift your entire body, some cosmetic changes don't seem so huge. Especially since being both intersex and a beta already meant I wouldn't be giving them any grandkids.

"Oh yeah!" Seb interrupts my thoughts as I pull into the cul-de-sac his brother lives on. "I almost forgot! I got our omegestrol refilled."

We both take omega hormones. Mine are because I'm a trans omega so they help me to present as an omega to other shifters. His are to treat creep. The condition affects shifters across species. It's a hormonal disorder that makes them infertile. For avians, it also causes them to present with alpha traits unless they're on lifelong omega hormones.

"Any luck with getting it changed back to the generic we were getting before?" I ask, hopeful. The brand we switched to a few months ago hasn't been working as well for Seb. His scent keeps slipping more toward the musky notes of an alpha. Like it gets lately when we run out of meds or need to ration doses between refills from the shortages.

Seb gets so dysphoric about the things creep stole from him that I've been worried about him not getting the correct dose. Even switching brands hasn't entirely gotten him back to usual. Beyond losing his heat cycle, most of the changes are subtle. His pretty hair is thicker and glossier and seems to grow a bit faster. His jawline is less refined while his aquiline nose seems even more prominent.

Seb's scent changes when his hormones aren't in the correct range. That's the most obvious warning that he's not doing well. His shoulders and arms bulking up from his usual flights around town are the second most noticeable change. That and the sexual effects. We've been going through more bottles of lube since he buys a ton to compensate for producing less slick and having a higher libido.

That last might be his depression worsening more than the creep advancing. I don't have firsthand knowledge, but some omegas with unmedicated creep even develop an alpha's knot. That's rare though, and it usually means the shifter in question can get an omega pregnant.

Seb's creep might not be quite that out of control, but the new formulation we're on doesn't seem to agree with either of us. It gave me a bunch of digestive issues and headaches. The worst of the weird cramping and headaches I got around New Years when we first made the change have settled down now that I've been on the new meds a while, but I've noticed that I still get the headaches on occasion.

The cramps were weird. Kind of like the very brief menstrual cycle the doctors of my youth were able to stimulate for a few months with intensive estrogen therapy to jumpstart the puberty that was never going to happen on its own. That was before I asked for testosterone instead.

It's a weird dichotomy that my inner omega is euphoric at the symptoms that mimicked a heat even while I have visceral memories of how much I'd hated the super femme branding around my short-lived use of Blake's stash of menstrual products.

Seb shakes his head and my heart sinks. "Sorry. I asked, but it looks like no dice on switching back to the other brand. The manufacturer still has it on back-order, I guess? I asked them to call if they get our usual brand back in stock, and they said they would. They also suggested talking to our prescriber about blood tests to assess if we need a dose adjustment, so that's not super helpful since your doc won't even prescribe shifter HRT in the first place and I don't really want to pay out of pocket for extra labs. But it's better than nothing for now, right?"

"Right." I swallow down my disappointment and the urge to nag him about his health.

"I wish I could do more to help, Rollic." Seb pats my thigh. "I'd like to shake sense into your doctor about this, or at least make him refer you to a shifter specialist."

My doctor here is a static endocrinologist, like the one I saw as a kid. He won't prescribe me omega HRT since he doesn't feel comfortable handling any potential interaction between shifter medication and the testosterone I've been on since my teens. So I can't exactly ask him for bloodwork to monitor the medication that Seb gets for me through some sort of arrangement I carefully don't ask too many questions about.

The static human endocrinologists my parents took me to see warned us that testosterone meant for static humans hasn't been studied well in shifters. It might cause unpredictable and irreversible changes in an alpha or omega shifter. My parents were willing to accept those risks since shifter specialists were too few and far between for them to take me to another state for an appointment with yet another specialist who they didn't think would change anything.

"It's fine. I'm just worried that he'll drop me as a patient and there is other routine monitoring I need him to access for me related to my weird genes. Helping me get the meds is more than enough."

It's more than anyone else has ever done for me. With the possible exception of my boss. Harvey took a chance on me when I first moved here and now I've worked my way up to the head manager position at the local grocery store that he owns. He even covered the costs for me to get an associate degree so I can take a more active role in the business and maybe even take over running the entire store some day. It's nice to have people who believe in me.

"You deserve more than you ask for, Rollie," Seb says, exasperated.

It's not the first time he's called me out on that. I rarely ask for anything, and generally only from him or Harvey. It's just so much easier not to risk finding out that help still isn't coming, no matter how much I need it. My parents' toxic beliefs that betas like me are an aberration have always been an unspoken understanding hovering like background radiation over my life and coloring every interaction.

It's why I had to leave when I graduated high school. I came to Four Corners and met Sebatian. Even then, I'd been steeping in that morass for so long that I didn't even realize how many of my gaze's attitudes I'd internalized until I saw other ways of living. My move to this tiny map dot town in Maine is the best choice I ever made.

"Maybe. Good thing I've got you looking out for me, huh?" I stick my tongue out at him. Seb rolls his eyes at me. He rolls his shoulders, a subconscious move that reminds me of his bird form resettling his feathers. He's the best choice I ever made. Whatever capacity I can have him in my life is everything to me.

I'm so glad I didn't listen when my family told me I was making a mistake moving here. When I told them I was moving to a shifter community after high school, Mom got a pinched look, like she was constipated. Dad asked if I was so sure that was a good idea. My sister asked me why in this shocked tone, as if I'd told her I was taking to my fur and living among the local static raccoons fulltime, or something equally outlandish.

My brother took all the attention off my plans when he ran off to go puke because he was already carrying his first kit and it was a rough pregnancy. We were in the same class at school and by all accounts we should have been close, but we weren't. Once I learned the truth about my health history, the suspiciously close timing of our birthdays felt too much like he was our parents' redo since I was defective.

"Always. You and me, Rollie. Omega solidarity," He winks at me, softening the fervent intensity of his tone that makes his words feel like he's making promises to a mate. Except I'm pretty sure Seb has sworn off mates, or anything serious with anyone he fucks regularly. What we have is more than I ever thought I'd have growing up. A partner in every sense.

"Solidarity," I echo, taking one hand off the steering wheel to offer a fist bump without taking my eyes off the road since there are a bunch of kids in the neighborhood.

Seb helps me to understand myself. He takes care of me and lets me take care of him and we just fit together so seamlessly. My family made that seem like an impossible dream for me. They made it so hard to sift through the complexity of my identity as an omega. Sometimes I still feel like maybe I really am just ashamed of being born a beta. Maybe I just *want* to be an omega instead of actually being one. How can I know? I've gone in so many circles about that issue in the therapy my parents insisted on sending me to—to accept the facts as they saw them—that it's kind of become absurd.

The therapy was okay, but it was a static therapist who just didn't understand how integral a part of me it is to be a shifter and express my secondary gender identity as well as the primary one I claimed for myself. It was all such a giant messy tangle in my head until I spilled my guts to Seb.

He looked at me with such utter sincerity there was no room for doubt as he asked me, "Why does that distinction matter so much to you? If being an omega makes you happy, who cares why you feel that way?"

He was right. It doesn't matter if some unquantifiable part of me is biologically omega, whatever that might entail. Whether I've got faulty hormone receptors or low hormone production. Whether I should have been born with functional gametes instead of the infertile static human parts I got. And even those were wrong until I went on hormones.

Like my parents, I had an easier time accepting that part of myself. It's just that primary gender isn't as central to who I am. It didn't matter to my family. It's more about how I chose to present to the static world, where being a shifter sets me apart more than being trans ever could. So, it was comparatively easy to change that versus something that my family has been telling me for years is fundamentally broken about me. Like maybe I just want to be an omega so I won't feel broken instead of out of any innate sense of myself. Except I do feel innately omega in a way I can't entirely put into words.

He sighs. "I still wish I could do more. You're my best friend, Rollie."

"That goes both ways. You're my BFF forever, Seb. Say the word and we can bounce early," I offer him an out that I know he won't take.

I have to park down the street from Bram and Ty's cute little house since several cars I recognize from the rave are already here lining the quiet street. I smile at him, wishing I could support him more through the next few difficult hours of celebrating something he desperately wants for himself. Facing the dreams that creep stole from him along with his fertility.

"I'll be fine. I truly am happy for Bram and excited to meet the new nibling in a few months."

"I know. You can be delighted for him and hurting for you at the same time."

"Yeah." Seb acknowledges, shrugging his shoulders again, like he can let the hurt roll off his back like water from his feathers.

Seb has been my guiding light for so long. The one who makes me feel seen and heard. Who makes it so I can breathe when the world seems too vast and the weight of my place in it seems too heavy to bear. I want to do that for him in turn. I can't tell him that I adore him with every fiber of my being in so many words, but I do my best to show him. He reaches to open his door, the bangles on his wrist clinking together. I devour the sight of him wearing my bracelets, because he knows how I feel on some level, and he sees me as family.

Seb cuts through all the bullshit in my brain. None of the tangled vestiges of my internalized issues with my past matter when he lays the facts bare. What matters is that when I smell like an omega, I can breathe easier. When other shifters assume that's who I am, that I belong with the other omegas and I can relate to their heat cramp woes and they treat me as one of them, I just have this giddy sensation in the depths of my soul.

Like for the first time, I belong and they can see me for who I am. And who cares why that is, so long as it brings me joy? Who does it hurt?

The first time Seb handed me a dose of omega hormones, I cried. And since being on them, I've never felt more like myself. More happy and fulfilled and just...real. I owe all of that to Seb. I'd do anything to make him as happy as he makes me.

If I could battle creep with my bare hands and give him back the life that his diagnosis stole from him, I would. I rub the bracelet charm he handed me before we left the house, taking strength from it. We can't fix the world for each other, no matter how much we might want to. For now, the best I can do is to paste on a smile and take his hand as we walk into his brother's baby shower. Ty greets us at the door, and I watch my best friend in the world paste on a sappy false smile to hide his pain while he watches Bram get everything I know he'll never admit he wants with all his heart.

Chapter 2

Seb

I TAKE A HIT off the popper and wiggle my ass at the alpha who is currently fumbling with a condom. The dose helps me relax my body enough to take the double penetration promised by hooking up with a gator shifter. It also lets me eke out a bit more slick from glands that haven't worked quite right since my creep diagnosis. What is the hold up with the condom?

Oh. Gary is struggling with the sticky latex. The issue seems to be stuffing both dicks into the same condom, probably because his drunken coordination isn't up to the fine motor task. I watch as he tries to line the latex up around both tips and one slips off to the side yet again.

Fuck me. I shouldn't do this. Brush off his ineptitude and inebriation.

I shouldn't reach for the sticky latex and toss it aside. Kiss away his half-drunk protest as I straddle him and sink down on both of his thick, bare hemipenes. He invited me home to fuck before the last round of shots at the bar, grinning as he pounded them back and told me the whiskey helps him to last longer. Shifters metabolize booze a little faster than static humans, especially bigger species like gators. He knew what he agreed to.

So I only have the slightest twinge of doubt as I lower myself onto him, taking both his cocks to the root. It doesn't matter that we aren't using protection. It doesn't matter that he might not be fully present. He said he wanted it like this and I don't want him to notice and get all soppy on me if I take rough sex too far for my broken body to handle.

I want it to hurt, and I don't need a therapist to lecture me about healthier coping mechanisms. Fuck that. This is better than some of the other things I've done to blunt the voice screaming at the back of my head that I deserve so much worse than this stranger would dream of doing to me.

Gary can't knock me up; that's impossible, even if I smell like omega slick. I always smell like slick when I miss a few doses of my meds. Slick and alpha pheromones.

And he's not an avian shifter, so it's not like he can give me anything else either. All he can give me is another meaningless fuck. A moment where I pretend at a connection to a mate I'll never have. This stranger lets me play at riding the edge of a heat that will never be the real thing again.

Never let me be what an omega should be—I shove the thoughts that sound far too much like the ex-almost-mate who broke my heart aside. I close my eyes against the sting of tears, and fuck myself harder on Gary's twinned lengths. Cling to his broad back as I ride him. I want to drown out the stench of my wrong, wrong, wrong pheromones in this alpha's cum. Want him to fill me up, knot me, and make me feel like the omega I used to be. I want to fill my nostrils with slick and jizz and alpha and omega and sweat and musk and—

"Harder, fuck me harder!" I demand, as though he holds the power to stop my spiraling thoughts. He doesn't.

I score my nails into his back, part of me flashing to the sense memory of my sharp raven talons digging into the flesh of a fresh kill with the local wolf pack. I was so proud to help provide for my family when I first landed that job and pulled my clutchmates in on the scheme. It all seemed so grown up as we scouted for the young wolf shifters, just learning to hunt. Marin was a year older and impossibly cooler and he made me feel so damn special.

For just a second, it's not Gary I'm clawing at as my memories superimpose the wolfishly charming grin of my first heartbreak over the pleasantly broad face I'm gazing up at. I don't see Gary hovering over me, only the young alpha who promised me the world before creep broke me. In that instant, I hate the alpha moving inside me almost a fraction as much as I hate myself; I want to hurt him as much as I want him to hurt me. I want his word to cut to the bone, as unerring as Marin's ever were.

"Ow, that fucking stings," Gary growls as he slaps my hands away from his back.

The smack, more noise than force, startles me and banishes thoughts of my ex-alphahole. Gary pulls out of me and bodily flips me onto my stomach. For a dizzying moment, the world spins as his mattress bounces under me and my brain catches up with the sudden disorientation just in time to stop a startled shift into my feathers as a reflexive response to the momentary sense of falling.

I shouldn't be disappointed that all Gary did was toss me effortlessly into a different position. One where I can't lash out at him again. Splayed belly-down on his sheets,

I'm at his mercy. My dick is totally fine with that, so I nestle in and get comfortable.

Garys' sheets reek of his reptilian scent, like he hasn't changed them in a while. Good, if my nose is full of him, it's easier to pretend all the traces of alpha pheromones in the air are coming from him. Not my scent. Not the result of my condition progressing.

I know I'm looking more alpha lately for a few reasons. It's my own fault I've been rationing my hormone dose more to give Rollie enough O. I get breakthrough symptoms regardless, and he's so much happier presenting as an omega. Whatever side effects the lower dose I'm taking brings, it's worth it to see Rollie confident in his place among shifter society.

I'll just have to hope my creep symptoms aren't progressing on top of taking too low a dose of O. I can't afford to pay out of pocket for testing again now that the deductible cap on my policy has reset for the year. Damn it. I can hear Marin's voice in my head, calling me a stupid slut for not planning better. I meant to get the tests scheduled before the holidays, but then it all got away from me and I didn't. Marin hated sniveling excuses like that.

"Behave," Gary grunts as he grabs my ankle to haul my ass to the edge of his mattress.

"Make me." I muffle the words in the gator's rumpled bedding, imagining how much worse I deserve to be roughed up for all my failings.

"That your way of saying you want it rough?" Gary asks, reading me far too well for a stranger I picked up in a bar.

I nod. Depending on how things go, I might have to look him up next time I have an itch that needs scratching. The hemipenes that were stretching me to my limits before he flipped me over are a major perk.

Gary wrenches my head back by the hair. The sting brings tears to my eyes. "Not good enough, omega, I asked if you want my knots to wreck your hot little hole?"

"Yes. Fuck me, alpha. Stuff me with both of your dicks. Make me hurt—" I whimper as he pins me more forcefully in place.

A painful wrench of his hand in my hair lights up my scalp. I moan and arch back toward him, hoping he'll take me again. Harder. Hard enough to drown out my thoughts and the ghost of Marin's voice. I need this alpha to let me just feel.

"Fuck, you smell good," Gary groans as he sinks back into my ass. I hate my scent these days, hate the sickly sweet synthetic slick I use to make up the difference when my body fails me yet again.

The alpha growls low in his throat, animalistic, like he's caught up in a rut. I sob as he thrusts in hard. Not at the burn of the alpha's two reptilian cocks driving into me, stretching me open all over again, or the punishing thrusts.

Nothing could hurt as much as knowing I'll never get to share a real rut with an alpha mate of my own. Or, hell, share a true heat with any lover. I bite my fist to hold back the sobs and rock back to meet each thrust, willing the alpha to hurry up and knot me already. Make me feel whole. Please, I just want to feel like a normal omega again. Just for a moment.

Except, by the time he comes the synthetic slick isn't nearly as slippery as when we started. The relaxing effects of the drugs have long since worn off, and the sharp stabbing ache of his dual knots swelling inside of me, stretching me more than my creep-ravaged body can bear, is only a further barbed reminder of everything the disease has stolen from me.

I feel broken as I endure the tie while the alpha moans and fucks his load deeper inside of me, oblivious to the discomfort I've gotten so very good at hiding over the years.

It's not enough. It doesn't help. Nothing helps. He falls asleep before his knot goes down enough to pull out, snuggling me close as though I'm his teddy bear or something. Oddly apt, I'm nothing but a comfort object to him.

When he finally slips free of my aching hole, I squirm out of his bed, find the clothes I didn't bother to change out of after Bram's baby shower this afternoon. I pad down the hall to his kitchen and dress in the dark. After a moment's hesitation I pause to rummage for a pencil to leave a flirty note for him to call me the next time he's horny along with my number on his immaculate kitchen counter.

Gary wasn't the worst fuck, and there are things I could do with two knots. Glorious, messy things I want to share with Rollie. My Rollie who won't ever be my mate. I don't deserve a mate, let alone one as wonderful as Rollie. Still, it's always fun when he agrees to pick up alphas with me, and Gary's natural inclination toward gentleness commends him for that. Rollie hasn't ever said explicitly that he's only interested in alphas, but his family is so traditional I don't think he's ever let himself consider that he might want a mate who isn't an alpha. I consider myself lucky to get to share him with them as often as I do.

I'll have to vet the gator more before I suggest a threesome with my sweet bestie, but the idea of both of us tied on the same alpha's dual knots has my abused ass valiantly attempting to slick up and my dick coming to attention. Yeah. Gary is worth feeling out if that's the payoff.

I sign my note with a lipstick kiss, making sure to get my scent on it for good measure. Alphas like that shit. Ball is in his court, and maybe he'll be a better fuck when he's sober, the delicious ache that comes with every step has me hoping for another round. Two cocks and only having to deal with one alpha is a bargain. And the fantasy of sharing him with Rollie is tantalizing.

It's easy enough to slip silently out of the fifth floor loft apartment that I'm not sure I'll ever set foot inside again. I wince and sit gingerly in the back of my Uber to Four Corners, the novelty of the ache wears off with the prospect of the long drive home to look forward to.

I stumble over the address I give my driver, starting to rattle off the address of my flock's apartment complex on autopilot even though it's been years since I moved out. It's too painful to be surrounded by my rave, the way my clutchmates and I always intended. Just like our parents raised us there along with a boisterous sub-flock of raucous cousins. Most of the raven shifters I grew up with are mated and raising chicks of their own.

I visit all the time, but I need to have a retreat from the constant reminder of the dreams creep stole from me. Being surrounded by family who mean well, but can't help being their obnoxious, loving, nosy selves day and night is too much to bear. I love my rave too much to be bitter toward them, but I can't help that I need a space of my own sometimes. When Bram and Ty got serious, Rollie offered me the haven I needed without me having to spell it all out.

I give Rollie's address to the driver. I've lived with him since I moved out of the apartment I shared with my brother. It's been years now, but it still doesn't feel quite like my home.

Part of me misses curling up next to Bram after a night like tonight. I used to climb under his covers and bury my nose in the sweet comfort of his pure, uncomplicated avian omega scent, so like my own, and yet subtly unique. He always used to let me cling to him until I relaxed enough to sleep.

Now he sleeps next to his mate, his belly round with their third child—no, fourth; he'd be livid if he ever caught me not counting his step-daughter, Myra. And she is his kid, even if not by blood. It's obnoxious how perfect my brother's family is.

So I go home to Rollie's cute little house instead of Bram and the flock apartments. Everyone teases us that we're practically mates, but I know better. Rollie can do so much better than me. It never ceases to astound me that he hasn't already had enough of my bullshit and told me it's time to find a place of my own. I know I should move out, for his sake, but I'm not strong enough to deny myself the taste of what it would be like to share my life with a mate who sees and accepts all of me.

The driver seems really into his podcast, so I mess around on my phone to distract myself while we drive. Rollie texted me earlier to confirm he got the message about who I was leaving the bar with. So I guess I already have contact info for Gary the next time I'm craving a double knotting. I don't have the energy to get into it with Rollie about how he told me the shower was a bad idea. He knows how I need to find a physical way to let out the emotional pain when life gets too intense to handle.

I text Rollie anyway. So he won't worry about me. It's a bit of a drive from the trendy heart of Old Port, where my hookup lives, to Four Corners. I wince internally at how much this ride is going to cost me, but I promised everyone who matters I wouldn't drive drunk again after the last time. That's one promise I haven't broken. I rarely drive at all since getting my license back. I never intended to get on the road when I got behind the wheel that night. Or to hurt anyone but myself. My intentions didn't matter in the end though.

Seb: You can delete his deets. On my way home.

Rollie: Stay safe

Seb: For you? Always ;) *kisses*

I shut off the screen and press it against my forehead, hating that I did this again. I said I was going to turn over a new leaf in the new year, but I blew that promise to Rollie right out of the gate.

My alpha du jour's knots hurt more than usual tonight. The way it's not supposed to for an omega. It feels so different from how things used to be and I hate the changes. And I still smell wrong, only with an added layer of reptile musk because apparently drunk and high Seb makes terrible life choices.

I'm sure Rollie will be thrilled to scent an alligator shifter on me. The gator had such a pretty twang to his voice at the bar though. And I had high hopes he knew how to put his unique reptile shifter attributes to good use. Too bad for me he seemed to think all he needed to do was dual wield his dicks to be amazing in bed.

I try not to wake Rollie as I let myself inside. His door creaks. I've been meaning to get some WD-40 for that shit. The sound makes me pause, waiting with bated breath for some sign I woke Rollie. There's no noise from within.

I slip off my shoes by the door and pad softly toward the bathroom to take a shower. I don't want to smell alpha musk. Not my own and not a stranger's. I want to scrub myself raw until I can erase all the changes, scrub until I find the omega that used to be under my skin. He's still who I am, even if the part of me that hates myself insists that's not true.

The bathroom vent and the hot water should be enough to drown out any sounds I make. The white noise should be relaxing. Rollie doesn't knock before he lets himself in.

"You okay in there?" he asks, and he knows me too well for me to bother lying.

"Nope."

"Want company?"

"Mm."

My best friend steps under the warm spray with me, heedless of the water soaking the pajama pants slung low on his hips. He wraps his arms around me and holds me while I fall apart. I bury my face in his shoulder and I fit against him the way I can't seem to fit into my own life anymore.

He smells so good. Like the coconut scented lotion he uses as though it's going out of style and something subtly spicy. Cinnamon and sugar and fresh cookies and everything good in the world. His scent has gotten sweeter since I started slipping him half of my prescription.

I should get a higher dose. My doctor prescribed it because my bloodwork keeps coming back too low. And I would, if I could afford it. The problem is that hormones are expensive. There's a program Bram's boss suggested that subsidizes my drug costs, but it only covers valid prescriptions. The zoo has specialists who could prescribe Rollie his own meds, but they only accept patients on the zoo health plan and their immediate families.

Bram tried to get Winny and I covered that way, but it means mates and dependents, not siblings or roommates. It's one of the many reasons my brother keeps bugging us both to apply for jobs at the zoo. He doesn't get why being on display like a model specimen of alpha raven shifter virility might bother me.

It's almost funny that the very condition that drives my need for the zoo's cushy benefits is what makes working there feel impossible. My scent and my call and even the way my feathers look in the sunlight is wrong with my hormones out of whack. And my doctor at the low-cost clinic already seems suspicious about why the standard dose of O she gives all her avian creep patients isn't helping me the way she thinks it should. She's told me that all her other avian patients with creep do just fine on fifty milligrams daily. So she wants to run more specialized labs I can't afford before she'll up my dose again.

Of course, I haven't told her that I've been taking half that amount, sharing the pills with Rollie so he can take the lower dose of omega hormones recommended for trans omegas. Nevermind that the formulation for avians isn't quite the same as the one for raccoons like him. It seems to be working regardless, especially since I started giving him a higher dose.

Neither of us has told anyone. I could stop. Tell him to see a different doctor to get his own meds, but he won't and he's so much damn happier since we started this.

He's finally getting to show the world the omega he always has been inside. My discomfort isn't enough for me to take that away from him. Not after feeling how truly awful it is to appear to be something I'm not. When other shifters scent me and think 'alpha' it makes me cringe. It makes me want to scrub another layer of skin off. It makes it impossible to tell Rollie he has to go back to feeling that way about presenting as a beta again.

I can't take away his happiness. I won't. Not when no amount of hormones will actually fix the root cause of what's wrong with me.

I could take all the hormones in the world and it still wouldn't restore my normal heat cycles. Wouldn't let me bear a clutch. It won't give back my first love and the mating and family I thought I could have. It won't restore the innocent belief I had in people before the alpha I loved with all my heart stomped the dreams I thought we shared into oblivion. Even if there was an actual cure tomorrow, that betrayal will still haunt me and shape me into someone the starry-eyed version of me from before creep wouldn't recognize. I'll still be broken, and Rollie doesn't have to be.

So I sob in Rollie's arms and wish I knew a better way. A way to get us both what we need.

Chapter 3

Rollie

"Hey, you're home!" Seb bounces up off the couch and toward me, reminding me of the way he hops across the floor in his raven form. I can't help smiling at his enthusiasm.

"Yep, what's up?" I ask, turning to hang my keys on the hook by the door. "Did you want to go out tonight?"

"We're going to a barbeque at the rave. You know how Elric's fledging party was supposed to be next week? Well, the forecast changed; it's going to be stormy most of next week, so they moved it to tonight."

"Oh?" That's typical short-notice planning coming from the rave. Of course we're going regardless. Fledging parties are important milestones for raven shifters.

"Yep, Elric and some of the other cousins. Can't believe they're finally making it official." Seb grins.

From what I've learned about the tradition Elric really did take their time to make their adult name and pronouns government official. I've seen raven shifters ranging from as young as eight up to seventeen among the fledglings celebrated at these parties, but most of them are roughly middle school aged. And it's unusual for a raven shifter who is so settled in their identity to wait so long to declare it. Cory, the baby of the family, is almost old enough to consider when he's going to have his ceremony, now that he's been using he/him for over a year.

"How is Elric feeling about making it official?" I ask with a sympathetic smile. "I know they've had a hard time setting a date."

"Yeah, our moms nudged them along, but they seem excited now that the date is set? I saw them last night for supper, cause you had the closing shift." Seb makes a face at me, showing how little he appreciates the disruption to our usual mealtime routine. I shake my head at him, I missed having dinner with him too, even if expecting family dinners to include us both feels perilously close to treating what's between us like the mating I wish it was in truth than I have any right to. "Elric seemed more excited when we talked about the party last night. It helps that the paperwork is all done except the signatures, and Mom reminded them it's okay to make a change later on if they need to. Plus Elric has always put it off by saying they want to wait for their favorite cousin and she is declaring tonight too, so it all aligned just right."

"I think they also feel weird about not changing from their birth name, you know? Most of us at least try on a few other options, but not Elric. They just always felt like themself I guess? And they said it feels weird not to feel weird about that?" Seb shrugs. "I don't know, I think it would be nice to just, have been hatched feeling all the way like me and never wavering from that certainty, you know?"

Seb looks so wistful and I understand that sense of longing to the depths of my soul. His experiences with his identity not matching his body are so different from mine, but the raw pain of it is the same.

It hurts not to feel like myself, and Seb is one of the few people I know who understands that reality on a visceral level. His creep related dysphoria over his body's inexorable drift toward unwanted alpha traits and the loss of traits that helped him define his omega-hood isn't the same as my dysphoria over being trans a man and a trans omega, but it's similar enough that we've connected on a deeper level than I have with any other person in my life. Seb understands all of me in ways I'm not sure anyone else can. And I understand him.

I don't have a vivid enough imagination to conjure up an alternate past where I was born in a body that wasn't the source of so much shame and trauma. I can't untangle the lies about myself that my parents and doctors used to control me. Or the ways being raised as a beta by parents who saw that as a deep character flaw shaped me. But Seb's wistful longing for a simpler path, a life where being ourselves didn't have to hurt so much, that strikes a chord deep in my heart.

"Yeah." I croak, choked up about it. Ugh, I'm not going to get all soppy about impossible what ifs, we have a party to get to and a little sibling to celebrate.

"Anyway. You'll come with me, right?" Seb asks, sounding weirdly insecure. As if I'd miss something this important.

"Of course, I always want to support you and your sibs," I assure him.

"Sweet, you're the best!" Seb dances in close to brush an excited kiss over my cheek, then whirls in a swish of his silky silver blouse. "I'll grab you something to wear, we have to change."

He's so pretty and sparkly already, I don't see why he'd want to change. I press my palm to the lingering warmth of his kiss, wishing I could memorize the feel of his lips on me. Wishing I could run my fingers over the soft planes of his chest, feel the way the slinky fabric would move under my hands until I can tug on his piercings. I want to have him under me, writhing with lust and need. I almost choke on the moan I have to swallow down at the mental image of him coming apart for me, the way I've watched when we share an alpha lover, hoarding those memories like a raven's treasure trove.

For all that we've toed the line between friends and lovers, we've never quite crossed it without a third to spread our focus away from each other. I push aside the heat of desire and trail Seb into our shared bedroom so that I don't have to take my eyes off the most alluring shifter I've ever met.

"Hmm, I'm thinking blue? To bring out your pretty eyes?" Seb paws through his closet and tugs out several colorful shirts, visually eyeing up how well they'll fit me. He clicks his tongue and flicks through hangers until he finds something with enough stretch to fit me comfortably. "Try that?"

"Do we need to bring anything to the party? I can pick something up from the store." I tug the shirt on, and while he's thinner than me, he's also taller, so the hem hits me at mid thigh. Seb tugs at it, purses his lips and then cinches a gaudy belt made of interlocking metal loops around my hips to emphasize the curvier figure that my omega HRT gave me.

"Hmm, yes! Hot. And also, nope, nothing except your iced tea. Between my moms, Ty, Bram, and all the aunties and uncles, there's going to be a ton of food. Do we have a batch of your iced tea?" He licks his lips and I chuckle.

"I made more sweet tea last night since you were out late with your sibs, yeah. We can bring it."

"Good. Turn?" I twirl for him to examine his handiwork, which has me facing his vanity mirror. I give myself a dubious glance, but before I can really take in the look, Seb tugs me around and shoves a pair of leggings at me. "Put those on. We aren't looking to pull at the rave, right?"

His eyes dart appreciatively down my body and for a split second, I'm dead certain that he wants me all to himself. The same way I want him. Our eyes meet and I can't find the words to ask.

Seb swallows hard, throat working and no words falling out of his verbose mouth. As long as neither of us brings it up, there's hope that we can be each other's forever, but once I say something everything will change. I'm not ready. So I stare—helplessly and hopelessly in love with my sweet raven. The best treasure I've ever found.

Seb clears his throat. "So, uh, yeah. Fledging party, gotta save pulling an alpha for the after party." He grabs a tight pencil skirt and slips it up his thighs over a thigh-length pair of skintight shorts.

"Yeah?" My mouth is dry just watching him get dressed. Damn, I want to help him take every scrap of his clothing back off.

"Yep. Elric might never forgive me if I steal the spotlight by hooking up there." Seb forces an awkward chuckle. He flits over to his vanity, picks through his costume jewelry, carefully arranging a collection of his favorite rings and bangles on his fingers and wrists. I have most of his favorites memorized. Gifts from his family and loved ones. The bangles I gave him. Pieces that remind him of important moments and places. He's a walking temptation, and he's putting on my bracelets.

If we had more time I'd shift for a cuddle before we have to leave. It's easier not to give away my reactions to him from behind my furry mask. As it is, my face flushes with unbearable heat and I turn away to wriggle into the tight leggings. Not my favorite clothes, but Seb likes the way I look in them. Besides which, he's never steered me wrong in how to dress if I want to get my brains fucked out.

Sure, he said we aren't planning to pick up at the fledging party, but I can tell from the charged energy buzzing under his skin and his utterly tantalizing outfit that there is an excellent chance we'll end the night on the prowl. When Seb's in this kind of mood, he usually needs a good hard fuck to get it out of his system. If I thought it wouldn't make things weird between us, I'd offer to help him take the edge off before the party. But I'm too chicken for that.

I gather my courage in both hands, bolstered by the fact he's dressing me up like he wants to show me off to one of his alpha fuck buddies. I know this song and dance.

"So, am I invited to this after party?"

"Obviously." Seb covers his hands and wrists in sparkles, does a quick touch up to his eyeliner, and then plucks up two bracelets that match the belt he's lending me. "Here, put these on and let me do your hair and eyes?"

I let him guide me to the little chair in front of his vanity, close my eyes and tip my face up. This is one of my greatest guilty pleasures. Seb's fingers gently reposition my face. His voice is a breathy whisper as he tells me just how he wants me to move.

"Open just a little?" He says, the tickle of his makeup brush making me clench too much for him to apply the eyeshadow.

"Tickles." I grunt as I obey.

It's hard to sit still with Seb's whole focus on me. All but impossible not to squirm, even though it is natural as breathing to trust myself entirely into his gentle hands and the soft command in his voice. My mind races with lust-fueled images of Seb giving that exact command with his steady hands holding my thighs open instead of holding my face still to be his canvas.

Open for him, let his cock slip inside of me. Fuck. It's just as well that I don't have the slick glands that most omega have because I'd be making a sopping wet mess of myself for him. As it is, the long since atrophied pussy that only Seb has ever fucked—and even then, only a handful of times when we're with a third—pulses with heat and want and a trickle of moisture that isn't nearly enough to make sex comfortable without extra lube.

It's plenty to make my arousal loud and clear in my scent. Seb notices. He has too. His breath catches and he inhales sharply.

"Mm. Almost done. You look good enough to eat, Rollie."

It has to be my imagination that the saccharine scent of aroused omega gets thicker in the air. His vanilla and lime aroma layered in lust. Even if I'm not imagining things, that doesn't have to mean it's aimed at me.

"Yeah?" I ask, voice shaky. I try to force away all thoughts of tumbling into bed with Seb. Later. With a third between us. Plausible deniability that there's anything more between us. An alpha buffer to keep our safe boxes around sex and love unsullied.

"Take a look." Seb spins me back toward the mirror and I gaze at myself.

My eyes perfectly framed with retro style smoky make-up. Seb somehow created a glittery reflection of my animal form, as if my raccoon is gazing out of my human face. The same way his perfectly coifed hair is a reflection of his glossy feathers. I reach toward the reflection, heart swelling that he sees this part of me and thinks it's worth taking pride in. Not a part of me that I'm not worthy of claiming because I don't fit the way my family thinks I should. Seb gnaws on his lip. "We aren't going to have any trouble picking up after the party tonight. What do you think?"

"I love it." I stand and hug him. Trying to let him hear the part I can't say aloud. I love him.

I love that he embraces every part of me. Even the parts I don't know how to embrace fully. The parts I had to leave behind in a sense. I couldn't stay in the raccoon shifter community where I grew up. It took turning my back on my gaze to find acceptance and build a life as an equal among my own kind.

Seb knows all about my complicated feelings toward my inner raccoon. I love my furry side, but I don't always know how to relate to other raccoon shifters and it can be awkward to feel disconnected from that heritage. Seb sees that, and he makes it a beautiful part of me.

I might be reading too much into his simple artistry, except for all that he can seem superficial, I know Seb. And he isn't the vapid featherhead fuckboy he pretends to be to keep everyone at arm's length. He knows exactly the message of loving acceptance that he's sending, and he means it. I don't think I'm ever going to stop falling for this shifter.

"Good." Seb rubs my back for a while longer, and we can both smell how turned on I am, I'm sure of it, but he lets me stay in his embrace until I have my emotions back under control and step out of the circle of his arms. "I was thinking, now that you've been on your omega hormones for a while, would you want to try having heat sex?"

"Huh?" I blink at him, mouth going dry with the mix of want and nerves and wary distrust because that isn't actually possible, right?

"I mean, not the real thing." He waves away the notion with a flustered flap of his hands. "A medically induced one that isn't fertile. Like they use in porn shoots and stuff. I've considered bringing it up a few times, but I wasn't sure you'd want to, since it might feel dysphoric? But then we were watching that really hot omega mates double heat porno a few month back, and I was planning to bring it up around the new year, cause that's when raccoon mating season usually starts, right?" Seb rambles adorably.

If I didn't know him so well, I'd swear talking about sex with me is making Seb nervous, but that's absurd. My best friend is a proud slut and we've had enough threesomes that he has to realize I'd gladly reenact any part of that particular video with him.

I vividly recall the night in question. He walked in on me jerking off to a selection of my favorite adult films when he came home from a night out with his clutchmates early, and just plopped down beside me to watch together. Hottest night of my life, watching him jerking off next to me while the real-life mates—two omegas—fucked the night away on-screen.

"It is." I nod, dazed that he put that much thought into this and confused about what he's actually offering.

"Right, so I thought it might feel more natural that way? But then we had the drug shortage issues and side effects from switching to the generic and it took a while adjusting to the new brand, but now that we're back on an even keel, I was thinking it might be fun to try having a heat together."

"Yes!" My heart is pounding, joy bubbling through me. I can't agree forcefully enough. A million times yes. A chance to have Seb all to myself, and as a cherry on top, while we're both in heat—or as close as either of us can go to the real deal? Sign me up.

Seb's next words temper my exuberance before I can jump on him and get started without the synthetic heat hormones to complicate matters. I have to be dreaming because this offer is taken whole cloth from my fantasies.

"Awesome! I was hoping you'd say that. So, I made a few arrangements. You know Gary? The gator alpha fuck buddy I told you about? The one I've been seeing since Bram's baby shower? He got his hands on some synthetic inducers. Plenty of people use them and they're safe. It's practically a rite of passage for old mated couples to use them to spice things up without risking pregnancy, and I thought it might be fun to share. If you wanted to feel what it's like."

I lick my lips, nerves jangling for entirely different reasons. It's still heat sex with Seb. And some alpha I don't know or care about. One who gets to have Seb all to himself in ways I can only dream of...nope, not going there. Better to focus on the practicalities, since heats and slick go hand in hand and I don't want to come out of the haze of lust with a chapped ass.

"What about slick?" I wave vaguely at myself to remind him of the requisite glands that I lack.

"Not a problem." Seb shakes his head and grimaces. No longer producing enough slick is one of the creep symptoms he hates the most and I could kick myself for reminding him of it, but it's an important detail to discuss if we're really doing this. "Picked up a gallon of the artificial stuff. I know it stinks of artificial omega pheromones, but it's less noticeable with an alpha in rut to cover up the smell. Plus, if you're cool with going bare, they come a lot when they're in rut. That's kind of why I suggested it with a gator, almost no chance of any cross species STIs to worry about for any of us once we get going."

Neither of us mentions the other risk. Because neither one of us is going to end this fake heat pregnant. My womb has been broken since forever and creep fucked over his. So that makes screwing around with his gator friend safe for everyone involved. As far as his fuck buddies go, the gator doesn't leave bruises, and from what Seb has said, the main reason he keeps going back to Gary is the novelty of screwing a reptile shifter with their unique anatomy.

"That works. You have the inducers, like, we're sure it is what he says it is?"

"Yeah. I had my med person check them out. It's legit, I don't take risks with you, Rollie." He holds up a pill case and rattles the contents.

"I know." I bite back a retort that I'm fully aware he only takes risks with himself. I'm grumpy that I misinterpreted his offer, but I still want to share this experience with him.

"So, can I tell him you're down to fuck raw?" Seb checks.

My stomach rolls and pitches at the reminder that he's not just asking to share a heat with me. If I agree to this, then it means fucking one of the alphas who goes along with the games Seb plays to hurt himself. It's not my place to tell either of them what to do. And the gator doesn't know Seb the way I do. Doesn't see what giving in to his more destructive impulses does to him.

Seb is going to do this either way. I can see it in the glimmer of need in his eyes and the carefully selected outfit, the way his scent changes when he's in one of these moods. It's not that I don't want to fuck some stranger, per se. It's just that if I had the option, I'd kick that alpha to the curb and spend my heat with Seb and only Seb. I want to smell Seb in heat, not some random alpha's rut. But that isn't what Seb is offering me. And it will still be fun to share him with his friend. The details don't matter as long as I get to be a part of his pleasure without sacrificing our friendship.

Seb means the world to me. I would follow him anywhere. Even into a stranger's bed. I've done it before. And I genuinely do want to experience a heat with him. Even if it is a synthetically induced one that wouldn't happen naturally. Even if he invites an alpha along for the ride. If that's what it takes to make him feel fully omega and leave the trauma of his diagnosis behind for a while, I'm on board.

This isn't something I'd have asked him for, but now that he's put the possibility in front of me, I want to feel that rush of instinctual need. The soul deep knowing that he's going to be there with me for every hot and sweaty second of it. I want to let the lust consume me so I don't have to overthink what I'm doing during this threesome. A chance to have him without second-guessing how much of my heart is showing in my every touch and needy moan. There is only one answer I want to give.

"Rollie?" Seb is studying my face, the pill bottle still in his hand. All his excitement has slipped away and worry furrows his brow. "You don't have to take any. Or do this with me or at all if you don't want to."

"No, it's not that." I lick my lips and shake my head. "I want to. I'm a bit nervous to have my first heat is all. But I want it to be with you."

A slow grin lights up his face and he sashays closer, bending to tuck the vial of pills into the breast pocket of my shirt. "Good. Me too. Hold onto these for us?"

I nod, wishing I had the courage to lean forward the few inches that are all it would take to bounce up on my toes and kiss him. "Yeah. I will. Um. When are we doing this?"

"Tonight. After the party, I'm going to text Gary on the way over there and arrange for a static human rideshare to pick us up around midnight, so we can be ready to go by the time we get to his place. Sound good?"

"Yeah. That, uh, sounds really good." I squirm in anticipation. Tonight. I'll get to kiss him in a few short hours.

"One more thing?" Seb says, reaching out to brush his fingers along my jawline.

"Yeah?" I ask, leaning into his gentle caress. He seems to have put more than his usual level of thought into this, and I'm not sure I want to probe too deeply into why. Was inviting me a last-minute impulse? A surprise that he intended to share with me all along? I don't know and I don't want to find out that my part in his plans is as an afterthought or addendum. He says it was the porn that inspired him, so maybe this really is something he arranged for me?

"Can I give you the first dose at the party?" Seb asks, fingers still cupping my cheek, like a lover. I close my eyes because that isn't what we are and I can't ask him for more than he is able to give me, but for as long as the heat inducers last, we can pretend. Pretend that we're both just like any other omega.

"Yes. That's probably a good idea. Um, from what I've read about trans omegas and synthetic heats, it can sometimes take a higher than usual dose to get much effect." That's the reason I'd have never brought up the idea of trying this if he hadn't made the offer first.

"I know." Seb is gazing so intently into my eyes, I can almost hear the love in his voice and believe he feels the same way about me that I do about him. The moment of connection passes and he goes on, "Same goes for avians with creep. I've got it covered. Gary got us plenty of the most potent synthetic heat inducers on the market. Enough doses for us both to last several days if we want. Or you can stop taking them whenever you've had enough of our three-way fuckfest. That's part of the fun of a synthetic heat. You have more control over how long it lasts."

"Yep," I force a weak chuckle and nudge him away. His scent, tinged with anticipatory lust is getting me all hot and bothered without any need for pharmaceutical help. Seb smirks knowingly, holding my gaze as he takes a slow step back.

"So, sounds good about dosing me at the party. As long as it's after the kids are in bed I don't mind being a little horny and drunk around your flock. It's been a while since we shared an alpha. Can't wait. We should, uh, get to the party, right? Don't want to miss the fledglings doing their announcements."

"Yeah." Seb agrees. He grabs his phone, fingers flying as he taps out a message. Probably confirming our plans for later tonight. "Elric might end us if we aren't there for his turn."

Us. Not me. Because that's how seamlessly I've allowed Seb to fold me into his family and their unconditional love. My heart melts for Seb even more. Elric won't end us. They're probably the least high strung of Seb's five siblings. It's still a big deal for us to be there to support the kid, and Seb won't ever forgive himself for disappointing his sibling if we're late. So we grab the heavy three-gallon jug of sweet tea that I made for us when I was too restless to sleep after my shift last night without Seb home, and head over to the flock's building.

The first time Seb invited me along to a fledging party, it was for his sister, Bryony. I wasn't sure what to expect. The raven shifter flock in Four Corners collectively own a large apartment building where most of them live in various family groupings. The building has a large interior courtyard open to the skies where the flock loves to host large gatherings.

Fledging parties are different in that the actual ceremony at the start is just for people the flock trusts like family. So when Seb invited me along for Bryony's party a couple of years into our friendship, that was when I knew for certain what I meant to him. The sort of friend you can call on like family. It was also when his cousins started to tease us about our future mating. That might have been the first jarring tumble I took into loving my sparkly raven, even though I didn't fully understand what the rite of passage meant to him.

Seb explained the entire tradition with a sort of sheepish reverence. It was before he moved in with me, but he'd stayed over at my first tiny apartment here in Four Corners that night.

I was still learning to read his more subtle cues back then, but I could tell from his hunched shoulders while he mumbled a mile a minute that, for some reason, he was ashamed of how much weight he still placed on this ceremony. It took living with him and getting to glimpse under the shining carefree facade to his vulnerable hurt parts to understand why it matters so much.

Seb's fledging party was a time when he had a choice in asserting who he is and how he is seen among his flock. The antithesis of everything that creep took and takes from him daily. It was exactly what he needed as a touchstone to remind himself of who he is, and I suspect he saw how much I needed something similar in my life.

At Bryony's ceremony, I was just coming to grips with my desire to be seen as an omega. My sense of identity was clashing with the ingrained beliefs my family had passed on about the immutability of how I should present among shifters. I'd internalized so much of what they told me for years.

Wasn't it enough that they'd let me transition my primary gender from female to male? So that the static humans see me the way I want to be seen? Why do I want to change even more about myself?

I was nervous about agreeing to attend. Afraid that a party celebrating how permissive the rave is with their young might stir up the old wounds my family carved into my psyche so deeply that I had to leave them in another state to breathe freely. I left everything I knew behind to live my life on my own terms. Despite my misgivings, I went to Bryony's fledging to deepen my friendship with Seb.

More than supporting Seb and his family, it was healing to see shifters lovingly encouraging kids who were exploring the sort of identity issues that created impenetrable barriers between me and my family. The announcements were met with raucous celebrations all around.

Regardless of what each young shifter announced, they were all applauded and congratulated. And then the parents and aunties brought out the food. A couple of elders broke out bottles of a deceptively potent homemade alcoholic infusion for a toast that had my head spinning after a single shot and Bram and Winny giggling over Seb failing to warn me. Someone turned on the music and the actual party was like any other flock get-together.

Boisterous, and playful. Ravens in and out of their feathers dancing, showing off, and lounging about the courtyard, sharing food and gossip. Passersby wandered in from all over the town to join the festivities as word of the party spread, bringing more refreshments and live music with them. The hatchlings chased each other with playful shrieks on foot and on the wing.

Elric's celebration follows that same pattern. When everyone invited is present, the new fledglings file in to stand solemnly in front of their gathered family, glittering with an assortment of their favorite treasures proudly displayed on their fancy clothes. Elric has baubles from each of their siblings and favorite cousins. I get a little teary when I see they're wearing a gift from me too, an enamel pin of a ghost on a van that I got for their hatchday from their favorite paranormal investigations vlog.

Once the official proceedings end, the fledglings disperse into the crowd, half of them bundle their treasures into cubbies so they can take to their feathers and fly, the other half flop into a cuddle pile with older siblings and cousins to devour snacks and punch. We congratulate Elric and Seb gives his sibling a huge hug and a card from us both.

Then we leave him to celebrate with his peers. All of them are touching and teasing each other, and reveling in their new status as no longer being counted among the hatchlings. We end up gravitating to Seb's usual group of cousins along with his clutchmates.

Honestly, watching the flock interact, from the hatchlings to the adults fussing over the food, it's not that much different from the way Seb sometimes seems to just need to be around people, connecting and touching each other. When Seb's family despairs of him settling down some day, he just gives them a laconic grin and promises a distant someday, but this is what they want for him, this connection that he holds himself on the outskirts of reaching for.

Seeing him with the other ravens, I get it. He needs this level of connection, even if he can't seem to let himself have it in healthy ways. The unending string of alphas, occasional flings with other shifters that burn hot and fast until they fizzle out, and the various ways he's tried to numb this need are all trying to fill something that he won't let himself have. He's not that different from the rest of his flock. Even the prickly loners like Seb seem drawn to these get-togethers.

I stick by his side, watching other ravens stretching their wings in a warm evening breeze. The whole flock dotes on the children who are constantly underfoot and underneath the laid-back supervision of all the adults present, even if all of them don't want clutches of their own. And the flock loves to gossip, so I end up being a popular source on the latest Four Corners small town drama.

I see it all, working at the market. I don't generally share any of the negative gossip. But the flock is content with fueling speculation about who is getting mated soon and which families are expecting or who needs an extra meal delivered during hard times. Ravens can be extraordinarily stealthy about leaving a basket of groceries or a nice casserole if they want to be.

Tonight, I don't have much to say once we settle in amongst a cluster of Seb's favorite cousins and clutchmates. Snippets of old gossip, mostly. That's okay, his family is full of their own stories and jokes. I'm happy to sit and chat with them for hours. Time slips away, I lose track of how many times Seb's cousins refill my glass and jokingly prod him about when he's going to make me an official part of the flock.

I'm tipsy, but not so drunk I can't think straight when Seb gets back from the snack table and settles into the seat beside me to share some trail mix. He leans in close, the heady cloyingly floral scent of liquor clinging to his skin. He offers me a folded napkin packet of food.

"You still want to?" Seb murmurs into the shell of my ear. His fingers are a live wire trailing up my forearm.

It takes me a long hazy moment to parse what he means as I nibble on some dried berries from the handful of food. The synthetic heat. Oh, yes. I nod.

"Yes."

The moon and stars are high and most of the hatchlings have already been corralled off to bed or settled in to nap on their parents in their feathered and human forms alike when Seb reaches into my pocket and taps out two doses of the heat inducer, pressing one into my palm and taking the other before he caps the bottle and tucks it back into my pocket.

"Take it, my sweet trash panda," he murmurs into my ear. I turn to catch his scent under the alcohol. His sweet vanilla lime is an aphrodisiac all on its own, even if his words didn't have me imagining him asking me to open my mouth to take something far more substantial than a pill for him. I take the first dose.

And wait. Can I feel it working? Is that twinge of desire just the lingering effect of being so close to the shifter I adore above all others or is it something more? Seb does something on his phone. Ordering our ride? I lose track of the conversation going on around me until Bram nudges me with his elbow.

"You got awful quiet, everything alright?" Bram asks into a lull in the conversation as two of the cousins wend their way over to the refreshments to bring back another round of drinks. Which means all eyes turn to me when I don't marshal my muzzy thoughts into an answer right away. Bram either doesn't notice, or else he does and takes pity, guiding me to an easy topic, "What's new at the market?"

"Nothing much. Mrs. Leopard has been showing off pictures of her new grandkit to anyone who will look. And you know the milk cooler in the back that's been on the fritz for ages? Seems like the time between repairs keeps getting shorter and shorter so I think Harvey is going to need to replace it soon." I could go on about what a hassle the whole thing is, but other than Seb, Bram, Ty, and Winny giving me sympathetic looks, the raven shifters around us aren't interested in my dairy dilemma. Not that I blame them. Most avian shifters, even the kids in their human forms, aren't big milk drinkers.

"Anyway, it's just too bad that we don't have room for a few more freezers along the back, because with the summers heating up we can't seem to stock enough of the frozen novelties in the little chest freezer by the checkout." I wrap up the work talk with a wistful sigh. And look over to see Seb's cousins no longer bored with talk about the market, they're watching me intently.

"Oh, that does sound nice, a whole ice cream aisle like at the big stores?" Lydia, one of the more vocal cousins, asks. "My kids would love that."

"I mean, yes?" I realize it's the wrong reply as soon as the word leaves my mouth. Yes, that is what I had envisioned, but no, it isn't happening. The flock is already abuzz with their own speculation, but I try to salvage the situation. "It was just a suggestion, but I don't think there's room for it. Harvey said we would need to do a major renovation, and it's not in the budget at the moment..." I trail off, no one is listening past mention of renovations. Heck, most of them tuned out when I said *yes*.

The raven shifters around me light up with enthusiastic glee, all talking over each other in their excitement. They take my pipe dream future planning for an expansion that isn't happening and run with it. Imagining all the new things they can get. Dairy free ice creams. Popsicles made with real fruits. Things that are a pain to get from nearby towns without having to worry they'll melt on the drive. The possibilities they come up with are endless and as the rumors my slip of the tongue inspired spread across the party I just know this isn't going away anytime soon.

"Oh, yes, of course, nothing official," Lydia gives me a knowing smile and a wink, then raises her voice in a sort of warning to the others who are busy passing along their version of the remodel like the gossip is gospel. "We won't tell anyone that *our Rollie* let any company secrets fly, will we?"

The other shifters nod and voice their agreement and I resign myself to the fact that this rumor isn't going away, maybe ever. But at least they want to keep my name out of it.

The flock is good at spreading random acts of kindness. They are superhuman about spreading local gossip. The whole town is going to be talking about Harvey remodeling the freezer aisle for the non-mammalian shifter kids by the end of the week. And word is definitely going to get back to my boss. Who knows how much I've wanted that expansion to be a part of the store's future vision. Crap on a stick. It's a good thing I know Harvey likes me.

Harvey has been giving me more responsibility as a manager lately. We meet to discuss the business and his vision for the market's future. But I'm under no illusion that he's going to add a brand new ice cream section big enough to hold non-dairy offerings for my best friend and his family just because that's the first upgrade I would make if it was up to me. And not just to make the avian shifters I love happy. It really would be a sound investment, based on the sales numbers I've run, at least I think so.

Ugh. Why am I thinking about spreadsheets at a party? I guess the heat inducer had nothing to do with the lust Seb brings out in me. Good to know. I might still blame the meds for how hyper aware of his presence I am.

I thunk my face against Seb's shoulder and he wraps his arm around me to steady me.

"Drink too much again?" Seb asks sympathetically. I glance up at his bemused grin and snuggle into his neck, scenting him. He smells so good, a tantalizing blend of sweet lime, vanilla, and feather dust that I want to breathe in deep enough to imprint it in my soul.

"Maybe I drank just enough," I whisper into the shell of his ear. Then I nip his lobe, not quite daring a kiss, but needing to taste him. I might need to lay off the drinks before I say something I'll really regret. Like begging Seb to take me to bed without the hassle of meeting up with the alpha he invited to squeeze in between us and pin the veneer of staying *just friends* on to. Fuck I want him all to myself.

Seb startles and turns to face me. "Horny much?" he teases. "Is it working?"

"Yeah." I grin coyly up at him, watching his face as my fingers dance along his collarbone, smoothing the silky silver fabric against his equally soft skin. It feels as amazing as I'd fantasized it would. I bite my lip to keep from blurting out the humiliating truth that he brings that out in me, even if I didn't just take a heat inducer.

Seb is watching me, his teasing smile slipping toward a more serious expression, his eyes scorch into me with naked lust, his fingers tighten on my shoulder. I imagine what it would feel like to lift my leg up a few inches, just enough to slide my thigh over his lap. Enough to straddle him.

"Not here, Rollie, love. Soon." Seb reads my mind.

I bite back a sound between a protest and a needy whine. He's right, even if I want nothing more than to grind my needy little omega cock against his. For the two of us to scent the air around us in the thick, sweet pungency of omega arousal. A beacon to every shifter around us of exactly what I want from Seb. What I'm all but certain we both want right now.

Part of me wants them all to know what my inner raccoon knows in the depths of his furry little soul. Mate. This is the shifter I want to tie my life to for always. And I can never be what he wants in a mate. That cools my ardor enough to act rationally. I don't push for more.

Seb has one hand on my shoulder, holding me so close, that every inhale makes it harder to remember where I end and he begins and why acting on my attraction in this moment is a terrible idea. His other hand goes to my thigh, sending so many mixed signals that I feel like a one shifter traffic jam. His thumb caresses my thigh even as his palm presses my leg down, pinning it in place, preventing me from climbing into his lap the way every one of my omega instincts is telling me to. Climb onto my mate and have him inside me and...

"Not here, Rollie." Seb repeats as he nuzzles in close to my ear, the words a barely audible whisper, soft enough that it's possible nearby shifters, with their better than static human hearing, might not be able to make out what he's saying under the music and laughter of the party still going strong around us.

Right. I take a deep breath and put a little space between us. Enough that I can inhale without taking in quite so much of his scent. I'm not entirely sure what that was, but a moment to cool down and ground myself clears a bit of the buzz from my brain. Apparently the meds are as potent as promised.

But we're still at the rave party. And sure, it's late enough that most of the young children have gone off to their beds, but we're still sitting in the middle of the courtyard. Surrounded by Seb's extended family and the entire local raven shifter community. Shit.

That splashes more cold water on my lust. I scoot away from Seb, needing space to pull myself back together.

"Sorry. Not sure what came over me there."

"It's normal for it to hit hard the first time. Sorry, I forgot you've never..." Seb sighs and shakes his head. "It's all good. Let's get out of here so you can let go and enjoy the full experience, okay?"

"Yeah." I nod.

"See you lot later, I'm taking my poor lightweight mammal shifter home and putting him to bed before you all poison him with your hospitality," Seb announces to his laughing cousins. It's a running joke when I come around, even though I've gotten used to their deceptively sweet alcohol preferences. They call out condolences, joking about whether my hangover or their cousin is going to give me the bigger headache tomorrow.

Seb flips them off, then he stands and offers me his hand with a flourish, like some gallant prince charming in a fairy tale come to sweep me off my feet. I take his hand and let him lead me away from the party. We leave the mostly empty jug of iced tea with the other drinks. Seb will fetch the jug home after the party.

Seb grabs the overnight bag with the massive bottle of lube he packed for us from the entry hall as we walk through the building and out to the main road to the highway. We walk along the shoulder toward the outskirts of the town. There's a gravel turnaround next to the sign marking the town limits. Static drivers like to use it as a pick up or drop off spot for rides out to Four Corners, so they don't have to drive around the shifter town.

"Sorry." Seb rubs sheepishly at the back of his neck. We wander most of the way to the sign before Seb adds, "I didn't think it would hit you that hard that fast. Our ride is about five minutes out and then it's another thirty to Gary's place. Think you can hold on or need to take the edge off?"

"Take the edge off how?" I arch a brow at him. Everything I've read about heats implies that coming doesn't really do much to sate the rising tide of need. Maybe it's different if it's a synthetic one? I don't want to think about that. I want to pretend like this is real. Like I'm just like any other omega, eager to enjoy this time with the shifter I love.

"Touch yourself for me?" Seb suggests.

I shake my head. I don't want to touch myself on the side of the road. I want to drop to my knees and go down on him until he's dripping with his own natural slick. But I know he's sensitive about that. Dysphoric. Because his body doesn't respond the way he's used to. Doesn't do the things he thinks it's supposed to. The same way mine doesn't. And I could spiral about how much that hurts and what it means. Or I could kiss him.

So I do the latter. I close the distance between us and I kiss my sweet raven until our ride pulls off the highway. A lone car takes the exit ramp and pulls up next to the welcome to Four Corners sign at the edge of town. It bathes us in the glow of its headlights.

The driver idles the car on the shoulder. A moment later, Seb's phone pings with a familiar app notification. He messages back just as the driver leans out the window. "You Seb?"

"Yeah," Seb steps away from me, his fingers catching mine just before he steps out of reach, pulling me along in his wake. I know Seb does this all the time. That using ride services is safer than driving when he's in one of his spirals and he knows what he's doing to mitigate risk. I still don't fully trust outsiders. Most statics don't give shifters much thought in their day-to-day lives, but I still worry. There are good reasons that shifters stick together in communities like Four Corners. Good reason, especially for small, non-threatening species like raccoons.

"We're ready to go now," Seb says.

"No fucking in the car." The driver wags his finger in admonition, like we've already broken some unspoken rule. "I charge extra if you're too far into the heat to control yourself or your mate, got it?"

"Yeah. I read your rules for shifters," Seb waves the rude driver off and opens the door for me.

I slide dubiously into the backseat. It's covered in a thick plastic seat cover that crinkles and sticks to my skin and I get the distinct impression this guy is not a fan of shifters, even if he is perfectly willing to take our money. Great.

Seb scoots in close and places a comforting hand on my thigh, but even that isn't enough to have me feeling amorous in front of a potentially hostile static. There are ads playing on the radio, a soft undertone of normalcy juxtaposed against the driver's thinly veiled hostility and the heat and comfort of Seb's thigh pressed against mine.

Seb confirms the address. Our driver grumbles something about premium pricing as he pulls away from Four Corners and onto the highway. He cranks the music when the ad break ends, so at least we don't have to sit in awkward silence or make small talk.

I stare out the window as the ubiquitous Maine balsam firs that have become an integral part of the smell of home give way from lining both sides of the road to rocky stretches of the Atlantic coastline. Even at this hour, the glow of Portland's lights blots out the endless expanse of stars as we approach our destination.

Seb pays the driver in the app and waits until he pulls out of sight to lead me the last couple of blocks from the brightly lit gas station where the driver left us to Gary's home. The swanky loft deep in the Old Port has a buzzer, but someone propped open the security door, whether for us or their own purposes I don't know and don't care.

Seb leads me past an elevator with an out-of-order sign to a dank stairwell that reeks of more than one shifter alpha and sex. Seb certainly has a type. Too bad that type is horny alphas who don't ask too many questions or get attached.

Gary's apartment is on the fifth floor. Seb pauses in front of his door and smiles at me.

"You ready?"

"Yeah?"

"Want another dose to get us back in the mood? Sorry the drive over didn't go quite as smoothly as expected. My usual guy had something come up, and he passed it along to a friend who needed the premium rate. If I'd have known he was that much of a statics first type I'd have gone with a random driver. Or a shifter."

I wave away his apology. "It's fine. But yeah, I could use another dose to get back in the mood, how about you?"

"Sounds good."

I grab the vial of pills and take one for myself and hand the rest to Seb. He swallows his dry. I copy him, gagging a bit on the chalky texture and bitter taste. Seb smiles at me.

"I can't wait to see you begging on a knot," Seb murmurs to me, leaning in closer with every word, but not dropping his voice at all. He's speaking loud enough that the alpha I can smell just on the other side of the propped open door can probably hear every word. "I've told you he has two, right? Imagine how good it's going to be with him buried inside both of us at the same time? Fuck, I can practically feel your slick dripping into my hole while his knot swells already."

I moan softly and Seb kisses the corner of my mouth.

"You want that? To have him tied to us both?"

"Yes," I hiss the answer. I want that and so much more. I want everything with him. All of him. "I want him to take you with both cocks while you're buried inside of me. Coming into my..." I stumble over what to call it. Squeeze my eyes shut because if I'd been born anatomically an omega son who my parents could accept, then I'd only have one hole. A cloaca. Not the vestigial opening to a malformed womb and ambiguous other bits that mean I'll never fit neatly in any primary or secondary gender category, among static humans or shifters.

Seb lifts my chin so that I have to look at him instead of dwelling on my trauma. It's like he can see right into my soul and wipe away the pain.

"I know, darling. You want me to breed you, the way only another omega can, right? That hole is all mine, off limits to any alpha's knot."

"Yeah." I agree. Thankful that he's making sure our alpha du jour knows that hole is off limits to him, even if I let Seb fuck it raw while he watches. There was a short-lived moment when it seemed like I might be able to carry a pregnancy like a static, but the treatments to make it possible ended with my doctor telling my parents that my ovaries were basically post-menopausal and useless. Seb nudges my shoulder, shaking me out of those dark thoughts of the past and what neither of us will ever have.

"Good. I want to be the only one who has you like that," Seb says, his chest puffing up with a pride that doesn't look at all feigned.

His obvious desire makes my own chest ache with a hopeless need for him. The lust from earlier makes a resurgence, not as strong as before, when I was surrounded by shifters I trusted in a place I felt safe, but still there. And I don't want to talk about this anymore, I want to act. I want Seb and Gary to take charge and fuck me. Breed me, even if it's only ever going to be a kinky game.

"Please. Need you. And um, need our alpha," I tack on, because what is taking the damned gator so long?

The door creaks open and a toned alpha muscle jock in nothing but a pair of low-slung lounge pants leans against the frame. "Ah, I'm so glad you made it, pet," he purrs at Seb who slinks up to him and drapes his arms around the alpha's neck to grind against him and kiss along his chiseled jawline.

"Promised I would, didn't I?" Seb asks archly as he rakes his fingers over the alpha's sculpted chest and abs. "Say hi to Rollie, it's his first heat so you better be nice to him."

"Oh?" Gary's eyes flick over me with keen interest. He straightens to his full height, nudging Seb aside and beckons me closer. "Let's have a look at you, lovely."

"Mhm, remember? I told you I was bringing my friend." Seb's eyes narrow in warning, and neither of us needs him to spell out that Seb already told Gary that I'm infertile and this is a synthetic heat for both of us.

I flush at the hollow compliments, but approach Gary obediently. His overpowering alpha pheromones waft over me when he leans in close to scent my neck. Alpha musk is thick in my nostrils as his lips brush my ear. It's not unpleasant, but I miss how Seb's sweet scent fills my senses when it's just the two of us, alone in our bed. Sharing him is better than not getting to smell him in heat at all.

I shiver as Gary's breath tickles me, my breath catching in my throat. "Um, Seb says you're a lot of fun and it's been a while since I've ridden a nice fat knot." I wince internally at how awkward my attempt at flirting sounds. Seb makes it seem so natural and sexy and I sound like a cheesy porno.

"Ah." Gary's gaze goes hooded. "That's right. First timer sharing a heat? Seb says you boys are both good with me nutting inside you?"

"Yeah." I swallow down my reaction to his crude language. He's objectively hot, and he's got that raw alpha appeal Seb likes. His movements are languid as he drapes an arm around each of us and guides us inside his apartment. He shuts the door behind us with his foot, and I hear the lock clicking into place as it latches.

Gary fondles Seb through his shirt, fingers twiddling his nipple piercing as he shepherds us through his open concept living space and into his bedroom. I can't tear my eyes away from where he is touching Seb, the silky silver material of Seb's shirt bunched and twisted under his thick alpha fingers. Gary's other hand rubs along my biceps, fondling me absently as he focuses on making Seb squirm.

I don't mind not being his focus, too busy hanging on Seb's every breathy moan. He's told me that sometimes it feels like those piercings have a direct line to his dick, but I never thought that watching him hump an Alpha's leg while he plays with them would go right to *my* cock. My breath catches in my throat, the need hardening my cock has me hanging on every pinch and twist of Seb's nipple. Gary chuckles.

"You like that, huh? Sebby, he likes watching me torture your tits." He changes his grip to twist the other side. "You want to make him gasp and beg for us too, huh, Rollie? Sebastian, on your back on the bed so I can watch your lover tease you, yes?"

"Please, alpha," Seb whines. Gary kisses his cheek and releases me so that he can swat Seb's ass.

"On the bed, Sebastian."

Seb scrambles onto the huge mattress that's been stripped down to a fitted sheet and flops gracefully onto his back, crunching up enough to gaze at us. He squirms against the narrow confines of his skirt until it rucks up his thighs toward his hips, his legs falling open and oh, he smells indescribably good, like an omega in heat. A pure distillation of himself, but more. His sweet omega arousal is like candy and I breathe him in, wishing I could taste the wet patch on his tight biker shorts where his slick is leaking between his thighs. I want him so much I could burst.

"Now?" Seb whines, squirming more. Gary drops a heavy hand on my shoulder, holding me back as he shakes his head theatrically.

"Not until you're dripping for me, omega." Gary tsks disapprovingly. "Turn around, I want your face hanging over the edge here so you can swallow my cock like a good little slut while Rollie mounts you and plays with you. Neither of you is getting a knot until I say you're slick enough for it. Got it?"

"Yes, alpha." Seb obeys with alacrity, turning so that his shoulders are lined up at the edge of the mattress, his mouth opening eagerly in offering. I glance between the two of them, frozen. It's not that I'm not turned on, just, this isn't anything like the heady thrum of overpowering lust that the first dose set off inside me. When I was breathing in Seb's scent and pressed against his body. I'm not going to get slick regardless, but I don't even know how to begin to pretend like I might and I'm out of my depth.

"What's the matter? Did you get enough of a dose, boy? I want you out of your head with need before you get my knot. I'll make sure you're slick enough for it," he nods his head toward the overnight bag Seb dropped by the door of the bedroom. I swallow hard. Okay. So, Gary gets it.

This is part real, part game and I knew that was what I was agreeing to from the start. It's just hitting me harder than I'd anticipated.

I thought being in heat would make the awkward bits between coming easier.

"Um, I don't know?" I shuffle my feet and pat the pocket with the meds in it.

I've played similar games with Seb before, with other alphas. Just. Being in heat isn't a game I know how to play, and a part of me is starting to regret agreeing to it at all. Not the heat sex. But this part of it. The roleplay that feels like going through the motions of something so integral to being an omega that I'll never actually get to experience.

It's like the marks from a childhood injury I couldn't leave alone until it scarred. An itching, angry scab that I couldn't help picking at until it bled over and over and over until it left a permanent mark on my shoulder. One Seb kisses late at night when he sneaks into our bed and I pretend he didn't wake me up.

I curl my toes and close my eyes and try not to ruin this. It might be the only chance I get to share a heat with Seb. I'd do anything for that. And if I take more of the inducers, then it won't be make believe, a role I'll never really fill. If I take the meds, then I can just be an omega like any other. Like Seb. We can both enjoy the no strings pleasure of a synthetic heat, round after round of coming our brains out with a dominant alpha.

Can I even take another dose so soon, though? Maybe I'm not already consumed with lust because it's not going to work. Maybe the meds are telling me I'm not omega enough for this at all.

Gary steps back, running a hand through his hair. "No pressure," he says. But he's eyeing Seb like he wants to devour him and they both smell horny as fuck.

I need to either take another dose or leave them to it. Shit or get off the pot. I glance at Seb. I don't want to leave without kissing him. I want this. And beyond all the impossible things I want with Seb, I like the idea of both of us being pinned under the alpha he picked for tonight. It felt nice to have his arms around us both, taking control and making it easy to just act on my attraction without shame or worrying I might upset the status quo with Seb.

Seb notices my hesitation and winks at me. "It's okay, Rollie, you can take up to four to kick things off and then another couple every few hours as needed. Or we can go home. Your call."

"I want this," I say, for myself as much as the two of them.

Saying it firms my resolve. I do want this. Every part of it, even the alpha telling us what to do and making his interest in both of us clear. I fish out two more tablets and swallow them. Then I put the lid on the bottle, set it on Gary's dresser, and climb onto the bed with Seb. I straddle his hips to grind our cocks together as I stretch up his body and tease his nipples through his shirt. Seb bucks under me, grinding us together and making our alpha moan.

"Damn, you boys are sexy together. Can't wait to double stuff your tight little asses. Open, Sebby."

I get my first glimpse of Gary's hemipenes. Two hard alpha cocks that jut thick and glistening over the waist of his pants, stacked vertically over his balls. He strokes both shafts idly in his meaty fist as he watches us. Seb wriggles under me, reminding me to keep teasing him. I pinch his nipple then lean in close to lick the hot little nub as Gary slaps his dicks against Seb's cheek. Seb turns his face to chase after them, tongue outstretched in his eagerness to get a taste.

I'm desperate for a taste too. I lick Seb through his silky shirt, kissing and sucking his tender nipple through the fabric. Seb responds beautifully to the contrasting textures, I can feel him trembling under me, he writhes under me and I ride him, both of us seeking the friction we need to find release. It's not enough and every desperate motion perfumes the air with more of Seb, more of the sweet scent of omega and the answering musk of the alpha watching us.

I push the neckline of Seb's shirt aside enough to expose the other nipple so I can watch how tight his nipples get as I gently twist the hoop on the other side. Seb whimpers and arches into me, our hips rocking together as the heady swell of lust builds between us and I can almost forget Gary is in the room with us until he voices his admiration of us.

"Damn you boys are a vision. My very own pair of sweet little omegas, so ready to take my knots, aren't you?" Gary moans, and I glance up to see him gazing at both of us, not just Seb.

I watch in fascination as he lets Seb lap over the crown of one of his cocks, then drives deep into his throat, making him gag. "That's it, Sebby, you love it rough, don't you? Get it nice and wet omega, wet enough to fuck your lover, yeah? I'm gonna double stuff you both with my cream."

Seb moans his agreement, then gags on fat alpha cock as Gary thrusts in even deeper, one hand resting on Seb's throat to hold him in place while the other continues to work his neglected second cock.

And I can't help moaning too, because yeah, the alpha's lines are still corny as hell, but whether taking a double dose did the trick, or it's just smelling Seb in heat and getting to touch him, I'm too horny to overthink my place in this tableau. My place is with Seb, as long as he's here I'm safe to relax and enjoy the way it feels to have a hard cock pressed against mine. I can rut against him and kiss and tease and lick his chest, work my way up to his neck, so I can inhale his scent at one of the pulse points where it is strongest.

I listen to Seb deep throating the alpha who smells so good a few inches away. Seb clutches at me, his hands gripping my ass to grind us together more firmly. The alpha makes more lusty sounds, a sort of rumbly growl that has my inner omega wanting to present for him. When he runs his fingers through my hair, I lean into the caress. I let him gently guide me to lay over Seb in such a way that Gary can nudge the crown of his second hemipenis against my lips.

"You too, Rollie, taste your alpha, little one," Gary urges, but he doesn't thrust in, or force the issue. He isn't rough with me the way he is with Seb. I give him a tentative lick and he groans. "That's it, omega, take it for your alpha."

I open, and it feels nice to have his cock in my mouth, to know that his every thrust is mirrored in Seb's mouth too, both cocks surrounded in our warmth. I shudder at the thought of him behind us, fucking us both. Of feeling just what Seb is feeling as our alpha knots us. I moan around the cock and if my mouth wasn't full of him I'd be begging to have him mount us properly.

I hump more furiously into Seb and he holds me tight, urging me to fuck him harder. Like he wants to share every moment of this with me the same way I want to share it with him. I want our clothes out of the way. I can feel how wet I am for Seb, not omega slick, but the natural fluids that are only really noticeable when I'm out of my mind with lust since starting T. I want Seb there, thrusting into the wet heat. And I want alpha too. Inside both of us.

I might not produce omega slick, even on omega HRT since I was born without the glands to produce it, but I want our shared alpha. To be fucked so thoroughly that I can't tell where I stop and the two shifters with me begin. I just want to float on the heady rush of pheromones that feel like a fever flush of pure unadulterated need.

"That's it. Such good boys. You're so ready for it, huh? Need to come on a knot, don't you?" Gary teases, punctuating his words with gentle thrusts into our mouths.

The alpha's fingers in my hair tighten slightly, not enough to hurt. From the way Seb whines, he's probably in that floaty place he goes when he's into something like this. I kind of want to pull his hair too, the way I know drives him wild, but the angle is awkward all around. Alpha eases his cocks out of our mouths, a string of saliva connects him to Seb's lips as Seb gazes up at us both with an adoringly lust-filled look in his eyes.

This is the fleeting high Seb is always chasing. This innate need to be wanted and worshiped and used. I want to give Seb that, to be enough for him, I nuzzle in behind his ear kissing and nipping until he whines, begging to be used.

"Fuck us, please, Gary. I need it so bad." Seb squirms again, but this time I can tell it's because he wants to get up, reposition himself for the alpha.

"Strip each other for me, then I want you on top of your lover, Sebby, with his ass propped here." Gary plops a rolled-up towel on the edge of the mattress and pats it gently to indicate just where he wants me. So that he can stand to fuck us both at the same time. Seb licks his lips greedily and nips at my shoulder, hurrying me along as I reluctantly peel myself off of him.

Seb tears at my clothes while I watch Gary grab the lube, a synthetic omega slick that's supposed to smell amazing to alphas. It's a sickly sweet to my omega senses. I help Seb squirm free of his clothes, rubbing over his slick hole, teasing him enough to get him back to needy whining instead of that desperate lust-driven need to obey.

Seb kisses my neck and inhales deeply. "You smell so good in heat, Rollie," he murmurs.

"Mhm, you too." I scent him, capturing his lips in a quick kiss. I continue to finger him open, loving the way he moans right into my mouth.

Seb's fingers trace over my cock, rubbing the swollen head of it before dipping into my pussy.

"Mm, you're so wet. You're never this slick outside your heat, are you baby?" Seb kisses along my neck.

I nod, groaning incoherent agreement. It's not just sexy talk. I really am slicker than usual. The way a heat should feel. It's nice, even if it's not exactly what I've fantasized about. The meds can't grow nonexistent slick glands, but they do seem to work to max out the amount of slick we've each got to work with naturally.

"Ready for his knot?" Seb asks me.

"Yeah." I smile at him, yeah. I'm ready. I want this.

Seb guides me into position, then covers me with his body and nothing has ever felt so good as the floaty pleasure of Seb's fingers on and inside me as his weight pins me to the bed and the heat pheromones drive the pleasure beyond the highest heights I've ever imagined.

I was a little afraid this would be like the drunk sex Seb sometimes talks about enjoying. Like I'd be out of control and out of my mind, unable to really understand what I was agreeing to or doing. It's not though.

Or at least, this synthetic version isn't like that for me. It's like permission to turn off the part of my brain that constantly second-guesses how much I'm revealing with Seb and I share an alpha. The heat lets me just enjoy being in bed with someone I want in the depths of my soul. To have the sort of sex that seems too wonderful to even ask for outside a heat, when sex doesn't feel so damn necessary. It lets me act and react in a way that is more myself and less the accumulated residue of every expectation and stereotype that I've been taught to be ashamed of in myself.

Seb's fingers stretching me open are so good, I can't wait until it's his cock filling me. Except Seb eases his slick fingers out and adjusts his position to slip them into my ass instead, preparing me for our shared alpha.

"No! Seb, need you," I whine a protest. I want Seb to push his cock inside of me, my wet pussy clenches on nothing and I squirm to try to get him to take me. I'm so greedy for him to fill me up.

"You two ready?" Gary asks with a low chuckle that reminds me that he's here with us.

"Yes, fuck me," I demand. Gary can fuck me too, as long as I also get Seb inside me.

Seb echoes my words and the alpha's big hands spread my ass cheeks, his fingers gently replacing Seb's inside of my ass so he can make sure I'm ready for his cock.

"Sebby, his little bonus hole is dripping for you, dear. I want to watch you fill Rollie up before I take both of your asses," Gary teases. He steps back to watch.

"That true, Rollie? Need me inside you?" Seb smirks as he lines himself up and teases his cockhead over my slippery pussy lips.

"Yes."

"Yes what?" Seb teases, pushing against me, but not quite inside.

"Please!" I whine, hips bucking up to chase what I want and get him where I want—need—him.

"Please what?"

"Please fuck me, Seb. Fuck me like only you can." Like I only ever want him to fuck me.

Seb pushes inside of me at last. I arch to meet him, Seb fucking me is the best feeling in the world. I have enough of my senses not to blurt out that I love him and I never want him to pull out of me, but only just. Seb fucks into me a few times before pinning me to the bed and murmuring in my ear.

"You feel so good, Rollie. And you're going to feel even better with a fat alpha cock in your other hold. I want to feel him thrusting into us both, making you wild, knotting us both, like we're one tight little hole for him to fill up and breed. You want that, Rollie? Want us both to come inside of you?"

"Yes. Please. Now." I whimper and squirm under him.

"Hush, be patient now, feel me inside of you." Seb teases, moving the barest amount inside of me. "Gary, want to get in on this?"

"That would be my pleasure, you ready for that, Rollie?" Gary asks.

"Mhm," I agree, more than ready.

Gary steps closer again, fingering my ass gently. He uses a syringe thingy to apply enough artificial slick that I can feel it dribbling out of me. Like it would during a natural heat if I had proper slick glands. Seb kisses me, his cock moving inside me as I listen to the squelching sounds of alpha roughly prepping him too. I can feel Seb's slick dribbling over my groin. And then alpha repositions us so the angle works for him to get his hemipenes inside both of us comfortably without Seb having to pull out of me.

Seb kisses me as Gary fucks into us, every thrust driving both his and Seb's cocks deeper inside of me. It's been a while since I've been with an alpha, but not so long that it hurts to have him inside me. And Seb is holding me, rubbing my cock and kissing me like a lover as our alpha grunts and thrusts and comes inside of us both. His dual knots swelling and locking us both to him.

Getting fucked like this is a revelation. Like Seb and I are one omega with two holes for our alpha to fill. Like we're one heart beating in tandem. Like the synthetic heat coursing through us both might consume me and leave only the parts that belong to Seb.

I come so hard I might actually black out for a second. The first round blends into the second and so on until I lose track of time entirely and nothing matters but riding the crest of each orgasm with Seb and Gary.

Nothing matters but sharing this heat and making it last as long as possible. I want to curl up right here in Seb's heart with his cock buried inside me, a knot firmly locked inside of each of us.

I never want it to end, but of course it does. The closeness persists for the ride home with the static driver Seb knows and trusts. Both of us are sated and saturated in the scents of our sex marathon.

That closeness lasts as we climb into our shower and wash away the evidence of the fake heat. Slick and jizz and pheromones swirling down the drain along with all the cozy feelings of forever and mate and love until Seb distances himself. He calls me a good friend for joining him and making sure he didn't do anything stupid during the heat. He curls up in our bed with his back to mine, barely touching me. Back to only allowing himself the scraps of what he wants in unguarded moments.

So. That's it then. We shared an amazing heat and we're back to this again. This veneer of friendship covers over a chasm of unspoken longing and love and dreams neither one of us dares to speak aloud. I can't give him the mating he wants. I can't give him a clutch. And he doesn't see me as anything but a friend he can rely on. I won't ruin that by telling him I want sex to be a regular part of that friendship.

I've seen the distance sex puts between him and his other fuck buddies and I'd rather have the vulnerable sweet side of him with only an occasional side of sex than make him come every night. So I go back to loving him the only way I know how. Quietly, in deeds more than words, and with all my heart. The same way I can feel his love for me.

Chapter 4

Rollie

LIFE GOES BACK TO normal after our shared heat with Gary ends, but even as the last of the snow melts and mud season turns to spring, I can't help feeling different. It seems silly, but there's this subtle sense of having partaken in something if not sacred, then at least special.

It's like I have a whole new insight into the smug way my younger brother sashayed between classes and took his place as a de facto ring leader among the other omegas in our grade after being among the first to get his heats.

I didn't understand it back then. How all my peers sorted themselves into groups I wasn't welcome to be a part of—alpha or omega, it made no difference. I didn't belong on either side of the widening divides among my classmates.

I still don't quite understand why how others view me matters so much, just that it does. It's not that I subscribe to any view of the world that means I'm more of an omega based on a weekend of phenomenal heat sex. There was just something about it that made the experience momentous, so it's jarring that nothing in my life changes in any material way as a result.

Part of me wants to ask for a repeat, but I'm not sure what Seb will say if I do. I don't want to come across as too eager and scare him off by acting clingy. Seb doesn't let lovers get too close. He's already moved on to other fuck buddies, I've only smelled Gary on him a handful of times since our weekend with the alpha.

I know why; Gary was far too sweet with us for Seb's tastes. Not that I keep close tabs on who Seb fucks. That's his business as long as he's being safe. Following our rules about drinking, and using a rideshare if he isn't in a state to fly or drive, and sending me information if he's going home with a stranger.

What matters to me is that he mitigates the risks he takes. That, and if I'm entirely honest, the fact it's always me he comes home to. I'm the one he curls up next to when he dreams. That's always been enough for me. Seb is enough. I just don't know how much longer I can keep telling myself that I don't need to define what we are to each other. During our heat, he felt like my mate, and I can't let go of just how wonderful that was.

I keep looking for signs something might have changed for Seb too, but there's nothing concrete. Just a growing restlessness under the surface that might have more to do with the increasing alpha pungency of his scent.

The ongoing medication shortage has really been messing with both our hormones. I've been getting more headaches and weird mood swings lately. And weird dreams that disrupt my sleep, but that could be partly because Seb has been sleeping poorly too, waking me with his tossing and turning. He's depressed and edging toward the sort of downward spiral that scares me.

Seb blames his moodiness on being tired from picking up extra odd jobs around town as a distraction from the dysphoria, and to save up for extra blood tests. He watches hatchlings at the flock building and does deliveries on the wing. I put in extra hours at the market to cover heat leaves for several of my coworkers.

Plenty of shifter species plan their heats for the spring to align with natural cycles, so it's natural to need a dose adjustment this time of year. Seb claims the generic hormones we're taking are the same as what we've been on for years without any issues. That's clearly not the case though. I can tell the more pronounced alpha traits are taking a toll on him and I've been feeling more and more strange since the change in meds.

Something is off about the new brand of hormones, no matter how positive a spin Seb puts on the entire situation being temporary. I know the facts don't quite add up, but my only other option is to stop the meds and go back to presenting as a beta. Feeling wrong in my skin. My static endocrinologist also manages my testosterone and the other hormonal imbalances related to my messy genetics, so I don't dare to find out what will happen if he finds out I've been skirting the law to get my O. I can't risk losing my T and the other meds I need over this.

It's less scary to take Seb's reassurances at face value. Sure, our side effects lately are strange. Just not quite strange enough to merit risking other aspects of my health. Not strange enough to press Seb on where he gets our meds. We're just still adjusting to the brand change. That has to be all it is. Nothing to fret about.

Life goes on. With spring comes a slew of raven birthday celebrations. Seb and I attend family dinners together as usual. I tease Seb about complicated raven traditions when we pick out gifts for his youngest niblings, first for Leighton's birthday and then Kyrie's hatchday. I follow their alpha parent's lead, calling them twins, despite their asynchronous birthday celebrations.

Seb keeps brushing off the continuing side effects from the new medication, always telling me it's temporary until the shortage with our usual brand is resolved. Pretending neither of us notices how miserably dysphoric every new alpha trait makes him. I recognize the signs of a crash coming with him, and family parties with his young niblings always hit him hard, though.

I keep asking if we can talk about it, but there's always something more pressing going on. I have to put my foot down and insist that we are discussing it after Kyrie's party, but he still claims that we're just both overtired from picking up extra hours. He's not wrong, even if it feels like an excuse. I don't have time to press the issue before the party though, because the dairy cooler has been acting up and Harvey calls me in on my day off to cover a shift while he works out some logistics.

So instead of spending the day of Kyrie's party with Seb helping his clutchmates prepare for the party, I spend the day covering an extra opening shift for Harvey. The cooler we've been battling to keep running is making a new weird sound; it's a matter of time before we can't put off replacing it any longer. My boss spends the day in the office tracking down a replacement and calling around for quotes for a last-minute installation to compare with the latest repair quotes.

To complicate the issue, as I expected, rumors about Harvey renovating the market to expand the freezer section have spread around the entire town on raven's wings in the months since Elric's fledging party. The workers Harvey has called in to assess repair costs for the faulty refrigeration unit have only fueled those rumors. Harvey commented on the gossip with a knowing smile in my direction the last time we worked together, but he doesn't seem to blame me for starting it.

I even caught him looking speculatively at the area across from the dairy coolers and taking measurements after hours, like he's sizing up how to rearrange things. I make sure my projected profit spreadsheets for expansion are up to date, just in case. But Harvey isn't in the store for most of the day as I handle managing the day-to-day operations for him.

Seb calls me during my lunch break and I all but pounce on my phone to answer it. Mel, who has only picked at her sandwich, raises an amused brow at my overeager reaction as she wraps up her untasted food and shoves it back into the breakroom fridge. She waves at me as she heads back to her register.

"Hi?" I answer the call and wiggle my fingers at Mel in a wave, mouthing that I'll be right out to join her and the other young cashier working with us today soon.

This is Mel's last shift before she's scheduled to start a week of heat leave, so I've been keeping an eye on her. I suspect I'll need to send her home early today, but not yet. Her scent is a little different from usual, but not yet that overripe off-putting omega sweetness I associate with a heat that would have me bundling her out the door. I have time to finish my food and take a quick call for now.

"Hey, Rollie! I assume since you answered you have a quick second?" Seb's voice pours over me, warming me to my toes.

I try not to examine the giddy swoop of pleasure low in my belly at the sound of Seb's voice. I shouldn't miss him when I saw him a few hours ago—fast asleep in our bed—but I do. Or maybe that's the wrong word for the melancholy of his presence in my life and home feeling transient. It's not that I feel like a placeholder, it's just that I can't see a way to be more than that and give him the life he deserves, full of love and family and kids of his own to dote on.

"Sure," I agree, no need to point out that I will always make time for him. "What's up?"

"Awesome! So, I just have a quick favor, since you're there anyway. Bram is in a mood because Kyrie is teething so he used the last of the juice to make ice pops for them. Ty was supposed to pick up more juice for the party since Kyrie and Leighton have both been obsessed with it and no other flavor will quench their thirst, but he went to, like, three stores after his shift last night and none of them had the right stuff, and the market wasn't open by the time they got the kids fed and settled for the night." Seb pauses to take a breath.

"Sounds rough," I comment, to show I'm listening.

"Yeah, so now Ty is at work with the car, and Bram is stuck at home with both babies since they gave their second vehicle to Bryony as her graduation gift. So my brother is being a total featherhead and grumbling that he's going to walk over there with both babies to pick up their juice himself even though he's ready to pop out the new baby if he sneezes too hard, so if you have a couple of bottles of that guava nectar juice stuff you can bring home with you, that would be a godsend?" Seb rambles the whole story, parts of it likely verbatim from his brother.

Bram would without a doubt walk across half of Four Corners at full term with two toddlers in tow to make sure Kyrie's celebration is perfect. I have to suppress a laugh at the mental image of Seb's clutchmate balancing as many bottles of his coveted fruit juice as he can carry on his big round belly as he pushes the twins in their stroller.

"I'll check how many we have in stock now, give me a second?" I pack up my lunch stuff, scarfing down the last bite of my blueberry muffin as I stand to put it away.

"No problem. And it's not like there's any rush, so long as I can promise him there will be juice at the party Bram will find something else to stress about. Pretty sure he's nesting and if it's not stockpiling the perfect juice, then it will be something else, so he's lucky we love him too much to duct tape him to his chair and make him relax. Winny and I claimed the two earliest due dates in the betting pool, so she's been texting to tease me that we're going to be neck and neck on predicting the kid's birthday."

Seb's fondness for his siblings is sweet. Most of the time, I love listening to him talk about his family, but today I can't help the ache of longing for connection that his words always inspire in me. It's easier to focus on the task at hand than what might have been with my siblings if they'd seen and accepted me as an omega—or even just looked past my beta status and embraced me as a fellow shifter despite not fitting the binary alpha/omega mold our parents expected us all to fit. It's impossible to know, since the insidious shame of never being enough kept me from even considering that I could fit in with my family and my shifter gaze back home.

I stride to the juice aisle and stop in front of the correct section without having to really look. I've spent enough time in Bram and Ty's home to know which brand of juice they get, so I locate the juice in question, snap a picture to be sure and send it to Seb.

"This one, right?" I ask, lifting one from the shelf to scan at the register with my employee discount. Actually, I'm pretty sure I can find an entire unopened box of them in the stock room and really make Bram's day.

There's a pause as Seb checks the picture. "Yeah, that's the right one! He wanted at least two bottles, but I can pay you back if you want to grab as many as seems reasonable?"

"I've got it, don't worry, tell your brother the juice is covered."

"You sure? I'm good for it, Rollie," Seb insists.

I sigh and roll my eyes. It stings that he doesn't want to accept my help, if I'm honest. But I know it's not about whether he sees me as family, no matter how much a tiny part of me wants to read rejection into his offer to pay. He's told me more than once how sometimes he's convinced I'm going to get sick of him outstaying his welcome in our home. Well—he says *your*, not our, but it is ours in every way that matters.

I might be the one listed on the mortgage for our modest home, but he contributes to the payments and I made him sign a lease agreement when he moved in. At the time, because I listened to my alpha sister telling me to cover my ass, but now I'm glad I did because it means I can point to it and show Seb his name on the contract giving him the right to live there when he says shit like that. It's our home. I want it to always be *our* home. Even if I'm a selfish asshole to want to tie all his charming radiance to myself.

"Fine," I huff out a sigh and roll my eyes at him. "If it's that big of a deal we can go halfsies on the twin's juice. I promise it's not a big deal to me though. I love your niblings too, you know."

"I know." Seb says. His breath catches, like he's going to say something else. Maybe assure me that they see me as family. I know they do. If not the toddlers, then their parents at least. Bram treats me like I'm mated to his brother, and Ty acts like I'm as much mated into the noisy flock as he is. He doesn't offer reassurances, probably because Seb doesn't think I need them. "They still aren't twins though. Clutchmates aren't twins. No matter how many times you and Ty try to say it's the same difference."

That level of nuance is beyond me when I've already been at work since opening with no end to my day in sight. It makes sense to ravens though. I've heard his reasoning, but Bram carried them at the same time and birthed them at the same time, so it really shouldn't matter that Leighton was born in their human form and Kyrie—born in their egg in raven form—hatched roughly a month later. They're twins.

"Agree to disagree. My lunch is over, but I'll stick the juice in my car now so I don't forget it, okay?"

"Sounds good, thank you Rollie. You're a lifesaver."

"Anytime, Seb. I'll be there to get you in a few hours, right?"

"Yep. See you soon. Thanks."

He hangs up, and I listen to the dead air for a moment, wishing for one more moment of connection. Then I go have Lou, one of my favorite coworkers, ring up two cases of juice for Bram's twins. I load them into my car before getting back to work. It's a long, slow day, but that could be because I'm antsy from watching the clock.

I can't wait for my shift to end so I can head over to the party with Seb. His family won't mind if we're a bit late, but I need to be there to support him if this is one of those nights when the reminders of everything he wants and can't have worm their way into his psyche.

I have to ring up a customer, and work picks up steadily from there for a bit, but my day passes in mindless monotony, repeating the same motions and the same small talk. I have too much time to think.

The whole twins versus clutchmates thing is a minor detail, but the key to it is that it means Seb and his clutchmates each grew up having their own hatchday celebration. And now each of Seb's niblings have their own day to be celebrated too. It's the polar opposite to how I felt overlooked and forgotten next to my younger brother growing up, even though we were never wombmates despite sharing a birth year.

Each toddler getting their own party feels remarkable to me, but that's just the way Seb and his family do everything. They treat each other with loving acceptance and a knack for making each member of their family feel special. Like Seb planning to let me experience a synthetic heat with an alpha he knew would treat me well.

It was a gift I didn't think I could have. An experience so intrinsic to how I was raised to define being an omega and yet seemingly impossible for me to know firsthand. Seb saw something I couldn't have articulated about myself and he gave me a chance to embrace being as fully omega as I have ever felt in my life.

The enormity of being understood so deeply is a warmth nestled in my chest. And a growing pressure to gather my courage and ask Seb for what I truly want—a lifetime in his bed. Whether it's the platonic cuddling we've shared for years or something more overtly sexual. It's a thrumming *what if?* that buzzes just under my skin. I should have said something on the phone earlier. Called him out on why he felt the need to repay me for something as trivial as juice for babies we both love. I should talk to him about all the things I want from him. The future I scarcely dare to dream for us.

What if we really could be the mates his entire flock already accepts us as? What if I could be part of a shifter family for real? An omega mate? Enough?

Whenever I think about it lately, my heart pounds a giddy staccato. As I stand by my register during an afternoon lull, I allow myself a brief fantasy of Seb kissing me at the next flock barbeque. Or openly spooning up against me under our pile of colorful mismatched quilts and fuzzy blankets and decorative pillows. Our bed is a riot of colors and textures and shiny beadwork and sequins. A sensory feast of treasures fit to line any raven's nest. A perfect cozy den for two.

I shake myself out of horny raccoon thoughts about snuggling into my den with my mate and try to clear my head. What the heck? I'm not normally so easily distracted at work. Oh. I inhale deeper, testing the air. Mel.

Her scent blockers must have worn off because I can smell the overripe sweetness of her heat pheromones from three aisles away now. She needs to call her mate for a ride home. My mind wanders to thoughts of the shifter my raccoon is convinced should be our mate. Which might mean her pheromones are getting to me—they never did when I was presenting as a beta. Must be the O doing its thing for me, I'll have to tell Seb.

And I'm back to wishing Seb could be my mate. Pure folly. I can't ask him to settle for a broken shifter like me. No matter how much I want a future where I can pull Seb into our den with me, he deserves better. I long to be wrapped in Seb's arms as we exchange lazy kisses that lead to even lazier lovemaking. But then reality slaps into me, because I can't give him the type of traditional mating he wants. No clutch, no alpha. Just two broken omegas clinging to each other while we drown in our own fears.

Even considering the possibility of risking what we have by getting too greedy makes my belly flip sickeningly. It's like tipping over the peak of a rollercoaster into freefall the one time my parents took us to an amusement park for my birthday.

As if celebrating the occasion with their stereotype of how static human families do it would make me embrace the life in exile they imagined was best for me. Seb is the first shifter who made me feel like I belong with my own kind. The contrast between him and my family couldn't be more clear. After our disastrous first ride on the roller coasters, I puked all over my siblings. They didn't take being in the splash zone nearly as well as Seb did the night we met.

Seb is the kindest person I've ever had in my life, even if there is something weird going on with him and our medication. I trust him. He'd tell me if there was anything I needed to worry about. He's everything I picture when my inner raccoon wants nothing more than to inhale the sickly sweet scent of heat pheromones wafting across the store.

I need to focus. Mel. My employee needs to get home to her mate. I probably should have just sent her home at lunch when she had no appetite for lunch. That's a classic sign of an impending heat. I would have noticed her scent changing sooner if I hadn't gotten so distracted with Seb.

"Mel?" I call her name and her head whips toward me with a feral intensity in her eyes. Her badger shifter nature has her ready to meet any perceived threat.

"Hm?" She asks, some of the bow-string tension leaving her muscles when she realizes it's me and I'm not a threat.

"When was your last dose of scent blockers?"

"Dunno? Morning break?" Mel's eyes widen, expression sliding from puzzled to *oh shit* as she gets why I'm asking. "I'll go take another dose. Sorry, boss."

"Yeah, good idea. Might be time to call your mate for a ride too," I suggest in a tone that brooks no argument.

Mel bites her lip. "I can probably make it until five if I just have an extra break to take more scent blockers and a heat suppressor. We were hoping to time it for after my mate drops our kids off with my in-laws tonight, but these things are never as precise as we'd like, you know?" She glances dubiously toward the clock, but I'm already shaking my head. It's easier to focus when I can see the feverish gleam in her eyes.

"No, don't worry about work; do you have a ride home?" I wave away her offer to tough out the rest of the shift. Harvey is firm about enforcing our heat leave policy, and sending her home is the right call, regardless.

"Yeah, my mate was antsy about letting me come in today. She says my scent was already changing at breakfast. I only took the scent blockers to humor her." Mel grimaces. We exchange one of those omega-to-omega looks as she rubs at her lower belly. "I thought she was just being a typical over-protective alpha. Sorry, the cramps are getting to me, you know how it is."

Mel is a newer coworker who isn't familiar with my history so it doesn't even occur to her to question whether I know what she's going through firsthand. Thanks to Seb, I do know. I can reassure her that I've been there and truly mean it.

In the past I've tried to extrapolate the crampy feeling from my handful of pubescent periods to the way I've heard the prodrome of a heat described, but truly understanding the way heat hormones affect my entire body and the heightening of my already shifter-sharp senses as primal instincts come to the fore is new.

"I know, it's intense. You'll feel better once you're home," I assure her. "For now, close your register, go wait in the breakroom and call your mate. I've got things handled out here. I'll come check on you if she's not here in the next fifteen minutes, deal?"

Mel hesitates, then nods and does as I said. "Deal."

Even as I give Mel a sympathetic smile and make sure she has everything she needs to wait for her ride in the breakroom, I can't help a giddy swoop of joy in the pit of my stomach that I can truly relate to an experience I never thought I would have for myself. A shared lexicon, all thanks to Seb.

Mel's mate picks her up less than ten minutes later. With only one other cashier on duty, I have to call Harvey out

119

from his office to help close out Mel's cash drawer properly once she's gone. He notices the way Mel's scent lingers and spends the rest of my work shift in the front helping out until I'm steadier and my thoughts stop looping back to getting Seb naked. Harvey notices my clock-watching and sends me home early.

"Why don't you head out too, Rollie? I know you have a family party tonight, right?"

"Yeah. Sort of. I mean, Seb does," I stammer over correcting him, mostly because I want it to be true so I can really be a part of Seb's family.

If I'm honest, Bram's kids feel more like my niblings than Alan's ever have. I've only been in the same room as my blood-related niece and nephew a handful of times and they largely ignore me to play with the silly animated filters when their omega dad makes them video chat with me to thank me for the holiday gifts I send them.

I can't bring myself to deny that I love Kyrie like family, but I can't claim Seb as my mate and his family as my own either. It's a bitter knot of words to swallow down.

"Ah, still haven't spoken to Sebastian about making things official?" Harvey nods knowingly and claps me on the shoulder as he eases me aside to take up my post behind the cash register.

"No." I admit. It's not like we spend a lot of time talking about my roommate, but he knows I live with Seb and the situation is complicated.

"Here, since I called you in on your day off, I got a little something for the birthday kid, they're avian right?" Harvey hands me a card with Kyrie's name printed on the back in his tidy handwriting.

"Yeah." I nod, choked up at the kind gesture.

"You know what I say about family, Rollie?" he arches a bushy silver brow the same hue as his wolf's wooly under-coat at me.

"It takes more than matching fur to make a pack?" I mutter the truism, unable to hide the hint of a smile at the familiar reminder that he sees me as part of his pack.

"That's right. That applies to feathers too; go celebrate with your flock, son. I appreciate you coming in today to help out." He squeezes my shoulder comfortingly. "And remember that I appreciate everything you do around here. I'm proud of how much you've grown into the man-agement role."

His kind words hit me like a sucker punch. Harvey has been a mentor to me for years, hearing that he's proud of me is—complicated. He had no obligation to take a chance on mentoring me to take over running the market one day. He has other business ventures, and other packless young shifters whom he mentors, but most of the stray young shifters he collects are at least his fellow wolf shifters.

Harvey's lovingly paternal role in my life is everything I wished my parents could be. It took finally moving here to snuff out the vain hope that if I was just good enough, they might love me. Harvey sees my worth more clearly than my actual parents ever have, and much as I love him for it, I'm still mourning what could have been with the raccoon gaze I grew up being a part of. Harvey notices my visceral reaction and hugs me around the shoulder.

Hazards of being close with wolf shifters—they're huggers. Raven shifters show affection with preening gestures and shiny trinkets, wolf shifters show it with touch, getting their scent on you. Raccoons...well—my home gaze always made it clear that I wasn't really one of them despite our shared form. Mostly I show I care with gifts, but I hug Harvey back.

It would have been easy to resent the animal form I share with my family and the gaze of raccoon shifters who made me feel like an outcast growing up. But just because they didn't accept me as one of their own doesn't mean my raccoon isn't integral to every part of me. Much as they might have wanted to, my family couldn't take my fur and all that it entails from me, even if they never made me feel like a part of their gaze.

I love everything about my other form from the warmth of my downy fur on a chilly night to the way my tail helps me to balance on narrow ledges, fingers made for climbing and foraging with my sharpened senses. And I love how Seb always lights up when he sees me in my fur. He gets all sappy about the darker band of fur around my eyes, calling me adorable whenever I look at him too long in my animal form.

I treasure the times I get to bask in his attention. Perching on his shoulders to keep him company on the days he cooks for us. How easily he pets my fur when I curl up beside him on the couch after a long day when human thoughts seem too exhausting to handle. Despite all that, Seb touching me all over can be complicated and confusing because of avian customs around preening. With Harvey it's simpler. His hug is fatherly and warm, and I let myself relax into it for once.

"I hope you know I consider you part of my pack too," Harvey says as he pats my back three times, drawing out the affection as long as I allow it. As soon as I tense to pull away, he steps back to give me space. "Your nibling is turning two, right? You know how we wolf shifters are; pups are a treasure, enjoy your family time and I'll see you tomorrow."

"Yeah. Thanks, Harvey." I'm all choked up, but he gives me a kind smile and pretends not to notice me brushing away tears. I clock out and text Seb that I'm on my way.

Kyrie's hatchday party is just like every other time we're around Seb's family lately. He's happy, while we're there, but I know to brace for another emotional crash afterward. Bram is clearly in full on nesting mode, bossing his mate and siblings around with setting up refreshments and fussing over the decorations. He's got the nursery looking picture perfect already, and he hugs me and tears up like I got him a one-of-a-kind masterpiece when I hand his mate two full boxes of the twins' favorite juice.

"You're a godsend!" Bram noisily kisses the air beside my cheeks, an affectation he must have picked up from the movies he's been binging since he's supposed to be taking it easy with the higher risk mixed species pregnancy. He hasn't been allowed to shift in months and his poor raven is cranky with it, Seb foists his box of juice off onto Ty at the first chance and greets his niblings.

It's obvious my bestie adores Bram's kids. Myra runs up to him and they exchange a complicated handshake.

They chat about her summer plans before her folks joke that they need Seb to teach them his interrogation skills. Bram laments that the pre-teen omega only shrugs and gives two-word answers when he and Ty ask about her day.

Myra flounces off, acting too cool to hang out with the adults and toddlers. She disappears into the living room to play video games with Cory and Elric.

"So, guess I'm all but officially not the coolest uncle anymore?" Seb stares after his niece, then turns and pouts at his brother. Cory technically still has to have his fledging ceremony before he makes 'uncle' his flock-official title for the niblings to use, but Seb's point stands. Especially now that Elric has their fledging officially entered into the flock records.

Bram laughs. His layers of bauble necklaces clack together when he fiddles with them. He claps Seb on the shoulder, hugging him awkwardly with his big round belly in the way. "Don't take it personally. She's having *a day*."

Bram's mate, Ty, snorts. Their skirt swishes around their ankles as they come to greet us, a toddler on each hip. Ty gives a rueful shake of her head. "I keep telling these cubs they should stay this little instead of growing into surly teenagers."

Ty's voice lilts up toward baby talk as she turns toward each toddler, kissing their chubby cheeks. Leighton squirms to get free, shifting into their raven form and swooping over to Seb's shoulder. Ty yelps as the kid escapes their grasp, clutching Kyrie tighter until the hatchday kid squawks indignantly.

"Still not used to that," Ty says, her free hand going to her throat, as if to calm her fear-quickened pulse.

I'm not used to avian shifter babies taking flight on a whim either—I sympathize with the startled expression on their mapa's face. Sudden shifts like that are less alarming with the older kids who are more than capable of running around on two legs as well as on the wing. Or with raccoon kits who have the sense to stay on all fours and clinging to their caretakers when they shift.

Seb coos to the little raven on his shoulder. Leighton tilts their head to demand Seb scratch itchy pin feathers for them.

Kyrie reaches for him too. "Unca Sev!"

Seb takes the kid from their parent, and lifts Kyrie up into the air, making them giggle with glee and throw their arms wide like they're flying.

"Wheee!" Kyrie shrieks. Leighton flaps in a croaking circuit of the room, unhappy with their perch moving on them. I watch Seb grinning at his giggling nibling. The way he looks holding his brother's child makes my heart ache for him. He should have this too. It's not fair.

I wish I could give him the life of his dreams. I can't. Even if it weren't for his creep diagnosis, I couldn't have kids with him, or offer to carry a clutch for him. The difference between us is that I've known since puberty that it's not possible for me. I've had time to accept that my happily ever after doesn't hold a baby shifter who looks like me and shares my form or my mate's laughing eyes. The thing about living in Four Corners is, I've seen that family goes so much deeper than a shared second form.

My parents raised me among other raccoon shifters, but I never felt as accepted among them as I do here in a mixed shifter community. Even though I presented as a beta when I first moved here, the better part of a decade later, everyone knows me as the omega I am. Four Corners and Seb's rave in particular, has welcomed me with open arms.

Even as I think that, Bram comes over and hugs me, just as warm with me as always. I hold out the gift bag Seb and I stuffed full of goodies for the hatchday kid.

Bram takes the gift, then he nudges me toward the spread of refreshments in the kitchen and dining room where most of the family has gathered.

"Glad you could make it, Rollie. How've you been?" Bram asks.

"Fine. Staying busy." I shuffle toward the snacks and grab a few juicy berries off a fruit tray.

"That's good. I don't suppose the shop needs extra help? I'm getting so sick of being on a forced sabbatical with the zoo until this stubborn little cub makes their grand entry. Dr. Martinez said if this clutch was in raven form then I could shift up to birth, but they're a stubborn little cub like their mapa, giving me grief already. We're thinking of Rascal as a hatch name." Bram rubs a hand fondly over his belly, his teasing words at odds with how clearly he already adores the new addition to his family.

I try not to wonder what it would be like to experience that. Or to watch Seb glowing with a new life growing inside him. I try not to let envy override the fact that I like Bram and I'm happy for him. Still, I'm guiltily glad it's not a lie when I say, "I'm sorry, we're not hiring at the moment."

"Too bad. I figured that was a long shot." Bram grimaces. "Harvey isn't my biggest fan anyway. You screw up one hunt..."

Bram mumbles to himself about wolf shifters taking hunting too seriously. Harvey is one of the pack's more influential alphas in addition to owning several of the Four Corners wolf pack's business ventures. I've heard the way the young raven shifters and their wolf counterparts gossip about each other. Both groups of shifters have a long-standing tradition of working together to train their youngsters in how to hunt in the animal forms.

"Mhm." I nod along sympathetically, not wanting to contradict him or badmouth my boss.

From what Seb's told me, there was more than one spoiled hunt that got Bram on the wolf shifter pack's no-hire list, but I'm not about to get in the middle of that drama.

"Oh! That reminds me." Bram touches my wrist, fingers brushing gently over the bracelet Seb gave me for the holidays in a gesture meant to make me focus on him. "Seb said he'd think about covering for me during my leave at the zoo, since Freya and Theron are expecting too. Theron gets broody with his clutches. So I got a couple of the cousins to apply, but if Seb takes even a part-time position, they have shifter medical specialists on staff to do a full work up."

"That would be good." I nod along, gently withdrawing from his hold to add a cookie to my plate. If Seb wasn't dead set against working outside the shifter community, then I might even try to convince him to hear his brother out about the job, just for that.

"Yes, so I've been meaning to see if you'd try to convince him to apply? He listens to you. And Dr. Martinez is amazing. He's even found ways to help avian shifters with creep have a clutch. Not carrying a pregnancy yet, but he's working with a clinic that has helped several avian shifters with creep who present as alphas successfully get their omega mates pregnant."

"That sounds like a major breakthrough." Hope for Seb soars inside me.

"Yeah, for now they've only found ways to make it work with alpha HRT, but maybe they'll find a way to stimulate ovulation too, now that there's some basis for hoping creep can be at least partially reversed?"

"Maybe." My face falls, the dim ember of hope for Seb to get his happily ever after crashes and burns at the mention of needing to take alpha hormones for the treatment.

If I know anything about Seb, it's that he would never want to purposely present as an alpha. Even if it meant siring a clutch of his own with a hypothetical healthy omega mate. I doubt he'd even consider it and I'm certain Bram has mentioned the possibility because sure as Seb will go to any length to bury his emotions until they fester and rot, Bram can't help blurting out every well-meaning thought that enters his head if he thinks he can help someone he loves.

"Well, the best part is that it's all covered as part of his compensation and Dr. Martinez is basically the top expert in the US, he works with the clinic that developed the protocol. And if he says that Seb needs a more expensive brand of hormone replacement, that will be covered by the zoo insurance too. Regardless, the doc will do a full workup on him to see why his meds aren't working the way they're supposed to. I know he's sensitive about it so I try not to pry into his medical stuff, but we all worry about him. So this would be perfect!"

"His meds aren't working?" I ask, alarm bells going off in the back of my mind. Something isn't adding up. Seb gets the meds for us both. Anytime I've had doubts about how he does that, Seb claims everything is fine. He says it's all under control and the way he smells like an alpha sometimes is just the expected progression of his condition. Or more recently he claims it's all a weird side effect from our change in suppliers. We don't lie to each other. Not about something like that, so I've let it drop. But it sounds like Bram is saying this isn't typical.

"Well, no? I don't know how much he's told you about creep in avian shifters?" Bram shuffles his feet, looking as though he'd rather fly away from this conversation if he dared take to his feathers. Well, too bad for him. I need answers about whatever fears and doubts have been eating Seb alive for years now. Since before he moved in with me.

"He told me that most avian omegas have one dominant ovary and creep attacks it. The other, under-developed, ovary sometimes starts to grow into a testicle if they leave it untreated. But he's on hormone replacement therapy, so at worst his other ovary should remain dormant. And the part that bothers him the most is infertility and not having heats anymore."

"Yeah." Bram nods. "That's a pretty good summary." He glances over my shoulder to where Seb is still playing with Kyrie.

Seb's got a big grin plastered all over his face as he focuses on his youngest nibling. My heart aches for him and the unfairness of life. I know he adores his brother's kids. And equally, I know how low his mood will sink later when we go home and the silence of our home emphasizes that he's never going to have a clutch of his own to make the rooms echo with giggles and laughter.

No raucous calls of a baby raven perched near the roof or the rough and tumble of a furry little cub playfully attacking his feet. No sleepy kits with their furry little masks napping in our colorful cuddle pile of soft things.

Our walls will just echo silence back at us tonight, emphasizing the absence. Not that we're even a couple. But maybe that's worse. Maybe I'm in the way of him finding a mate who could at least give him the companionship he keeps looking for in strangers' beds.

Bram rubs at his belly, as though he's thinking similar thoughts and needs reassurance that his picture perfect family is real.

"So, what's the problem?"

Bram bites his lip, shakes his head and then blurts. "I figured you knew? I mean, I can always smell alpha on him, even when he's not—you know—with an alpha."

"Isn't that typical with creep?" I ask. Seb told me it is. He promised I didn't need to worry.

"Untreated creep in an avian, yes. Not on HRT." Bram shakes his head. "Seb's hormone levels never seem to be high enough to keep him in the omega range. So he looks and smells more alpha, and the more it happens, the more his body will keep making the alpha hormones that make him appear more typically alpha."

"Oh." That's not what Seb would want at all. There has to be a way to stop it. A reason it's happening.

"I mean, I don't care how Seb presents." Bram flaps his hands in front of him, as if to wave away the very notion. "He's my clutchmate and I love him. To me, it's simple, as long as he tells us he's an omega, that's who he is, no matter what goes on with his health. But Ty says that's not enough when your body feels wrong, and she would know better than me." Bram shrugs. "They say being trans isn't the same as what's going on with Seb, either. More like being intersex, if he was static? Only that's not quite right either, since it's his secondary gender and that's a static human term. Maybe more like a beta? All I know is that his hormones aren't matching up with the rest of his anatomy or who he is in his heart, and it sucks."

"And the zoo medical people can help?" I ask, grasping onto hope instead of getting into the semantics of it all. Technically creep meets the definition for considering a shifter a beta, but that's an oversimplification and it's far from the point.

"Felix thinks so, yeah." Bram nods. "So that's why I think he should consider applying at Willowdale. They can make sure he's healthy. And who knows, maybe they could even help him have a clutch someday. For now they've only had success with using alpha HRT, but Felix says they're working on something to go the other way and it looks promising. If it works, he might be able to have a clutch some day."

"Don't tell Seb that!" I snap without thinking. False hope would only hurt Seb. And dangling an unproven miracle cure in front of him to manipulate him into doing what Bram thinks is best would be cruel, not to mention manipulative. I won't be a party to that. Not at all. "Not unless you know for sure it's real."

"Oh, no. Of course not." Bram looks taken aback at my vehemence, and I make an effort to smooth my face. He doesn't know that he stepped on a raw nerve with his meddling. Bram does it because he truly loves his family. It's not about saving face with other shifters or controlling Seb. He isn't like my parents. "That's why I told you. He listens to you and I really think they could help him." Bram looks sad as we both glance over at his brother.

Seb is on the ground now, with Kyrie and Leighton both clamoring over him in their bear cub forms, as though he's a climbing structure for their amusement. I wish I could give him the sort of family Bram is building with his mate. Even if I'm not a part of that picture. Even if it means encouraging him to take a job that forces him outside of his comfort zone and pushing him to meet someone who can give him the family he wants. Sick dread pools in my gut and I don't think I'm going to be able to eat any of the snacks on display in front of us.

"Yeah. I'll mention he should apply," I promise, stepping away from Bram and the refreshments.

I can't give Seb all his dreams, but if I can play even a tiny role in helping him get comfortable in his own skin again, that's more than enough. Especially if the nauseating realization taking root in the pit of my stomach proves to be founded.

Seb wouldn't hurt himself to help me, would he? Of course he would. I'd do the same for him in a heartbeat. Even if it means letting him go. I'm pretty sure I figured out where he gets our medication and why his dose isn't high enough to stave off his creep symptoms.

It was monumentally naïve of me not to realize the truth ages ago. Seb didn't find a way to get me a dubiously legal prescription of my own, he's been splitting his with me. Seb has been lying to me and hurting himself right in front of me for years. Fuck.

As soon as I can do so politely, I duck into the bathroom to shift in private. Then I retreat to the living room to spend most of the party in my fur. They ignore me for the most part and it's mindlessly soothing to watch the teens play video games and stream an amateur ghost-hunter exploring a haunted hotel.

I wait until after the party to bring up what Bram and I discussed with Seb. It feels wrong, an unsettled squirming in my gut, to have talked about him behind his back. But

I can't just sit on what Bram told me. Not when I keep circling back to the growing certainty that my happiness is being bought at the price of his health. Besides, this is the missing piece to the conversation he promised me we could have tonight. Now.

I should have questioned where Seb has been getting my medication before now. All the little details that never added up suddenly make sense. The fact he didn't need a prescription for me. That the pills for both of us come prepackaged in matching pill organizers. The fact our meds look the same even though his dose as an avian shifter with creep is supposed to be double mine as a mammalian shifter. The half tablets. Fuck. Was I truly that willfully ignorant about what he was sacrificing for me?

Tonight isn't the time to confront him for lying to me. I know that. If for no other reason, then simply because I know how triggering it will be to hear someone I love and trust admit that he took away my choices when he withheld important medical information from me.

I can't stay calm if we discuss that part of this while it's still so new and raw, but I also can't hold in the anger and shame at not noticing sooner. Or banish my fear of what this might have done to him. I glance over to see Seb's fingers clenches on the steering wheel, a partial shift turning his nails talon-like with the typical restlessness I expect of him when he can't stand to hear his own thoughts for another second. Yeah, he's already planning where to find some nameless alpha to fuck him senseless. We have to have this conversation tonight. Before he hurts himself.

"Seb?" I try to get his attention as he drives us the short distance from Bram's place back to our home. He is so intent on the road, I can almost believe he didn't hear me.

"Sebastian?" I repeat.

I never call him by his full name; it makes him flinch. He heard me.

My voice trembles with nerves because I don't know how this confrontation is going to go when we're both in the wrong place for a fight. My head is reeling, and it all comes back to the same cardinal point. Seb lied to me about something huge. Something that matters. He denied me a choice about myself.

"What?" his voice cracks like a whip and I flinch. "Are you going to ask me to stay home tonight? Tell me to be a good omega for you?"

"No." My mouth goes dry.

"Good. Because I don't think I can handle sitting at home and knowing I'll never have all of that—what Bram has."

"You could." My voice lacks conviction.

Seb shakes his head sharply. "No."

"Why not?"

"How would I support kids? Who would trust me with them? I have a record, remember? The DUI? They deserve better than I can give them." Seb turns his back on me.

I bite my cheek because there is no way on earth I could forget that night. No matter how much I wish it never happened. I have nightmares about sleeping through his phone call that night. Or hesitating before messaging his brother to call 911 and using the tracking app on his phone to send help that barely arrived in time.

Fighting about it isn't going to fix anything though, so I force myself to remain calm. I can't bring up the lies about our HRT when he's already this close to the edge. We need to talk about that part, but not tonight.

"You could get a job outside Four Corners." I keep my tone neutral. "Bram says the zoo needs more raven shifters. I bet they'd help you adopt. Or hell, your clutchmates would do anything for you. Have you asked them about surrogacy?"

Seb recoils like I slapped him. "I wouldn't do that."

"No?"

"No." He shakes his head vehemently. "Bram couldn't give up a clutch he carried. I know my brother."

"What about Winny?"

Seb shakes his head again. "No."

"If I could..."

"I'd have a clutch with you in a heartbeat if we could, Rollie. But we can't."

I don't bother arguing. I might smell like an omega now, thanks to the havoc switching to the generic formulation of his medication is having on us both.

The point we're both dancing around is that I still lack some of the necessary organs to carry kits. It's okay, the HRT has given me more than I dared to hope for. It's enough for me. I can even have synthetically induced heats now. Sure, they're not fertile and I have to use synthetic slick to help things along if I want to take a knot comfortably, but I get all the other symptoms. It's one of the most validating things I've ever experienced, even the feverish flush to my skin, and the unpleasant cramps and nausea leading up to it.

"What about the zoo?" I try again to give Seb a better way forward. I promised Bram that I'd ask, and it might actually be good for Seb to get checked out by the shifter specialists there.

"Did Bram put you up to asking me that?" Seb demands, voice flat. That's worse than annoyance or anger.

"He mentioned they're hiring to cover his parental leave. But I think you might enjoy having more of a set schedule."

"Less time to mope around your house, you mean."

Ouch, the fact he still doesn't see it as ours is a low blow. I press a fist to my chest, as if I can ease the non-corporeal ache those words cause.

"No, it's just one option. Something to give you purpose. It doesn't have to be the zoo. But everyone here knows you. They have...certain ideas..."

"I've got a bad reputation. I know."

"Yeah." I don't bother denying what we both know. It's one of the reasons he leaves the town for most of his hookups these days.

Seb takes a deep breath and lets it out slowly. "If you want me to apply for a job at the zoo, I'll do it. On one condition."

"What's that?"

"You apply too." Seb turns toward me, a challenge in his bright eyes.

"Me?" I ask, taken aback. "Who wants to see a raccoon at a zoo? They can see us in their backyards."

Seb rolls his eyes. "They can see ravens in their yards too. We're ubiquitous. Heck, this is Maine; they can see bears like Ty and deer and moose and all sorts of static animals out in nature, if they wanted to. The point of the zoo is that it makes it easy to see lots of animals gathered in one place. And maybe learn enough about us to get involved with conservation efforts for static animals. Or at least support shifter rights, because we made them smile for an afternoon."

I shrug. "Okay. If you apply, so will I." And if he can withhold key information, so can I. A promise to apply is not a promise to accept if they offer me the job.

"Really?" Seb arches a brow. "Even if it means quitting at the market?"

"Is that what you want?" I ask, his request making more sense. He's never liked me working there. I'm not sure what he has against the local wolf pack. I know Bram had some issues scouting on hunts when he was a fledgling. Winny mentioned that Seb's first heartbreak was a wolf shifter alpha. But surely that's not a reason to ask me to leave a job I love?

Seb sniffs, refusing to meet my eyes. "You stink of wet dog when you get home."

"I smell like wolf shifter, because Harvey is my boss," I say. Harvey and Seb are the two shifters who first made Four Corners feel like a place I could call home. Seb has to realize how much he is asking for with this request.

Seb grinds his teeth. "Right."

"And you don't like that?"

"I don't like wolf alphas." He sets his jaw. Right. I don't push for more details, Seb has enough exes for me to guess why. And that isn't probably not my business unless he chooses to share details.

"Okay. I'm still not sure they'll take a raccoon, but I'll apply if it will make you happy, Seb." Nothing says I have to take the zoo job, even if I get an offer. Or I could still work for Harvey on the side. That's tempting.

An additional consistent income would mean I can spoil my niblings more, get Seb something extra sparkly for his hatchday. Or pay off my mortgage faster. Heck, if I take the weekend shifts at the zoo and stick with my weekday managerial schedule at the market, I might even be able to save up enough to approach Harvey about buying into the business as a partner sooner. It's something he's mentioned in the past.

For now, that's still a far off future plan. Harvey runs so many of the local wolf pack's businesses here in Four Corners that he's always on the lookout for dedicated employees to invest in training.

Seb knows I want to build my career at the market. He just doesn't know that I have a real chance to buy into the business and maybe even own it entirely someday when Harvey is ready to retire. It's another gut punch for him to ask me to give it up because he doesn't want me to smell like another alpha, considering how often he crawls into the bed we share smelling like some strange alpha's cum and of a pain that has nothing to do with the physical.

"What will make me happy is if you get seen by a doctor who will actually listen to you and give you the help you need." He juts out his chin belligerently. "And stop believing the pretty lies some wolf alpha tells you about how he can make all your dreams come true. As soon as you can't give him what he wants he'll turn on you. That's what they do."

Ah, so Seb knows exactly what he's asking me to turn my back on by leaving my job. And he thinks he's protecting me. I shake my head at his misguided sweetness. Pieces slot together in my head. The ex who left him over his diagnosis overlaps with that first love he's so tight lipped about. The slightly older alpha wolf his clutchmates only whisper about with quietly seething hate.

Bram and Winny assure me that Harvey dealt with the situation as soon as he found out about it. Seb's ex is exiled from the Four Corners pack, no amount of digging gets me much more information than that. Seb has shared just enough for me to piece together that the voice that drives him to his riskiest behaviors probably sounds an awful lot like his ex. Or not him, so much as that hateful shifter's words wormed their way so deep into Seb's psyche that he can't tell they're lies.

Seb tells the story so clinically, it has to hide a world of suffering. He boils it all down to saying he almost got mated before his diagnosis. They figured out he had creep in the early stages because he was trying for a clutch before they made it official. His alpha didn't want a defective mate, so he dumped Seb in the parking lot after the testing confirmed creep. The math on that makes it even worse since we met in our early twenties and Seb had already had his diagnosis for years. I try not to dwell on it because I can't undo his trauma and feeling homicidal toward an alpha I hope to never meet doesn't help anyone.

"Bram says they have great doctors on staff, so that shouldn't be an issue as long as I get the job and can make the hours work. But I'm not quitting at the Market, Seb. You know I like my job and Harvey treats me well." It's on the tip of my tongue to assure him that Harvey isn't like his ex, but that will only plunge his mood into even worse territory, so I leave it at setting a firm boundary around my career.

Seb scowls. "You trust too easily, but fine. Keep the stupid job with the pack. We can still get you checked out by a shifter specialist. The zoo policy covers mates too."

"Mates?" I blink at him, my heart skipping a beat at him saying that in this context. It can't be as simple as Seb just offering my heart's desire to me, just like that?

"Yeah." He clears his throat. "We can tell them we're mated so you can get coverage with my benefits."

Oh. Nope. That hurts. A deep ache. Of course he didn't mean for it to be real.

"We aren't mated, Seb." My mouth goes dry. He can't know that I'd love nothing more than to be his mate. I've never cared about anyone the way I do him. Lying about that might just kill me.

Seb rolls his eyes and reaches over to shove my shoulder. "Duh. But we've been living together for the past two years and we sleep in the same bed."

We share a prescription. It's on the tip of my tongue to throw that in his face, but this isn't the way to bring it up. I need to be calm when we have that chat, and I'm the farthest thing from calm right now.

"So, you think we can just lie to them indefinitely? What if one of us meets someone?" I demand. *Him*, what if *he* meets someone who makes him want more than one night? Where will I be when he leaves me behind to build a family with some alpha? That will hurt regardless, but if he does it after I get a taste of the world seeing us as mated and being allowed and expected to encourage that perception? I don't think I can handle that kind of whiplash.

Seb snorts. "If some lucky shifter sweeps you off your feet, then we can fake break up. Or add him to our mating.

Polyam is a thing, you know. Pretty sure Felix, Bram's boss, is a squirrel shifter. So he should know all about that."

I sigh. "Stereotyping much?"

Seb snorts. "No, it's just how squirrels do things. Like how the rave all likes to nest together." Seb parks in front of our building and sits in the driver's seat without making any move to get out of the vehicle. "You mind if I borrow the car?"

Yes.

"No."

"Cool. I'll get a taxi if I have more than a beer."

"If you have more than a soda," I counter.

Seb sighs loudly, but he nods. "Yes, third mom."

"You want company?" I ignore his taunting. He's baiting me because he wants a fight. A fight or a hard fuck and I'd vastly prefer to give him the latter.

"I want to get every last thought fucked out of my head, Rollie." Seb echoes my thoughts.

I bite back my immediate response, *you don't need to go to a stranger for that.* Instead, I steal myself for the next best thing. The safe option that doesn't risk tipping over the familiar grooves of our friendship. "I could go with you. It's been awhile since we picked up together."

Seb stares at me for a long moment, and I'm certain he's going to reject the offer. "Yeah?"

"Yeah." I nod. "I want to get laid too." Another lie of omission, I want to get laid by him. Only him.

Seb blows out a breath and nods. "Alright then." A hint of a grin plays at his lips. "Let's go find an alpha to fuck us."

"Or, we don't have to find a stranger for that." The words slip out before I can think better of them.

Seb's head whips toward me so fast I'm surprised he doesn't hurt himself. "What?"

"I can fuck you. Better than some stranger. We were good together during our heat. I—if I could have a real heat, then I'd want to share it with you. Only you."

He stares at me and I can't read his expression. Neither of us breaks the tense silence at first. When we do, I'm not sure who moves first, but I lunge toward him and he catches me, his mouth crashing into mine, his fingers clench in the front of my shirt, twisting the fabric and dragging me halfway over the console so he can shove his tongue down my throat. I moan.

He tastes like cinnamon and sugar, sweet as the icing on Kyrie's hatchday cake earlier. I drag my hand down his chest, tugging at the hoop in his left nipple until he gasps into my mouth, a needy whine.

"I'd give you every one of my heats if I had any to give," Seb says. "In a perfect world where I wasn't broken, I'd give you a clutch, Rollie. I'd give you everything you deserve."

"I'd give you a kit if I could too. You aren't broken," I insist. It's on the tip of my tongue to tell him that he's all I want, but I'm too much of a coward for that.

"I don't want to fight. I know we have more to discuss, but I really need to get out of my head for now. Please? Make it hurt, Rollie," Seb's eyes burn into mine. He lets go of my shirt and grabs my shoulders, fingers digging in just this side of painful. Seb clings to me like a lifeline, and I'm not sure which of us is keeping the other afloat. "Please!"

I bite my lip, of course Seb is begging me for the one thing I'm not sure I can give him. I never want to hurt him for real. There's a challenge in his dark eyes though, and I want to meet it. I'm desperate to be enough for him. I twist the hoop through his sensitive nipple, kissing away his gasp in reaction.

Seb moans. He shifts his hold on me to push me back into my chair, following me over the console. He somehow folds himself into the cramped space between me and the dash, crawling into my lap to keep on kissing.

Our breathing comes in ragged asynchronous pants. When Seb straddles me, his ass rubbing over my dick, there's a wet patch of slick already forming between us and I'm so hard I can't think straight.

Seb kisses me with all the desperation of a heat. We make out like we're the only shifters on the planet as Seb gives me a lap dance. The omega I've been crushing on forever is slicking all over me like he's in heat and I'm his mate.

Except none of that can be real. Seb doesn't have heats. He takes dubiously obtained prescription drugs to simulate heats when he wants to get laid. And no matter what we're doing right now or what he suggested about faking it earlier, I'm not his mate. I still let him kiss me stupid and grind his ass against me until I come from the friction. Even then, I don't want it to stop, I want this moment to last forever, because once he comes we'll have to deal with whether this changes everything.

"Come for me Seb, want you to feel good," I encourage him when he arches off of me. I want him to believe he deserves to feel good, but I'll settle for making him come for now.

"Rollie. Can't...I need—" Seb grinds harder, and I know what he needs. I play with his piercings again, tugging and teasing and finally, when I can tell he's close, twisting just the way he likes best.

"Oh, fuck." Seb turns his mouth the crook of my neck, muffling my name with his lips pressed against my skin as he comes in his pants.

Seb grunts and slumps on top of me. I want to hold him, but I'm afraid to end this. Seb coming with me, no buffering presence between us feels like we've ventured into a fantastical topsy-turvy land where all my wildest dreams can come true.

My car smells like us and sex with a musky alpha under-current. As soon as the orgasm fades, Seb's nostrils flare. I know what he's smelling because I smell it too. I love his scent in all of its wonderfully rich variations, but it has always bothered him when he takes on those full-bodied musky alpha undertones. He shudders and scrabbles for the door, his breathing getting ragged again for an entirely different reason.

"I need to go." Seb leans against the door as he fumbles with the latch, all but tumbling out as it opens. "I'm sorry. I can't...I *need* it to hurt, Rollie." He glances back at me, his brows pinched tight, regret clear as he tries to wipe away his pained frown. He drops to his knees in the gravel of our driveway.

"Seb..." I reach for him, wanting to offer comfort. Desperate to know if it's fucking me he regrets or leaving. Before I can react, Seb shifts, his raven form bursts free from his shirt and he launches into the air on powerful wings. I stare helplessly after him as he flies impossibly fast, going where I can't follow.

Neither of us needs to spell out that the hurt he was seeking now makes me sick to think about. What he's going to find has nothing to do with kinky fun. If he just wanted rough sex, I could enjoy that with him. No, he's running away to find a stranger who won't know or care that Seb is looking for an alpha who will harm him without a second thought or a check-in later.

Sex when Seb is in this kind of mood is a way for him to self harm and we both know it. This isn't about anything good for him. He's not chasing a consensual good time, or something he enjoys. It's about punishing himself. He's running toward the same oblivion he almost found on the scariest, worst night of my life when he tried to kill himself.

I thunk my head back against my seat and groan out my frustration. My lap is damp with a combination of our cooling cum and slick, but my afterglow is completely banished by what just happened. Fuck. I can't keep doing this. I can't pretend I can fix this. Him. Or ignore how our broken shards keep tearing each other open.

By the time I collect myself enough to get out of the car, Seb is long gone, probably off to drown out the memory of kissing me with some nameless alpha. While I try to process tonight. Seb kissed me. Made me come and tossed me aside because I can't be the mate he needs. Seb has been lying to me for years about our medication. Or not lying, exactly, but withholding key information about my medical decisions when he knows how traumatic that is for me. I can't reconcile that behavior with the fact that I'm worried sick about him right now instead of livid at him.

I should be angry. We should be fighting. Or discussing or anything. But instead he ran away. He'll find some stranger who can give him the self-destructive things I can't. Some nameless alpha who has more in common with a knife he's using to cut himself open until he bleeds out than a lover. And I'll be left to patch up both of our bloody jagged wounds.

As I lock the car and go through the motions of my bedtime routine alone yet again, it crystalizes something. The time for accepting the status quo is over. We can't continue like this. I love Seb too much to keep letting him hurt us both by refusing to deal with his trauma. We both deserve better.

Chapter 5

Seb

I FLY UNTIL MY wings ache and the city lights go from a distant haze to right below me. It started raining as I flew and it's harder to fly with the water dragging at my feathers and the wind buffeting my body. The bar where I first met Rollie is one of my go to spots, so I'm not surprised that my raven thought to find solace here when I need to rest.

I swoop in to land on the railing of the fire escape. Rollie is still the best treasure I've ever brought home. I know I don't deserve him, even without Marin's voice ringing in my head telling me how thoroughly I fucked up being leaving the way I did tonight.

I shake my feathers flat, letting the water bead off of them and wishing it was as easy to shake off my current mood. I reclaim my human skin as I hop down onto the little platform outside the bar's second floor windows. I can't think properly in my feathers and I need to process what just happened. Besides, I deserve to be cold and shivering in the evening's drizzle. How could I hump my best friend like some sort of rut-crazed alpha and then run away from him?

Part of me wants to shift and go back to beg for his forgiveness. A bigger part longs to climb down the ladder and enter the shifter bar's back door. They keep a bin of clothes in various sizes there for situations like this. Shifters can be rough on clothing.

I could walk in, get pleasantly buzzed, and pick up an alpha. Just like I had planned before Rollie turned my world upside down. The thought of sleeping with someone else after what I just did has me feeling ill. Or maybe it's just the fact that I might have damaged my relationship with Rollie that has my gut roiling.

What just happened?

I kissed my best friend. I kissed him and I liked it and he liked it too. It can't happen again. Best to put the kiss out of my mind and find the alpha who is going to take me home tonight. And it has to be an alpha with the mood I'm in. No omega could compare to the one I left behind to fly here and a beta would just remind me of why I need to do whatever it takes to keep helping Rollie. Even if that means giving in to Bram's meddling and applying for a job at the zoo.

It can't be that bad if my air-head brother can make it work. I might even enjoy it. Maybe. If nothing else, it's probably a great place to meet other shifters. On second thought, if Rollie and I are going to be playing at being mated, I better not hookup at work.

That would probably get messy. I am not going to think about someone else getting to see Rollie coming the way I got to watch him tonight. His lips are so soft and yielding, his scent the sweetest I've ever inhaled. I can't let myself go there with him again. He deserves so much better than me. I need to forget what we did. I need to stop holding him back from the life and love he deserves. Tomorrow I'll call about the zoo thing, get both of our meds figured out and then, once he's stable on the correct dose and form of his medication...once he is ready to thrive as the gorgeous confident omega I already see him as, I'll have to let him go. This is what I deserve. A rough fuck in a filthy alley, time to remember that.

Resolutely, I climb down into the alley and push through the door to the back hallway at my favorite shifter bar. I dig through the bin of discarded clothing until I find a cute sequin-covered camisole. It's femme and shimmery and it will show off my back. I pull it on and keep digging until I find a pair of stretchy silver leggings that match decently well.

No need for pockets when I don't have so much as my phone on me, let alone my wallet or keys. I wince. Well, it's not like I need any of that to find a hookup.

I wish I had my phone, though. Just so I could let Rollie know I'm safe. And to get home later.

The outfit is a touch tight, designed for a more delicate build. But that just means it shows off my assets better. The shirt exposes my midriff when I lift my arms to dance my way through the crowd on the floor. My abs are flat and toned, my skin smooth, with none of the stretch marks my brother has now. I'll never have those.

Leggings aren't usually my favorite, but they make my ass look amazing and I can feel every inch of the alpha who grinds up behind me, nuzzling into my neck to scent me. His hands on my hips are a demand, moving me against him as he gets hard. Using me already. Just the sort of shifter I'm looking for tonight.

"Your place or mine?" he murmurs in my ear. I recognize the voice—Steven. He's an eagle shifter. Natural enemy. My raven recoils from his scent. Static eagles are a threat to raven chicks, and Steven is just the right amount of threatening to me. He'll do.

"Yours," I twist to tell him over my shoulder, letting him grind my body against his erection, all but dry-humping me in the middle of the crowd. His nails dig into my exposed flesh. His smell overpowers the notes of alpha musk in my own scent. Enough that I can pretend they aren't there. That I smell as sweet and lovely as Rollie.

I try to turn in Steven's hold, but he tightens his grip and keeps my back pressed to his front. I don't struggle. Not yet. I'll put up a token fight when we get to his place.

That will get more of a reaction. I want him to give in to a partial shift, just enough to use his wickedly sharp talons on me while we fuck. Pin me in place and take until I have nothing left to give. Like we've done before. Steven is smirking down at me when I glance up at him. He grips my jaw and turns my face for a brutal kiss that tastes of whatever beer he's been drinking. Doesn't matter, he lives a short walk away and does this frequently.

We dance for a couple of songs before he gets tired of foreplay and leads me back to his place. The sex is rough enough to clear my head. The sort of brutal fucking I deserve. He shoves me toward his bed and dives on top of me like the predator he is.

Instead of pulling down my pants, he tears the leggings open to access my hole and fucks me through the ripped seam. No condom, even though we're both avians so there's a miniscule risk of avian shifter specific STIs. Not enough of a risk for me to say anything. It feels good. Raw. He doesn't offer me lube, and I didn't have a chance to apply synthetic slick. Most alphas insist on rubbers to prevent pregnancy. Omegas can get pregnant from sex outside of our heats, but Steven knows that's not a concern with me.

It hurts when he shoves inside the first time, but I can at least still self-lubricate enough not to make it dangerous. Just uncomfortable without prep. Steven fucks me until I'm wet, the scent of my natural slick in the air is almost enough to make me sob in relief. Not completely broken. Part of me still works the way it's supposed to. I can still do this much for an alpha.

"Fuck, you're dry for an omega slut," Steven grunts as he drives into me.

I whimper. So maybe I can't. I can't—

"Feels good. Nice and tight. Almost like you haven't fucked every alpha at the bar." He gives my ass a slap. "Work my cock like the good little slut we both know you are, Sebastian."

So I fuck myself on him, using his dick just as much as he's using my hole. Until I drive him wild enough that he digs his nails into my flanks and drives in deep, pounding me so hard it hurts. Just the way I like it. We're both close to coming when Steven pulls out and flips me onto my back, looming over me.

He wraps one meaty fist around my throat, careful not to actually cut off my air, and the other around his dick and jerks himself fast. His knot is already starting to swell. I can't tear my eyes away from the precum drooling from his tip. My raven is enamored with the way it glistens in the low streetlight coming in through his bedroom windows. I want to lick it up, so I lean toward his dick, into the pressure of his palm.

"Fucking worthless slut, you don't deserve my knot, do you?" he taunts. I'm pretty sure it's meant to be sexy, but it just makes me feel even more empty than the loss of his dick inside me. Hollowed out. Marin's words on another alpha's lips.

"No, Alpha." I shake my head, tears stinging my eyes. Maybe he'll skullfuck me. I'm not ready for this to be over even though at the same time I want to shrink away from him, hide in someplace safe and far from here. My mind flashes to the sumptuous den Rollie and I have made together, my haven. I shove the thought away. I don't deserve that.

"You barely deserve my load at all tonight, slut." Steven slaps his cock against my cheek, the startling sound of it making me flinch. His grip loosens a fraction, pulling me out of the moment. "Open wide and stick out that tongue." Steven shoves his thumb into the corner of my mouth to force my lips wide. He barks a harsh laugh, the role firmly back in place. "You think you earned the right to suck me?"

Then he aims his cock at my face and cums all over me as I vainly try to lick him. He pumps himself hard. I just have time to close my eyes as the first jet of cum splatters over my face, coating my tongue and lips, dribbling down my chin. He moans as he keeps shooting. Alphas make a lot of jizz. Way more than statics. More cum splashes against my face, coating every surface in his sticky warmth.

I breathe through my mouth until he's done so I don't accidentally inhale the mess and choke on it. His alpha musk is overpowering, but I lap up as much of it as I can with him pinning me in place. He eventually releases me and I wipe the jizz away from my eyes with the back of my hand.

Now that it's over, I already know I fucked up by coming here. Oh well. Not like it matters. Avian specific STI testing is another perk of the zoo health insurance I guess. At least I don't have to worry about passing anything along to Rollie, even if I didn't have every intention of avoiding a repeat of what happened in the car. Maybe we'd both be better off if I just didn't go home. I cut that thought off before I can even follow it to the familiar conclusion. I can't do that to him or my family.

I wish Steven would get off of me already. It's no surprise that I'm not even hard anymore by the time he stands and lets me up. Steven walks across the room, turns then tosses his dirty boxers at me from where he dropped them in his haste to get inside my ass. He doesn't glance at me as he says. "Thanks, I needed that. Still having that slick issue, huh?"

"Yeah." I grimace; it's pretty obvious. And contrary to the games we like to play, he's actually a semi-decent guy. For an eagle shifter.

"Well, if you want to stick around for another round, we can use the synthetic slick to help you take my knot next time?"

"Not tonight." I wipe away his release on his boxers. "I should get going."

"You sure?" Steven cocks a brow at me, fisting the base of his cock like he's really like to be milking his knot right now.

"Yeah. Tell me to go?" I ask, because I don't want him to be nice to me and I don't like the sympathetic way he's watching me, his gaze taking in my limp dick and the evidence I didn't come yet.

Steven sighs and rakes a hand through his hair. "Are you sure you're good to leave?"

"Yes, my friend will start to worry if I stay out too late."

"Right. In that case, clean yourself up and get out, slut." Steven gives me a sad, lopsided smile that takes the intended sting out of the words now that the familiar roleplay isn't getting him laid. Well, fuck him.

I run my hands over the cum-sticky sequins on my new shirt with regret. I can't take it with me, much as my raven wants to keep our new shiny prize. The outfit is ruined anyway. I shuck it off, wipe as much of his remaining cum from my skin as I can, preening that mess out of my feathers is always a pain. Once I'm mostly clean, I shift.

I hop up to the perch he has installed on his window. Steven trails after me, he raises his hand like he wants to touch my glossy black feathers. I open my beak in a silent warning. He shakes his head at me and pushes open the vinyl flap covering the window—perks of fucking a fellow avian: easy window access.

"Stay safe, Seb." Steven looks like he wants to say more.

My raven can't get away from his eagle stench fast enough, so I just croak at him as I take to the skies. At least I'll be too busy focusing on staying aloft to think about what would happen if I just...stopped. No. I can't do that. I fly up away from the city, the effort making it obvious that I'll be beyond too exhausted to think about anything once I flap my way home. Just as well, my ass aches and I'm still horny and dissatisfied, but that all seems less pressing with the wind pushing against my whole body.

A strong headwind buffets me as I near the coast, tossing me around as easily as Steven did in his bedroom. For a terrifying moment, the human part of me wonders again what it would be like if I let it toss me beak-over-tail-feathers. Let myself crash down into the unforgiving waves below and never resurface. Good riddance to bad rubbish. No more making Bram take care of me or Rollie clean up after me. No more wrongness.

My raven fixates on the mental image of Rollie, smelling so good under me earlier. Rollie, frantic over me if I don't come home. That pulls me up short. I veer back toward the city and flap my way to safety.

Over dry land, the day's heat is rising up from the concrete of the highway. It's easier to glide here. On the wing, updrafts buoy me along like I'm weightless. All my human cares drift away and I refuse to think about how I could end myself. It's peaceful up here, with nothing between me and the vast starry sky.

Sometimes at night I can almost imagine myself drifting off into the glittering nothing of space. Part of the sparkling void that the earthbound can only gaze upon in awe.

My raven likes the idea that we're a shiny treasure, preening internally at the implicit high praise. My human side knows better, but I don't have to think like him as I soar above the sleeping city. The lights spread before me like someone spilled a trove of glittering jewels onto the ground.

I could admire the stunning view for hours if my stamina was up for that. It's not. There's a terrifying moment where I can't settle between the inner voice of an alpha who I'd give anything to forget telling me with smug satisfaction how that's the entire point, at war with the clear mental image of the devastation on Rollie's face if I don't return to our nest. I bank hard toward home and Rollie. No more thinking, only flying toward my safe cozy nest and the omega I don't deserve waiting in it for me.

Chapter 6

Seb

WHEN I WAKE UP the morning after Kyrie's party, Rollie has already left for work; the spot next to me in our bed is cool to the touch. He was asleep when I got home. I tried not to wake him when I crawled into bed next to him after scrubbing away the lingering traces of Steven's scent.

Rollie didn't wake fully, but he threw an arm and a leg over me, snuggling into me like I used to do with my clutchmates when we were younger and migrated into the same bed after bad dreams.

This morning, half asleep, I want to roll into Rollie's space and bury my nose in his pillows to inhale his sweet omega scent. Instead, I get up and trudge into the kitchen for coffee. Rollie left some in the pot for me. It's still warm.

There's a note next to my mug and I skim it as I sip my lukewarm coffee. I don't bother with creamer or sugar. Too much effort, even though I prefer it sweet. I don't deserve nice things after last night.

The note is simple and to the point: *Call Bram about the zoo job today! We can talk about the mate/insurance fraud thing and getting our HRT side effects sorted over dinner. You promised after Kyrie's party!*

Fuck. A promise is a promise and I can't have another night like last night. The siren song of the sea calling me toward the void kept replaying in my sleep. I'm afraid of what I might do if I don't find a way to block it out.

I've lost track of how many times before this week my brother has offered to help me get hired at the zoo with him, but I couldn't accept before. It is easier to parrot the same lines about exploitation that the elders caw about to warn young shifters against taking jobs in the static world.

Bram can't argue against their wisdom and experience with statics the way he would if I told him the truth; I shouldn't be anyone's idea of who shifters are. I'm a disaster and the only thing I can be relied on to do with any consistency is being a fuckup. Better not to pretend I can be anything more.

Better to self-medicate with sex and booze. Except getting drunk only ever makes my intrusive thoughts louder and meaner. Not to mention the choices I made while drunk scared the people who care about me.

Heck, I scared myself the one time I parked at the top of an overlook near the coast with a full bottle and stared down into the waves until the contents of that bottle were sloshing in my belly. The drop into the waves seemed like a peaceful way out. A hazy slide into oblivion.

I called Rollie that night. To tell him I loved him so he'd know when I was gone. The keys were in the cupholder when I dialed. I'm not sure what I said, but it hurts too much to ask him to relive what he calls the worst night of his life. Whatever I said, it was enough for him to realize what I didn't fully understand at the time. I called him because I needed help that I didn't know how to ask for.

Rollie texted my brother to call 911 while he calmly kept me talking and everything else about that night is a blur. I might never recall the details of how I went from the driver's seat to being back under my parent's roof for the better part of a year while I figured out sobriety and dealt with the fallout of the DUI conviction from that night. Moments stand out in startling clarity.

I recall the ocean brine and the roar of the waves crashing into the rocks. The triumphant high of finally jamming the key into the ignition. The engine rumbling under me as I put the car in gear and rolled toward the wooden barrier that wouldn't have stopped me from following through with my plan.

My ragged breathing echoed in the car as I told Rollie I was scared it would be cold. I remember begging him to tell me he'd forgive me while I nerved myself up to embrace the void that still lurks at the back of my head, a constant companion.

Rollie's voice telling me to hold on a little longer. Flashing lights and rough, urgent hands pulling me out of the driver's seat before I could do what I went to that remote overlook to do. I know from the reports that the police arrived before the ambulance. At the time, it was a haze of chaos and noise. It all added to the disorientation of waking up in the hospital with my righteously indignant family around me, my car impounded, and a court summons for driving under the influence.

I just know the only place I ever intended to drive that night was straight through the rickety wooden barrier in front of my parked car and into the ocean. Marin once told me he should do just that. Claimed he'd be doing the world a favor by ridding it of me as he swerved toward the guardrails separating the highway traffic from the bay. That night was the closest I've come to finishing the job for him. Not even Rollie knows that part. Rollie, who somehow cares about me and doesn't deserve to have that care thrown back in his face. If I can't take the job for myself, I have to do it for Rollie. To fix the medication situation if nothing else.

I call my brother.

"Hey, Seb, what's up?" Bram answers, out of breath, just before his phone kicks me over to voicemail. In the background, Kyrie and Leighton are squabbling and Myra is complaining about her oatmeal.

"Sorry, you sound busy. I can call another time." I'm an idiot for forgetting he's busy in the mornings these days. Obviously, my brother doesn't have time for my trivial bullshit when his kids need him.

"No, it's fine. Ty's just getting Myra out the door, and the twins are playing in their feathers, so it's a little chaotic, but I can talk. How are you?"

Terrible; worse now that I'm listening in on your perfect life. I ignore the question that doesn't have any good answers. "Rollie mentioned you two talked about the zoo needing more raven shifters?"

"We do! Are you interested? It would be fabulous if we could work together, Seb! Once this little one lets me shift again, we could all carpool. Actually, hang on, I bet Ty would bring you in to meet with Felix. Let me call and see if they can squeeze you in for an interview."

"Today?" I all but squawk at his eagerness. I'm not ready. There are probably still flakes of jizz in my hair and everything.

"Sure, why not?" Bram asks, and he has a point. I can't come up with a valid reason to put it off.

"Um, don't these things take time?"

"They do—usually. But I have an in with the boss and I happen to know they are down all three of us ravens this week, so if you can start ASAP, I bet the job would be yours by the end of the morning. You'll love it, Seb, all the attention, people pointing out your pretty feathers. I promise it's fun, and if the crowds get to be too much, there are perches where you can be less in the thick of things, make them hunt for a glimpse of you, ya know?"

That's...way too much. Bram is too much. But my inner raven likes the idea of being the subject of a live action 'Where's Waldo' for a bunch of admiring strangers. Besides, I'm doing this for Rollie. So he can get on the correct dose of omega HRT instead of my DIY approach, giving him headaches and making him moody. "Okay."

"Awesome! Just a second." Bram muffles the receiver, but I still hear him calling to his mate. "Ty, can you bring my brother to the zoo with you after you drop off Myra? Yes, Seb. Obviously not Cory. I'm going to get him an interview with Felix."

Ty's reply is too soft for me to hear.

"No, I know. I'll call as soon as I hang up, but he's going to say yes."

"Of course I'm sure. Here, I'll call right now." Bram's voice gets louder as he addresses me again. "Seb? You still there?"

"Yes." I can't help but be amused at my brother's unbridled enthusiasm. He's too sweet for me to stay jealous that he's got everything I want. I can ache for those things without begrudging him for having his doting mate and adorable children.

"Ty says he'll be right over. I'll call you back if the plan changes. Do you have a suit?"

"Yeah." I grimace. I had to get a suit to appear in court for my DUI conviction. That's an entire downward spiral I'd rather not dwell on. "I'll go change. Thanks, Bram."

"Anytime, Seb. I love you, bro."

"Yeah, love you too. Tell the kids hi for me."

"I will! Oh, shitake mushrooms, Leighton, honey, those curtains aren't strong enough to hold a cub..." There's an ominous creak followed by a loud crash. My muscles tense and my heart leaps to my throat at the implied threat to my nibling's safety.

The miserable toddler wail that comes over the line in the next heartbeat doesn't allay my fears, but it's better than total silence. The next few words are faint as Bram goes to comfort his child. "It's okay, baby, Daddy's got you. You're alright." Leighton's ongoing sniffling sobs imply otherwise. Bram yells to me. "Sorry, Seb, they're fine, but I've got to let you go. Good luck!"

"Bye, tell the brats Uncle Seb loves them." I raise my voice to be heard. Then I hang up; I doubt Bram's close enough to his phone to do it himself. Hopefully he follows through on calling his boss, but even if he doesn't, Ty can still bring me to the administrator's office to fill out an application.

Ty picks me up before I have time to blow up Rollie's phone with nervous texts about everything, from how sorry I am about last night to how nervous I am about applying to work at the zoo. I want to talk to him. To make sure we're okay, but I have less than fifteen minutes to dress up for a potential interview, so there's no time for everything we need to discuss. I scrawl a message at the bottom of Rollie's note that I called Bram and reaffirming our promise to talk tonight.

Ty is presenting masc today, his style is just as whimsical as ever no matter how he's presenting. Today he's wearing a mustard yellow blazer with teal accents and a duck print on a teal pocket square along with his usual gruffly unreadable expression. I'm sure Bram loved the ducks. I smile to myself at how perfect the grumpy bear's sweeter side is for my brother. Maybe someday I can be the sort of shifter who gets to have that kind of picture perfect life.

Ty and I make small talk about the kids and the party and my brother with ease. When we reach the Willowdale zoo where Ty and Bram met, Ty walks me to the main office where an efficient squirrel shifter with a baby napping in a Moses basket beside their desk greets me. I try not to react to the baby's presence. I can handle this.

The newborn makes my heart ache with longing I can't entirely ignore. There's something so sweet and pure about the scent of a baby. I'm not looking forward to Bram's upcoming birth. Having everything I want, but can never have shoved in my face again. Loving another tiny little shifter I can only ever hold for a few hours at a time before I have to hand them back.

"Hey, Pat, this is my brother-in-law, Seb. Bram called about getting him set up in the raven habitat?" Ty nudges me forward.

"That's right, pleased to meet you, Seb." Pat smiles at me, rising to offer a handshake. I oblige them.

"Happy to be here." I paste on a smile.

"Oh, yes, slight change of plans since we spoke. Felix is actually dealing with a minor plumbing emergency in the polar pavilion, so he can't meet with you right now. But Jolene handles the woodlands shifters and she can meet with you to go over the new hire orientation with you once you and I get your paperwork signed."

"New hire?" I repeat, not quite connecting the dots.

"That is why you're here, right?" Pat shoots a puzzled frown between me and Ty.

"Yes. Sorry. I just thought I needed to interview, or fill out an application..." Or else Bram isn't exaggerating about just how desperate they are to hire a temporary replacement raven shifter for my brother's clutch leave.

Pat waves away my concerns. "You're going to be filling in for your brother in Ty's habitat for the weekdays shift, right? Since the two of them vouch for you, I don't see where we'd have any issues."

"Um, I should probably disclose that I've got a record." I mumble the admission toward my toes. It's been an issue in the past. One of the many reasons I've mostly given up applying for jobs outside Four Corners and the safety net of our all-shifter community.

"Oh?" Pat quirks a brow at me, pausing in the middle of sliding the papers across their desk.

"Yeah. DUI. I've been sober since," I explain.

"Oh, well, that's not an issue for us. As long as you have reliable transportation for the duration of your contract?" Pat finishes sliding the papers in front of me.

"I do. So, it's temporary?" My heart sinks. For a second there, it felt like I was actually valuable to someone.

"To start." Pat nods and taps the papers. "I've got a parental leave replacement contract drawn up for you to sign today. If you want to stay on after Bram's parental leave, we can discuss terms for a new contract before this one expires; how does that sound?"

"It sounds good." I force out the words. I'll have access to the medical coverage Rollie and I both need. I hope. Do they offer that to temp workers? Better ask. "Um, what about benefits? Bram mentioned medical coverage?"

"Yes." Pat nods. "We offer full health coverage for shifters and their immediate families. That includes access to our staff physicians, all of whom are board specialized in shifter medicine. I'll email you all the details once you fill out your contact information."

"So, it will cover me and my mate?" I check, glancing at Ty in the hopes of conveying a warning to him not to give away my plans. His gruff expression reveals nothing.

"That's right. We cover mates and any dependent children," Pat says, smiling fondly down at the baby beside their desk.

"When can I sign up?" I ask.

"Right now, Ty, want to grab a coffee while Seb and I handle the contract? Then you can take him to meet Jolene outside your habitat." The coffee is an obvious pretext to give me privacy with my paperwork.

"Sure. Are there any honey crullers today?" Ty goes along with it.

"There are, help yourself." Pat points toward a break room. Ty shrugs out of his colorful blazer, draping it over one arm as he sweeps into the breakroom.

I draw up a chair within arm's reach of the napping squirrel shifter baby to fill out the paperwork. When I get to the insurance form, I write in Rollie's information under the line for my mate. If only that could be true. The bitter irony that I'm committing the same type of insurance fraud I once cautioned Bram against for our sister's shoulder surgery isn't lost on me.

I sleep in Rollie's bed, share his home, and most of our meals. From the outside looking in, it would be hard for an insurance company to prove anything except that I'm a shitty mate with all my infidelity. That's not untrue. I would be a shitty mate.

Still, for as long as it takes to get Rollie the care he needs, it might be best to keep up appearances. I'll just have to be more discreet. Or maybe stop fucking around. That's a small price to pay for Rollie's health. I sign my lies with a flourish and follow meekly after Ty to go do the job my brother loves.

It's not so bad; being admired in my feathers by a bunch of noisy tourists isn't nearly as exciting as being admired by alphas at a bar or club, but it's still a nice little ego boost. I try to ignore all the children running around outside the plexiglass.

The work could be worse. Bram was right that it's nice to be admired in my feathers. All I really have to do is sit around and preen for an admiring crowd. Ty even offers me some of the choicer bits and berries he forages from the enrichment toy another of the keepers delivers to the habitat a little before noon. I suspect that Bram asked Ty to be extra nice to me.

That, or my brother and his mate are both trying to lure me into liking this job. Which is fair, considering my past issues with sticking to anything for more than a couple of months. It's only the first day, but it already feels like this might be different.

Jolene is nice enough, if a bit busy and distracted. By my lunch break, she has my parking pass and security badge taped to the locker I'm using in the changing area. I hesitate before dialing the number for the zoo's shifter health clinic that she scribbled on the back of her card and handed to me during our whirlwind orientation this morning. It doesn't feel quite real to be able to call and schedule this appointment. My palms are sweaty and I crumple the little square of stiff paper in my fist.

I remind myself that I'm doing this for Rollie. Bram, incorrigible gossip that he is, says that Dr. Martinez can fix just about anything that's wrong with a shifter. Even help avian omegas with creep sire a child. It's not the same as bearing a clutch of my own, but it's something. Even if the thought of it makes me sort of shudder.

There's a typical pre-recorded message, and then I take a deep steadying breath as I punch in the extension for zoo staff to reach scheduling. It's too surreal to think that Rollie and I might actually get to see a shifter specialist who can sort out our HRT. I hate asking for help, but this isn't for me, it's for Rollie, so I hold the line as it rings and rings.

My mind wanders back to Bram's gossip about how this doctor helped his boss, Felix, and his trans alpha mate have their kids. What would be like to sire a clutch? Panic grips my chest at the thought. I don't like the idea of being disconnected from my clutch like that. It's not how I ever pictured having a family. For years, I planned to carry my babies under my heart, like my brother. Bram is so happy and round and glowing and I want what he has with a visceral yearning.

The idea of knocking up some omega who gets to have everything I wanted with my child is... too much. It makes my insides feel squirmy. I'm not an alpha. I don't *want* to be an alpha or have an alpha body. Even if it means I could have a clutch of my own some day. It wouldn't be the same. Would it?

For the briefest moment, I can picture Rollie round with a litter of my kits and, okay, I *might* be alright with that. Except Rollie doesn't have heats. He was born a beta, and while we haven't discussed his exact anatomy, male betas generally don't have a womb, so no amount of HRT is going to give him a fertile heat.

I know he's got some static human anatomy instead of a cloaca and that's not what I'm used to. It's possible I could be wrong, but as far as I know, Rollie carrying a pregnancy is impossible. The only omega I'd even consider going on the wrong hormones to impregnate isn't an option, so it's a moot point.

How is the phone still ringing? Jolene said I should be able to get right through on this extension. Then again, it *is* lunchtime. I flatten the crumpled card against my thigh and try to calm my unsteady breathing before I go into a full on panic. I huff out an aggravated sound that would definitely be a scolding squawk if I was in my feathers. So of course that's when someone picks up on the other end.

"Willowdale employee health, Terry speaking." The voice on the other end sounds bored with a thin veneer of customer service chipperness.

"Hi, um, I'm a new temporary hire, but I was told that my mate and I could book appointments regarding medication prescribing and testing for creep?" I wince at how tentative and rambling I sound. My voice pitches up at the end in a plaintive whine. If I have to smell like an alpha, why can't I also have their seemingly unending confidence to go with it?

At least I didn't stumble over calling Rollie my mate. The lie trips from my tongue far too easily, a seductive glimpse of a life I gave up on wanting when the alpha I gave all of my firsts to turned his back on me.

"Sure," Terry clacks away on a keyboard. "I just need your name and date of birth, as well as your mate's information."

I relay the information and Terry makes a tsking sound.

"Hm, it looks like you're not in the system yet. Have you received the medical coverage paperwork yet?" Terry asks.

"Um, maybe? I filled out a whole stack of paperwork this morning." I rack my memory for the specific paperwork.

Pat confirmed everything Bram told me about being eligible for healthcare through the zoo clinic. It still seems too good to be true, but Pat cited something about the zoo's mandate prioritizing shifter health. So that means even temporary workers are fully covered. Maybe I'd have believed in that earnest altruism in another lifetime, but I just skimmed the paperwork that the squirrel shifter pushed in front of me and started filling in the details on autopilot, taking the good for as long as it lasts and worrying about how to handle it ending when that hammer falls.

"Ah, that would do it. In case no one mentioned, our health policy here is..." Distantly, I'm aware of Terry reciting some practiced spiel about all the many and wonderful benefits of becoming part of the Willowdale family of shifters.

Terry clears his throat on the phone, drawing my attention back to the call. "Are you still there?"

"Yes, sorry. I, uh, could you repeat the question?"

Terry sighs. "I'm sure you've had a ton of policy thrown at you all day during orientation, so I'll keep it simple for now. For any urgent health concerns, I can put you on our cancelation list for an appointment. But if you just filed the paperwork, it can take up to a week for your information to be put into the system to schedule a regular appointment and to issue health cards good for any facility that offers shifter healthcare. If we call you with a cancelation at the zoo clinic in the meantime, as long as your mate is listed on your personnel file, the only thing you both need to bring to your appointment is your employee badge as proof of coverage. Any relevant medical records are also helpful."

"Oh, uh. I guess we should just wait for the cards to arrive once we get processed, then?"

"Not at all. Before you convince yourself it's not a priority, uncontrolled or poorly managed creep is considered urgent by our shifter specialists, so you and your mate are going on the cancelation list. Is there anything else I can help you with today?"

"Um, no, I guess not?"

"Great, in that case, we'll call when we have an appointment for you. Dr. Martinez tries to keep wait times for creep related care under a month."

I hang up, waiting for another month isn't that bad. Hope that Terry might call back soon is warring with the worry that this temp job isn't actually going to last that long. How could it last when I always fuck up every good thing?

The irrational urge to destroy that stubborn kernel of budding hope floods through me, driving me to just shove the shiny new employee badge into the locker that smells like my brother. Slam it closed, walk right out of the zoo. It would be so easy to go find some bottle to crawl into the bottom of, or failing that, a stranger to fuck all the emotions out of me until everyone can see me the way I do—nothing but used up garbage.

I stand there, leaning against the thin metal door until it creaks under my human weight. I draw in a deep steadying breath and my lungs fill up with Ty's concerned scent and Bram's sweet pineapple warmth. If I walk off this job, it would hurt them. And it would hurt Rollie.

I toss my phone into the locker. The low battery indicator is flashing as it drops below ten percent, so that will be dead by the end of my shift. That's what I get for not tossing the faulty charging cable that only works at just the right angle. Oh well. I shove my crumpled clothes on top of it, nudge the door shut and shift. Good thing Ty has an extra car charger for after work.

The emotions are different in my feathers. Clearer. My raven knows what it needs, what matters with a decisive simplicity my human side could never match. I ache for my flock.

I hop my way across the concrete floor of the employees only area, through the annoying plastic flaps that cover the bear-sized doorway even though there's an open window near the eaves with perches on either side for the ravens to use now that my brother and his workmates are a permanent part of Ty's habitat here.

I don't feel like flying. It's too much effort. Too lonely to fly when no one else here has the wings to join me, too desolate to call for a flock that won't call back. Instead, I strut my way across the packed dirt of Ty's well-worn path to his favorite napping den and flap noisily up onto his shoulder. Despite his furry bulk, I'm careful to be gentle with my talons as I tuck my beak into his fur to doze in the shady den through the afternoon heat.

Ty isn't my clutchmate, but the big bear alpha still smells like family. He only snuffles and nudges his nose against my tailfeathers when I snuggle next to him in the artificial cave. It's his territory. I shouldn't feel so safe invading an alpha bear's space while he sleeps. But Ty smells of Bram, and the overpowering alpha musk of him drowns out the wrongness of my own scent for a little while.

We stay like that for a long time. I only stir from my cozy perch when the keeper I've heard about in all my brother's work stories brings some sort of enrichment toy that looks like a large plastic barrel for Ty to play with and I flap my way up to the nearest perch with a good view of the crowd. My nap again, and the time in my feathers settles the edgy need to run away from my own skin. At least for now.

The announcement warning the zoo visitors that we're closing soon startles me out of my roost when it sounds over the zoo PA system. I fluff out my feathers with a disgruntled squawk and preen them irritably. Ty, who was snoozing below me before the announcement, snorts in amusement and I croak at him.

He rises up on his rear legs and uses the trunk of the tree I'm perched on to scratch his back. I flex my claws into the bark. A distant part of me recalls my brother mentioning some ridiculous territorial dispute over this tree when the pair started dating and how that somehow translated into feelings for Ty. My brother is welcome to his weird interpretation of how flirting works.

I stretch my wings and prepare to glide into the changing area to shift out of my feathers for the drive home. If I go now, I can probably avoid shifting in front of my brother's mate. It's one thing to touch Ty's bear, it's another to shift together, alone in an enclosed space.

Ty apparently had the same thought, because he doesn't come lumbering through the plastic flaps until I've shut my locker and opened the exterior door to leave. The bear sits on his haunches in front of his locker and waits patiently for me to shut the door behind me before shifting. Shifter senses mean I can hear him rummaging through his things to get dressed.

"Wait right there and I'll drive us home. Bram insists that you and Rollie are joining us for dinner to celebrate your first day," Ty says, knowing I'll hear him through the door vents

"Cool. Sounds good," I mumble back, suppressing a groan.

Bram is terrible at minding his own business. I've basically given up on expecting him not to meddle. Dinner to grill me about my first day at the zoo is tame compared to all but emotionally strong arming me into taking the job though. For all that he has boundary issues, I love Bram. And he's gotten better just by virtue of constantly being busy managing his kids' schedules. My human side is grumpy at being roped into an evening surrounded by his happy family.

My inner raven preens in delight at being included in the flock. At the chance to dote on my niblings and maybe take to my feathers with other ravens for a while. I haven't spent nearly enough time on the wing lately. Maybe that's part of why everything has felt so out of control.

Sure, *that's* the problem; I'm not shifting enough. It's not that I've cut my dose by another third to make sure

Rollie gets the right amount of hormones, since the conversion from avian to mammalian shifter dosing is different for this formulation.

"Ready?" Ty asks as he steps through the door, his blazer in place despite the heat of the day.

"Yeah, can't wait," I agree. And if I meant it to be snarky, I fall short, landing somewhere between earnest and eager.

"Good, we have a few things to pick up on the way first." Ty gestures for me to lead the way toward the employee exit.

The motion set his layers of bangles to clacking on his wrist. The mismatched collection is very clearly made up of gifts from my brother, but Ty wears them daily and smiles sweetly when he notices me looking at the gaudy collection large enough to rival my own. Or the one I've decked Rollie in for years. I swallow down how it makes me feel to acknowledge that Rollie and Ty both dress like they're mated to raven shifters in that sense.

I arch a brow and just barely bite back a snarky comment about him wearing my brother's heart on his sleeve. Just because I want to be able to claim Rollie with that same openness is no reason to take out my mood on Ty. With how kind Ty is being, that would be a poor way to repay him.

Ty seems to read my face anyway, but he only glances pointedly at the shiny rings on my fingers, each a gift from Rollie or one of my sibs. The hodgepodge of pins on my faded denim jacket is made up mostly of gifts from Rollie too. Priceless treasures, the lot of them. Okay. Point conceded. Raven shifter stereotypes might have a basis in reality, and Rollie might share that same impulse to collect treasures and share them with his loved ones.

I try not to think too hard about the collection of pretties on Rollie's bedside table. Or the way I never see him leave the house without one of my gifts displayed. It's too painful to think about the day when he finds a mate and stops wearing my affection so openly. At least that habit will make it easier to sell our little deception long enough to get the medication we both need sorted out.

Chapter 7

Rollie

THE MORNING AFTER KYRIE'S party, I wake up with a dull throbbing in my temples and lower belly. I want to chalk that up to hunger and sleeping poorly after our fight. More of the vivid nightmares I've been having—the ones where Seb never makes it home—kept me tossing and turning. It was almost a relief when Seb woke me from a particularly realistic iteration of that same dream when he slipped into our bed around dawn. Regardless, I sleep like crap and barely make it to work on time and I don't even have a chance to confront Seb about anything from last night.

When I get to the store, Harvey is already there, emptying out the refrigeration unit that's been on the fritz.

Looks like he tracked down a replacement on short notice after all. The damn thing giving up the ghost finally feels like a pretty good summation of how today has gone so far, and I've barely been out of bed for an hour.

I clock in and open my register to help with the line piling up for the single open cashier at this hour. At least when we're busy, I don't have time to dwell on how off I've felt all day. Like I'm coming down with a cold. Ugh, I don't have time to be sick.

There is so much Seb and I need to discuss after work. I just hope he's in a better headspace for a conversation after being out all night. Maybe we can have an early night, since neither of us got enough sleep after he kissed me and ran away from his emotions about it.

Everything seems to be going wrong lately, but I'm clinging to the hope that Seb will meet me halfway if I tell him what I need. If not...well, I can't bring myself to picture that outcome, but my stomach is in knots over the possibility.

The day seems to pass in a rush of demands from grumpy inconvenienced customers even as every hour drags. I'm on the verge of panicky tears over minor set-backs that I normally take in stride. It's got to be because I'm sick. Or tired. Or maybe because things with Seb and me feel so shaky. I wish I could take an extra break to call him to talk, but I don't think I can stop until I say everything that needs to be said once I start. It's not an option. Even if I wasn't extra busy with the fridge repair ongoing and workers tromping through the store to handle that.

It's not even lunch and it's already been a long day running to the backup refrigeration unit in the back storage area to get milk and butter for our regulars. Then again, maybe being busier than usual is just what I need to take my mind off the conversation I need to have with Seb.

As much as I long for his comfort, I can't get past the sense of betrayal over him withholding something so important. He lied to me. Sure, he did it to help me, but it reminds me of my family holding back the facts of my beta status from me for most of my life. They obfuscated key facets of who I am until they couldn't anymore. I don't know if they ever would have told me everything about my genetics and the experimental therapies they tried to make me 'normal' as a kit.

I only found out because a new endocrinologist who wasn't aware of how little I knew mentioned it while asking me questions. So my parents had no choice about coming clean. I'd already been confused about why my scent still hadn't changed the way it should have long past the age when my lack of development set me apart from my shifter peers. My little brother had smelled like an omega for years and I still smelled like a kit.

Whenever I asked what was wrong, they deflected. My parents knew I'd never develop on my own, so they tried to convince me to accept that I'd never be quite welcome amongst the alphas or the other omegas. Far from giving me the answers about myself that I'd craved and needed, my parents did their best to hide that they'd known what was wrong with me all along. When I did find out, it was easy to figure out why. They were ashamed I'd never fit neatly into a secondary gender they understood.

And much as I didn't want to, some part of me had internalized their shame and fear over what my lack of a clear role among other shifters would mean for me. Seb was the first shifter I let close enough to see those hurts. He was the first one to tell me—ever so matter-of-factly denying his own feelings about his creep—that there was never anything wrong with me and that I am exactly who I am meant to be, beta or omega.

So it hurts even more for him to hide something like this. The omission rubs against all those raw spots inside of me at not being trusted to know what's best for me or make my own choices with all the information at my disposal. I love my best friend more than any other shifter in the world, but it's going to be hard to get past this. To push back the worry about what else he might be hiding if he could hide this for so long. What other choices he might make for me, for my own good.

Ugh. I know that's my trauma talking, but I can't let it go.

Maybe I do need to mull things over more before we talk. Work doesn't require my full attention most days, and even running around more than usual, I still have room for my thoughts.

It helps that the most important part of my day-to-day duties is being friendly to the customers. That's a task made easier by knowing all of our regulars. Four Corners is a tight-knit community of shifters. Not that it's perfect, but it's mostly lived up to what I needed when I left home. The shifters here have accepted me for who I am since I first moved here and got friendly with Seb and his rave and Harvey adopted me into his pack and mentored me.

If it was anyone else who hid something this huge, it would have obliterated any traces of trust I had in them. But this is Seb. His word was enough to get me the job here at the market when I first got to town. Technically, I think he had his cousin Lydia talk to Harvey for me, since she's on better terms with the local pack than Seb is. We'd gone out a few times when I had the cash from picking up odd jobs and driving statics around for a rideshare service. So he knew I had cashier experience from back home and that the market was hiring.

Thanks to Seb and his flock, Harvey gave me a chance at a steady job in town. I started out bagging groceries a few hours a week purely as a favor to the rave and now I've worked my way up to full time and a title as store manager. Harvey lets me prove myself, and I work hard to earn his trust, but I know I'd never have gotten the chance without Seb.

Seb welcomed me into his community as a beta. He has earned my trust entirely. I have him to thank for helping me secure a rent to own contract on the modest little bungalow we share now because it had belonged to an elder in from his flock who preferred not to live in their rave housing. Her family needed to sell when she passed, and Seb knew I was looking for something affordable and close to the rave complex when my original lease ran out across town.

He's the only person I want in my heart and my home and my bed. He's the first shifter with whom I shared my first tentative wonderings about being an omega. He listened and encouraged me to explore what it might mean to embrace that part of me.

I need to confront Seb about the meds, but I can't quite reconcile this situation. The best friend who would literally sacrifice his own health to help me to feel comfortable in my skin, but who did so with all the little lies of omission that came along with that choice. Not to mention the way he pushed me away after what we shared last night. Coming with him in our driveway. Kissing like lovers.

How can I love someone with all my heart, and still be so unspeakably hurt and angry with him? It's exhausting, all my thoughts chasing each other in circles while I make small talk and answer questions about how long the repairs will take or making assumptions about the workers being here for the rumored frozen food aisle renovation.

We have our usual surge of shoppers after the knitting group that meets once a week at the yarn and bookshop on the corner finishes their meeting, so that keeps me busier for a while. Several of them show off their progress on projects and a bat shifter who is new to the area asks about special ordering specialty brands of nectar for an upcoming holiday. Harvey fields that request.

Mrs. Leopald, one of our regulars, comes in a little later than usual with her youngest grandson. The kid looks a little older than Seb's niblings in his stroller, between two and three years old. He spends most of the outing napping, his face cherubic under a fall of glossy dark curls. I can't help my mind's wistful wondering about an alternate universe where I might have a kit of my own to shop for, maybe even with Seb. I usually try not to consider that. It makes my chest feel too tight, like it's physically squeezing that hollow pit of a longing I've never really even dared to speak aloud.

Mrs. Leopald takes her time picking up kid-friendly snacks in brightly colored packages. Several other shifters she is friendly rivals with are shopping around midmorning too. They all coo over how adorable and sweet her grandbaby is and how lucky she is to spend time with the grandkids. She laps it all up as if it's the finest cream. She preens over having both her grandkits visiting for a week as the toddler dozes, a fuzzy rainbow spotted leopard something clutched in his pudgy fist.

He's less angelic when he startles awake, shifting into his fur and yowling at the strange surroundings. Mrs. Leopald hastily grabs a few final items and plops them into his seat as she scoops the upset kit into her arms, shushing him softly.

"Sorry, he's teething a bit, I don't suppose you have any more of the all natural real fruit low sugar popsicles in the back?" she asks.

"I'm afraid we don't," I say.

"Ah, well, I have a few at home and we can make more, I better grab another bottle of juice to make them. That new expanded freezer section can't get here fast enough, hmm?" Mrs. Leopald chuckles, inviting me to be amused at her exasperation. I flash a half-smile, but before I can correct her assumptions about the renovations, she starts unloading her groceries from the stroller onto the conveyor and bulldozes on with the conversation. "Would you be a dear and grab a second bottle of this?"

The question is worded like a polite request, but I know from helping her in the past that it is a demand and she won't appreciate me foisting the task off on anyone else. Scanning the other registers, I notice Lou, one of the more experienced cashiers, is working next to me. I catch their eyes and gesture for them to keep an eye on my till. Lou nods to me. I recognize the same brand of guava nectar that Bram's kids love, so I know exactly where to grab a second one for her. It's just easier than fighting.

I'm so focused on retrieving the juice that I don't notice the wolf alpha standing in the beverage aisle until I bump right into his chest. Colliding with a solid wall of muscles knocks the wind out of me and I inhale sharply.

Alpha musk fills my nostrils. For some unfathomable reason, it smells so much stronger than usual. Strong and off-putting. Weird. I exhale in a huff, catching a hint of a familiar omega's scent on him—Rose is a regular here. Ah, this must be the out of town alpha she's been talking about dating.

"Sorry! I didn't see you there," I apologize as I stumble back a step even as he reaches out to steady me.

The box of tampons under the alpha's arm bounces on the linoleum between us. It's not the most romantic gesture, but it shows a level of caring that makes me happy for the other omega. It's one of those little ways Seb and I care for each other, the kind gestures of support that make life easier.

"It's fine," he says. We both bend to retrieve the box. I get to it first and hand it to him with a smile.

"You're Kenton, right? From up near Bucksport? Rose has been telling me all about her new boyfriend."

"Oh, yeah, nice to meet you," he glances at my name badge, "Rollie."

"Likewise," I say.

Kenton is still watching me, and I realize he's waiting for me to hand back the box. "Oh! Here. Uh, good choice, we carry the generic stuff, but I always hated the crappy cardboard applicators," I say before thinking it through.

TMI. And it's not like that was even a thing I dealt with for long. Being both a beta and intersex meant that I had about a year of irregular periods before my body's doomed attempt at puberty fizzled out and I was given the choice of which primary gender to present as so I could blend in with the static humans around us.

For all their strict views on alphas and omegas roles in a family, my parents gave me free reign to decide whether to go on estrogen or testosterone to pair with the growth hormone injections the static doctors insisted that I needed without really explaining why or offering me a choice in the matter.

I turn away from Kenton self-consciously and reach for the guava juice I came here for. The motion hits me with a strong whiff of my own scent. Did I forget to use deodorant this morning? I must have skipped it in my rush to get out the door without waking Seb. If I didn't know better, I'd think some of the sugary sweet juice had spilled across the floor from how strong my scent is. I glance surreptitiously at the strange alpha, gauging his reaction to see if he notices anything weird.

Kenton's eyes dart over my body, nostrils flaring as he scents me, trying to make sense of how my words fit with my scent and appearance. "Um, good to know? Rose asked for this brand." His cheeks darken with a flush and he whips around, going back to comparing cranberry juice cocktails like there might be a test. "And pure cranberry concentrate? Do you have that here?"

"We sure do." I grab the little bottle of concentrate from the top shelf, half hidden between two larger juice cocktails. I point at the evenly spaced marks on the label marking out a serving. "Here, the instructions for how to dilute it are on the label."

"Thanks." Kenton takes the bottle with a tight smile, and another surreptitious huff of my scent into his lungs even as he shuffles further away from me in the narrow aisle. My heart sinks, he definitely noticed. At least he's being polite. I should check to see if I have a spare deodorant tube in my work bag during my break later. "You know—" he starts, winces then shakes his head at himself. "Nevermind."

"What?" I cock my head at him, hoping that I might have misread the reason for the sudden awkwardness. Maybe Rose said something about me? Well that's a whole new anxiety to explore later.

"Nothing. Just. You smell—" His cheeks flush as he burts—"omegas in heat are entitled to paid work leave. Just. In case you didn't know."

"Okay?" I'm not sure why he felt the need to spout employment law at me, but duly noted. "Thanks, nice to meet you, Kenton, tell Rose I say hello."

"I will." The alpha clutches his two items to his chest, turns on his heel, and flees back up the aisle so he doesn't have to brush past me. I shake my head at the weird encounter as I double check that I've got the correct bottle so I can get Mrs. Leopald sent on her way.

Kenton is standing in line at the furthest register from mine when I return to finish ringing up the order in my lane. I try to push the encounter with Kenton out of my head. I scan the juice and help arrange Mrs. Leopald's purchases in her reusable satchels while she fills out a check to pay.

I always enjoy seeing her latest bags, she sews her own out of scraps bits from her locally famous quilts, so they're always delightfully colorful and unique. While I finish bagging, she deftly maneuvers the wriggly ball of fur in her arms back into his stroller, he curls up in his own cozy wild cat themed quilt and she pulls down the firm but flexible mesh shade that will keep the curious kit securely in place for their walk home.

I hand over her bags, but her nose wrinkles when she leans closer to grab the second satchel and she tuts at me. "Are you quite alright dear?"

"Yeah, just tired. I was in a rush this morning." I hunch in on myself, wishing I had a scent blocker to help with my pungency problem if everyone's going to comment on it all of a sudden. It's not that bad, is it?

When she leaves I try to sniff myself again, and yeah, I smell a bit ripe, but nothing that merits public shaming...is it? I glance around the store and consider. There are enough people browsing the aisles that I'm going to be busy for a while if I don't act fast. Now or stinky.

With a sigh I dash out to the personal hygiene aisle and buy an emergency back up stick of deodorant, pay for it with my employee discount, and duck back behind a register to hastily swipe the vanilla and rose scented goop onto my pits. It's not ideal, but at least it's the shifter formulation that's meant to partially neutralize alpha and omega pheromones.

There, all fixed just in time to work through the mid-morning rush. Being too busy to worry about how I smell helps, and so does having more shifters' scents mixed in with mine. I fall back into easy small talk with everyone. My work smile almost starts to feel real as I banter with the regulars.

I have to correct at least a dozen folks loudly speculating that the repairs on the busted refrigeration unit confirm the rumors we are expanding the frozen goods section for the summer months. For many of our regulars, those rumors have been the biggest news for weeks and no amount of ignoring it or rebutting it seems to stop it from spreading.

Now that the idea has really taken root among our regulars, I'm considering pitching the expansion to Harvey again. I have data on our frozen food sales to back me up and everything. Plus, he looks contemplative when he overhears the speculation lately. As if it might just happen, if not this summer, then soon. I've seen him noodling around with spreadsheets and doodling out expansion plans, but he hasn't mentioned it at our weekly check ins. Unless paying more attention when I show him my analytics tracking just how fast our turnover is on various ice creams counts.

It's starting to seem like even if we don't do a full remodel, I might actually be able to get Harvey to take a chance on more dairy-free offerings for our non-mammalian shifter clients to enjoy, maybe by reorganizing our current shelf space or by adding a chest freezer near the registers.

Ever since promoting me as a manager last year, he's been more open to a lot of my ideas to improve the store. It's a novel feeling to know an elder I look up to is proud of me and trusts my judgment in such a tangible way. This must be what its like for Seb, knowing that his parents are in his corner no matter how badly he fucks up. Ugh. Why is it that every stray thought brings me full circle back to the infuriating raven?

Even with the expansion, if I'm entirely honest with myself, I want it so that we'll be able to stock more options than the freeze pops the raven shifter kids can currently get locally. Because I want to see Seb's eyes light up at getting to have a new treat.

I sigh at myself. I am so gone on a shifter who pushes all my buttons for better and worse, maybe it doesn't even matter what I say to him about sharing his prescription without being upfront about where the meds came from. Maybe. Ugh. Seb has a knack for making everything seem so much more complicated.

The scent-dampening deodorant seems to do the trick for a while. At least until toward the end of my lunch break when Lou mentions that Trinity was asking about picking up more hours if I need to take some time off.

They give me a sympathetic look and keep their distance, but I can't figure out why. It's not the only weird comment I get either. The weird looks and people giving me a wide berth continue until Harvey approaches me a short while later and asks if I need to leave early. I shake my head.

"I'm fine, just tired. Sorry, I'll do a better job focusing," I say, finishing bagging a customer's purchase.

Harvey doesn't let up though. It takes a few more probing questions until the pieces start to click together into a horrifying picture.

"You spent a lot of time with Mel yesterday, Rollie, right?" Harvey asks.

"Um, I guess?" I shrug, looking for the next round of groceries to scan. But there is no one waiting in my line. The closed sign is perched on the edge of my conveyor. I'm vaguely annoyed at my boss hovering like I'm a clueless new hire or something. I don't need a break, I just need to stop wool gathering so much.

"I'm not sure if your doctor warned you, but sometimes when you're um, close to your own season, being around another omega in heat can, uh, accelerate things?" Harvey stumbles over trying to phrase the suggestion delicately and I don't understand the implication at first.

When I realize he thinks Mel's pheromones triggered a heat for me I laugh. That's preposterous.

Harvey isn't laughing, he's watching me with a worried frown and sad eyes. He pats my shoulder gingerly, keeping his distance. "Why don't you take a break, son? Is there someone I can call for you?"

"Um, I guess? I want Seb." I can't smell him as he guides me toward the breakroom, which means he took scent blockers before approaching me. So he really does think I'm in heat.

Seb. If I'm really going into heat then something is really wrong. It shouldn't be possible and it can't mean anything good. I need my best friend.

Fear clarifies things for me. Seb offered to get the hormones for me, and I accepted even though I knew there was no way he could get a legit prescription on my behalf because it seemed like the only option for me to feel like the omega I am. It's the same reason that for all it presses on old wounds in the worst way, I know in my heart I will never hold Seb obfuscating the details against him. Seb is the only reason I've been able to transition toward presenting as an omega at all.

Shit. This whole situation might be my own damn fault. Or at least, we share the blame. And it should have been so obvious as soon as I learned Seb was sharing his meds with me, but it's only now hitting me, like a sudden downpour, that I'm probably on an avian formulation of omega hormones. The realization hits me hard. Avian omegas with creep require aggressive hormone therapy. Way beyond what most trans omegas would take.

What we've been doing has worked well enough for years, but we changed brands recently and something is apparently going very, very wrong with me. With both of us. Fuck. So much for being angry, I'm mostly just scared and I really need to talk to Seb so we can figure out what to do. My thoughts are muddled and fuzzy. Like when we took that artificial heat inducer after Elric's fledging party.

If I'm going into heat, I need Seb. My only regret about sharing that first one with him is that it would have been better without the alpha in the picture. Just Seb, thrusting a knotting plug into my hole until I begged him for his load and oh, fuck, I am ridiculously horny. But there's no way I'm actually in heat, right? Is this some weird form of creep for omegas with already broken ovaries?

I don't have answers. Or a way to get them. I don't want to call my stern-faced static endocrinologist and get lectured about all the ways getting illegal prescription drugs is a terrible idea and read the riot act about how the consequences of that choice are my own fault. I just want...I want Seb.

I want him to bury his nose in my neck even as he sinks his cock inside the tight little hole that I only trust him to fill. Alphas like that sometimes, watching him fuck me in the cunt. It's too atrophied for an alpha to give me anything but pain with it, but Seb fits just right. And sometimes I like to pretend like I'm a normal omega and he can breed me for real; he can't though.

Even if he wasn't a fellow omega, incapable of knocking me up, the doctor who put me on my synthetic puberty cocktail made it very clear that my static human reproductive parts were vestigial and couldn't actually produce a kit. My folks seemed almost relieved by that. I didn't notice it in the exam room when the future I'd imagined for myself with a mate and children came crashing down around me.

It seemed obvious that they were happy at the news in hindsight, when I overheard Mom on the phone telling her sister that it was just as well that I wouldn't pass along whatever is wrong with me to a kit. Tears burn my eyes and I don't want to think about that. How the parents who I had to rely on to make my medical choices for me called it a relief when it was a loss I was struggling to cope with, even then. I didn't consent to surgery to remove anything, even though they pushed for it for a while. That turned ugly until my grandparents intervened and I threatened to go live with them.

Just remembering all that drama has me even more on edge. Jittery, nerves jangling. Or it might just be another sign of whatever is going on with my hormones. It takes all my self-control to keep my breathing steady and normal. I press a fist over my heart to calm its racing.

A familiar rush of anxiety sweeps through me. My ears ring with barbs from my past. *Never going to find a mate. Who would want you? Defective. Not really one of us.*

A flush of heat suffuses my skin from my scalp down to my toes, too hot until sweat beads up and I'm so itchy in my skin, the intense need to shift and find a safe dark den is overpowering. I breathe and try to ground myself. I'm at work. Safe. Harvey trusts and respects me. My regulars like me. Seb wants me to be his best friend and his roommate. His family loves me. Lots of people want me and care about me just the way I am.

No amount of reminding myself of those facts helps. My raccoon is right there, just beneath the surface, demanding to come out and protect us both from foolish static human rules. Humans shouldn't run out of their workplace in the middle of the shift.

My inner raccoon shoves at me, and I can feel my fur starting to prickle over my skin even as the first wave of crampy aches rips through my focus and sends me to a more primal place. A place where getting away from pain and danger and fear is my top priority. Where logic doesn't matter nearly as much as my safety.

The raccoon part of me recognizes the reason my scent is so weird today. Why I feel just like I did during that artificial heat. I can't be in heat. I can't.

When a heavy hand lands on my shoulder I whip around to face the threat, cringing away from whoever it is even as I'm unable to control the partial shift that overtakes me. Harvey. I recognize his scent before the sight of his concerned face as he looks at me really registers. He immediately puts space between us when he sees my reaction.

"I'm sorry to startle you Rollie. Think you can keep your fur to yourself until we get to the breakroom?" he asks, voice gentle. He maneuvers me down an empty aisle and shields me from the view of any gawking shoppers with his body.

I nod stiffly and let him lead me into the employee only area.

"Lou is trying to call Seb to take you home, but if we can't reach him, who else should we call?"

I take a deep breath, which is a mistake because he's an alpha and my instincts should be telling me that he smells good and I want a big fat knot. Except the tiny trace of his alpha musk still present after he took his scent blockers is rank in my nose. Like Kenton earlier. Fuck. I breathe more shallowly, force my way back into my fully human form so I can talk to him.

"Hm?" I ask.

"You aren't working while you're in heat, Rollie. Is this your first—you know what? Forget I asked that. You are entitled to heat leave, the only question that matters is how we are going to get you home safely," Harvey says.

"Okay?" I'm not sure how that has anything to do with me. I can't be in heat. Can I? Something is wrong with me though.

"Rollie?" Harvey calls me back to the moment. "Is there someone else I can call for you?"

"Seb?" I hand Harvey my phone. I want Seb. So much. Need him. Want to feel his lips on my skin. Feel every inch of him pressed against me. Inside me. Making me...I moan at the mental slide show of all the times we've shared alphas. And last night, just the two of us making out together. I want him. Just him. No one between us. No lying or pretending. I want him as my mate. Seb will take me home and make me feel better.

"Do you have any blockers to take the edge off, Rollie?" Harvey asks, he still has my phone to his ear, but he snorts and takes a step further away from me. Like my scent upsets him. Or he's afraid I might trigger a rut if he inhales too deeply near me right now. Fuck, that's embarrassing.

Heats and ruts aren't like the statics portray them in static-made shifter porn. We can control ourselves when we're in season. Harvey won't hurt me if he does go into a rut. But he'll be horny for a while and it's inconvenient when it happens unplanned. Hence generous leave policies to prevent unintentionally triggering other shifters with our pheromones.

"Um, no. Sorry." I don't tell him that this shouldn't be possible. If I wasn't high on heat hormones I'd be more scared of what it could possibly mean. "Is Seb coming?"

I bite my lip, picturing how pretty his is when he comes, fuck I want to make him come. I want to make him come forever.

"Alrighty then. Let's go to the break room to wait for Seb, Rollie." Harvey says in his most alpha-hole 'I mean business' type voice. I follow him obediently to the break room. "Wait here, Seb or someone from the rave will be here to collect you soon, alright? Any preferences?"

"Winny. Or Bram... maybe Ty?"

"Alright, hang in there, son, you're going to be fine." Harvey leaves with my phone still to his ear. I guess that will make it easier for him to call my mate. Good. I can't focus enough to use it anyway.

"Yeah. Thanks." I force a tight smile and pace the room.

Now that it's silent and we're away from all the staring customers and my coworkers it hits me that there was a reason for all the weird looks and whispered comments. Oops. I might have made a scene. My raccoon doesn't care, and I'm inclined not to either.

After a few circuits of the room, I try to sit, but the anxious itchy need drives me back to my feet and I'm pacing again before long. This isn't my den and my mate isn't here.

I wait for what feels like an eternity before the door creaks open. The noise catches my attention and has my raccoon ready to bolt again. "Where's Seb?" I demand, whirling to face Harvey.

Except it's not Harvey at the door. Lou waves sheepishly through a narrow gap, the door is still mostly closed. I scent the air. Nothing. They took a scent blocker too, and they rattle a little pill in a paper cup as they hold it out to me.

"Hey, Rollie. I had an extra heat suppressor and a couple of doses of scent blockers in my bag, if you need them to take the edge off while you get a plan sorted out," they offer, letting the door open a bit more.

"What?" I sidle close enough to stare suspiciously down at the pills.

"Harvey says you didn't realize you were going into heat in time to take precautions?" Lou sounds sympathetic and they hold out the meds again. As casually as if they were offering me a tampon for an unexpected period.

I swallow down my suspicion and irrational irritability. This is almost exactly like sharing period products. And the meds will help. Probably. I sigh. What's one more dose of a medication that might not be what I'm told it is and might not affect me the same way it does normal people?

Ugh. Seb would be pissed if he heard me calling myself abnormal. That's my parents talking. I don't feel normal right now though. Which is laughable considering that heats are entirely normal for most omegas my age.

A giggle bubbles up my throat and I can't stop laughing as I reach from the little cup of medicine. I glance at the pills, the scent blocker looks like the ones I've used before when I don't feel like dealing with scents in an overwhelming situation. I wouldn't recognize a heat suppressor regardless. I swallow both pills dry and grimace at the way they drag down my throat. Lou hands me a bottle of water.

"Thanks." I grimace, but I offer the water back.

"Drink it, hydration is important during a heat." Lou nods at the bottle and stares until I chug half of it in front of them. You alright in here?"

"I will be. Did Harvey get a hold of Seb?"

Lou's face falls and they hesitate before shaking their head. "He left a voicemail. But he said to tell you that he called Bram and he's sending Winny to bring you home. Uh, here's your phone back, if you want to try calling Seb again once the suppressor kicks in."

"Yeah. Uh. Okay. Thanks." I take the phone and retreat out of their reach. Out of politeness, heat pheromones are intense. No wonder everyone was acting so weird about my scent all day. I take a deep steadying breath, and force my thoughts away from how stupid I was not to realize what was going on sooner.

Winny will be here soon. That shouldn't be such a disappointment. I love Seb's clutchmates. You can't love one of them without caring about all three of them. But I don't want Winny. I want Seb. At least I won't have to see Bram right now when I'm feeling so vulnerable. He's the living embodiment of everything I want in the world and will never have.

Guilt swamps over me for even thinking ill of Bram. That's probably part of why he is sending Winny instead of bringing the kids with him to drive me home or getting someone from the rave to watch them. He knows Seb and I want kids. Not together. That's an even more impossible dream than either of us having children with someone else. But...if I really am in heat and he's been smelling so much like an alpha maybe...no. I shake the ridiculously wild thought right out of my head.

The odds against Seb and I conceiving, even with whatever weird screw up happened with our medication have to be astronomically low. So low a doctor would tell us they're zero. Even if this really is a heat. It shouldn't be possible. And hoping it might lead to something even more impossible is asking to have my hopes crushed to dust all over again.

"You want company while you wait?" Lou offers.

"Not really, might want to shift. Tell Winny I'm alright with her picking me up in my fur?"

"Sure." Lou flashes me a wan smile. "Hang in there, it'll be much better once you're home and your inner animal feels safe with your mate."

"My mate?" I repeat, startled at the assumption from someone who knows me and Seb.

"Seb?" Lou gives me a look like I'm the one who is being weird.

"Oh. Yeah." I don't correct the assumption that he's my mate. I don't have the energy, and I know they're right on the outcome, if not on the details. Having him close will help with the anxiety and the cramps and just...everything. Seb will find me as long as I'm in our den, and then I'll be fine. Seb makes everything better.

"You'll be home before you know it and then I'm sure you'll feel better."

"Home?" I repeat.

"Yep, you're going to spend some time home in bed until you're back to yourself, Rollie." Lou agrees

Oh. Yes. Home is good. My inner raccoon approves of that plan. Home with Seb. I pull out my phone, unlock it with my face and then stare at the background image of Seb cuddled up in a puppy pile with his niblings. He's so pretty and nurturing and he'd be such a good dad. I stroke his face, wishing he was here so I could touch him for real.

Chapter 8

Seb

WE'RE ALMOST HALFWAY HOME when I remember to charge my phone so I can check for calls from the clinic or Rollie. I get several notifications as soon as I turn it on, but before I can check them, Bram's number comes up on my caller ID.

Weird. Bram has to know I'm with his mate and that we're on our way to his place. What could be so important that he needs to tell us right this second?

Knowing my brother, I assume he wants us to grab some last-minute ingredients for dinner and figured Ty must be driving. Which he is. But the car has Bluetooth, so calling me instead of his mate still seems odd.

"Hello?" I say, apprehension prickling my skin.

"Hi, Sebastian." Bram says. His use of my full name sets off all my internal warning alerts even before he gets super campy with the next sentence out of his mouth, drawing out his vowels for the first three words before blurting the rest in a rush. "Um, soooo...slight change of plans about dinner." He sounds...weird. like, he's forcing a chipper tone to disguise whatever news he doesn't really want to be giving me. That's not a good sign.

"Is everyone alright?" I ask, because that's the only thing I can think of that would upset my brother. My mind races with all the terrible possibilities, visions of carnage dancing in my mind's eye. Not the kids. If something happened to them, Bram would have called Ty, not me. And he wouldn't be coherent enough to play coy about it. Ty shoots me a quizzical look. I glance at him, then put the phone on speaker and drop it into the cup holder so we can both hear my brother.

"Yes?" Bram asks. "Mostly. I mean. No one is going to die or anything. The babies are napping and Myra is playing Minecraft with Cory in the den."

"Who isn't going to die, Bramble?" I grind my teeth, which isn't even nearly as satisfying a way to show my frustration as it is when I've got a beak to grind and clack at him. He has to realize that there is a world of misery possible between the lines of what he's not saying.

Is he calling about Winny? My heart sinks to my toes, our clutchmate has been through enough shit to last a lifetime. I'm trying not to jump to conclusions even as a slideshow of all the terrible things that could have happened to our moms and other siblings flashes through my mind.

I close my eyes and rub them until I see flashing lights. It doesn't stop the mental reel from spinning, each member of our rave flitting through my thoughts until the reel spins to a screeching stop on Rollie's face. Not him.

"What happened, bird, you're scaring your brother," Ty prompts his mate, low voice gruff and reassuring.

"Oh, no, it's not bad. Per se. Just. Um. Unexpected? We're going to have to reschedule dinner I think. I just got a call from Harvey, and you should probably call Rollie on your way home."

I want to reach through the phone and shake answers out of my infuriating brother. "Bram, focus. Tell me what's going on."

"He's in heat," Bram blurts.

That doesn't make any sense. None at all. Rollie can't be in heat. Unless he took something? Why would he do that without talking to me first? For some alpha?

He hasn't been seeing anyone, as far as I know. He'd have told me if he was. We tell each other almost everything.

Not about where the HRT comes from though. Or details about where I go when I can't drown out the voice of my own self-hatred. We don't talk about the types of alphas I look for at my worst. The ones who make my inner raven want to take to the sky and find our flock for a safety that the worst depths of my human side's psyche doesn't believe I deserve.

"No. He can't...that can't...I can't..." I can't actually finish the thought, the words choke me as I swallow them down. Bram babbles something absurd. False reassurances that everything will be fine once I talk to Rollie. I snort derisively.

I can't talk to anyone when it feels like I'm choking on air. This doesn't make any sense. Unless Rollie took a heat inducer to lash out at me? Except he wouldn't do that and even thinking it is grasping at straws because all the other possibilities scare me too much to consider.

I can't think logically about this. Fear tosses me along in an ocean of pain. If this is his way of telling me he's done with my shit, then Rollie might as well have tossed my heart in a blender. It's so far out of character I can't really bring myself to believe he's finally realized that I'm never going to be good enough for him and moved on. But the alternative that he's spontaneously developed a heat seems equally impossible, so I don't know what to believe.

At least if he took something to induce a heat, then he's not sick.

"Seb?" Ty glances at me, concern furrowing his brow. I'm glad my brother has Ty. Bram deserves the world, and Ty will happily give it to him. But in this moment, it just hurts to know I'll never have a mate who loves me. Someone who cares so deeply about my entire family that he looks at my clutchmates with that much kind compassion.

"Mm?" I try to sound normal. Like everything is fine. It's not fine.

Either Rollie is seriously ill because of the medication I gave him under false pretenses. Or I finally pushed him too far. My head is spinning either way. The only anchor tethering me in the storm of emotions is that this feels like a total vindication of the taunting inner voice that always spurs me toward my worst impulses.

The seductive voice of the void, telling me I'm not good enough. Whispering that I should just give up. Rollie would be better off without me. He's probably figured out that I'm garbage. Too useless for anyone to want me. I did something awful to the shifter I love and nothing is ever going to be okay again if I can't fix this mess.

I can't breathe. My seatbelt is choking me, so I take it off. Better, but I need out, need open skies and the wind under my wings. I scrabble at the door handle, heedless of the fact we're on the interstate going over seventy miles per hour in heavy traffic.

"What are you doing?" Ty asks, voice stone-cold calm. I shake my head and curl my fingers around the latch.

I can't breathe. I need to get out. Fly away from my life. Forget all this anguish at the bottom of a bottle and wake up in bed with some alpha I don't remember. Or never wake up at all; that's the quiet part I never let myself finish. It terrifies me how much a part of me wants it. Ty hits the automatic locks before I can get the door open. I tug on the latch and slap at the lock, nowhere near coordinated enough to actually get the door open.

"Whoa! Seb, stop that right this instant." Ty's voice booms like the one time we were walking to the park, and he yelled for Myra not to step into an intersection as a car ran a red light.

I flinch from his intensity and hunch low in my seat, reflex telling me the angry alpha beside me is a threat. Marin used to yell like that if I stepped out of line too. I'm trembling and even more desperate to shift and fly away, but I've only ever heard Ty raise his voice out of worry when someone he loves is in danger. He pulls into the breakdown lane and hits the hazard lights as we roll to a gentle stop on a straight stretch of road.

"Do not try that again, Sebastian. Understand?" Ty turns to look at me, angling himself away from me to look as unthreatening as possible as he does. I make myself look at him.

I nod woodenly and slouch deeper into my seat like a sullen teenager after being told off. I do not want to piss off the big loving bear shifter alpha, but as the adrenaline rush from the news about Rollie and Ty yelling fades, it's easier to believe that Ty would never hurt me.

No, more than that, Ty will go out of his way to make sure I don't hurt myself. The exact opposite of my type when it comes to alphas. I almost snort at my terrible judgment. Almost. It's the furthest thing from funny.

"What is it? What's going on?" Bram squawks through the phone. "I didn't mean to upset you, Seb. It's just, Rollie seemed really freaked too. Harvey couldn't reach you so he had to call me to come get Rollie from work. I guess he was too out of it to get home on his own and didn't seem to realize why. Did you give him something? Could he be having a reaction? I don't want to meddle, so I wasn't planning to say anything, but he mentioned something about you getting him hormones? If you two were planning to share a synthetic heat, then it seems like you got the timing or dosage wrong. Or maybe it was a bad batch?"

"Bram, Seb needs a minute to process the news. I'll make sure he gets home safe, okay?" Ty plucks my phone out of the cup holder, turns off speaker mode to exchange a few more reassuring words with his mate, then tells Bram he loves him before hanging up.

"Okay. First things first." Ty hands my phone back to me, scrubs a hand over his face, then meets my gaze. "Are you a flight risk?"

I shake my head mutely.

"Okay. Can you tell me what's going on with you?"

I can't, so I turn away and stare resolutely out the window at the trees lining the highway. I'm breathing more evenly now at least; no longer hyperventilating as I teeter on the edge of a panic attack.

"Can I talk about it then?" Ty asks.

I nod cautiously.

"Whatever is going on between you and Rollie is none of my business, but Rollie adores you. Bram says he was asking for you. Only you. Winny brought him home and made sure he ate, hydrated and got into bed with a second dose of suppressors for when you get there, so he can be lucid for you two to talk this out properly. But if you have any doubts about what he would want if he wasn't in heat or if you don't want to spend it with him, we have a guest room with your name on it for as long as you need it."

This isn't entirely mine to tell, but I don't know how to explain the depths of my despair over the situation without sharing all the reasons why it's so upsetting. And my family all knows that Rollie was assigned beta at birth, so I'm not outing him by talking about this. I shake my head, I'm tempted to just swallow it all down, deal with it the same ways I always have. Except I might not survive coping with losing Rollie with my usual methods.

I take a fortifying breath. And then another one. Trying to force the words into some semblance of order. "You don't get it. Rollie can't be in heat."

"Why not?" Ty's tone is neutral.

I groan. "Because he lacks the organs to actually have one?"

Ty shakes his head at me. "Because he was assigned beta?"

"Yeah."

"But he's on omega hormones now?"

"Yeah."

"So, his prescriber didn't mention whether this might happen?" Ty asks.

"No. Um. He doesn't have one. I, uh, I might have been sharing my prescription with him without telling anyone. And now he's having a heat and he shouldn't be and I might have really fucked up this time. I don't know what to do. He kissed me last night. Told me that if we could, he'd give me his heat and his kits and I—I don't deserve that. I don't deserve him."

"Is that what you told him? That you don't want to be his mate?"

"No. Worse. I came in my pants from making out with him, lost my nerve, and flew off to let a stranger fuck my brains out."

"Ah. So. Do you think he took a heat inducer to manipulate you into something?" Ty suggests, tone so bland I can't be entirely sure whether he's seriously suggesting that or if the question is meant to show me how absurd the possibility sounds when spoken aloud.

"No!" I snarl at Ty, taking out the visceral reaction on him and instantly ashamed of myself for it. "Rollie wouldn't do that."

"Well, then it must just be one of those things. Sometimes HRT causes breakthrough heats. It doesn't have to mean he's ovulating, or even that he *can* ovulate."

I snort at that. "Doesn't matter, considering I can't exactly knot him."

Ty arches a brow at me. "Last I checked, I've got three—going on four—cubs to teach where babies come from and you aren't one of them. I'm not here to tell you to be safe or suggest what you should do. But Bram will end me if I let you leave this car without doing everything in my power to make sure you're going to come home safe to us. Can you promise me that you're not going to make bad choices if I let you out here?"

I sigh. "Can you take me home? I should probably call Rollie first so we can talk before I get a whiff of him in heat."

Ty nods approvingly and gestures toward my phone. "That sounds like a good plan. Buckle up."

Ty watches as I fasten my seatbelt and I take a moment to compose myself.

"Bram isn't the only one who would never forgive me if something happened to you," Ty says, just when I have a handle on my emotions.

"Winny?" I guess, even as his actual meaning dawns on me. Aw, Ty cares. I knew that, but I can't help teasing him. "My moms? Your children? Bryony, Elric, and Cory?"

Ty laughs. "All of the above, but I meant that I care about you, Seb. Not just because my mate loves you with his entire heart, either. All you pushy birds seem to have nested in my heart too."

"We do that. Very insidious." My attempt to brazen out the awkwardness with humor falls flat, but it still makes it easier to pull myself back together after coming so close to shattering completely. I play at being a cocky little shit often enough that it feels natural. Like I'm back on solid ground.

"Mhm. Call Rollie." Ty nods toward my phone again, then he eases the car back onto the highway. It's just as well that we're far enough from the city that the traffic is lighter here. We're under twenty minutes from Four Corners now, so I don't have much time to procrastinate about making this call.

I swipe through my notifications first. Several missed calls from my family and Rollie's cell and the number saved as his work line. Wow, Bram wasn't lying when he said they tried to get in touch with me while my phone was dead.

The work calls were probably from Harvey. There's a slew of messages from the wolf.

Rollie: Rollie is safe in the break room at the market, but he needs a ride home from work. Everything is fine, but he's going into heat.

Rollie: This is Harvey, by the way. We'll keep calling until we find someone he trusts to get him home. I know things are awkward between you and the pack, for good reason, but Rollie asked me to call you, so I've been trying to get in touch.

Rollie: Answer your phone!**Rollie:** He's going into heat and he needs his mate. If you get this, call him back. I think your voice would help calm him down. This is Lou, his favorite coworker, BTW.

Rollie: Harvey told me not to be rude, but he had no idea he was in season, what the hell? You better take good care of him!

Well shit. Rollie really is in heat. It still doesn't feel real. A few minutes ago, I was bursting to tell him that I did it. I took the job, and I lied about him being my mate so we can finally see a shifter specialist about our respective hormones. The pride of being able to provide for him properly mingles with my guilt that I might have left it until too late.

All of my reasons for not working at the zoo seem so petty and childish now that Rollie might be sick from the medication he trusted me to get for him. Every excuse I gave Bram about not wanting to work among static humans and how degrading it felt to show off my bird form for gawking visitors stems from the toxic baggage of my past. A blend of my self-hatred and just how deep under my skin the alpha who I thought would be my future got with his ideas about what an omega can and should be. Marin saw me as broken when I couldn't give him the family we both dreamed of and a part of me still agrees.

Part of me still wants to punish that broken part of me that will never fit the idealized version of me that my ex put on a pedestal and promised the world. So I said no to the opportunities Bram gave me. Not because they were beneath my pride, but because I knew what Bram would never accept about me. I don't deserve good things. Certainly not a cushy job that brings more to the rave than I take from our pooled resources. What I deserve doesn't matter, Rollie deserves to spend his heat feeling cherished and adored. I can give him that. Even if letting him go afterward will break my heart.

I dial Rollie's cell. It rings for a long time. Long enough to feel like an eternity as tension coils through me. Is this how he felt when he spoke with me the night I called him to say goodbye and he saved my life? It's awful. I hate not having any control of the situation. I'm so scared and determined to do whatever it takes to make sure the person I adore above all others is alright.

The fact I'm not an alpha and servicing him through a heat feels perilously close to him telling me that's how he sees me. That what he wants from me is to revel in the parts of my body that make me wish I could shed it.

I was born with the requisite anatomy until my body got its wires crossed a few years after my heats started. Most people don't argue that omegas with creep aren't real omegas. No amount of saying I'm still an omega even without my heats and fertility helps with the dysphoria when I get a whiff of alpha musk emanating from my scent glands though. Nothing really helps with how broken I feel when I can't slick up properly no matter how turned on I am, but sharing the prescription omega hormones I need to keep my condition stable gives me the illusion of control over it. And it means that my dysphoria has a purpose, a reason for the suffering and loss.

The only thing that matters for now is taking care of Rollie. Not just because I love him. As a best friend and my chosen family and so much else besides that. I love him as the mate I know I won't ever deserve to share my life with. This impossible heat is my fault, and if fixing the situation hurts, it's nothing less than the penance I deserve. I just need it to not be a harbinger of some worse health concern that my stumbling efforts to help him have caused.

I can't help the nightmare slideshow of all the frantic online research I did about weird heats when my creep symptoms first started. All the terrible possibilities that loom over us now because I thought I could help him. This isn't the same as that. We can fix it. My own impotent terror doesn't matter as long as Rollie is alright.

"Seb?" Rollie fills my name with galaxies of longing, vast as the starry sky. His need calls to me with the same intensity as the night sky too. His voice lands on my ears like a soothing balm to all my worry, anger, and fear.

"Yeah, it's me. Are you okay, baby?"

"Mm, no. Need you."

"I know. Bram says you're in heat?"

"Yeah. It's not like last time."

"No? What do you mean?"

"No. Hurts more. All crampy and I didn't get slick. We need lots of slick. Need your knot in me. Want you to breed my pussy and fill me up with kits. Eggs? Dunno. Want your babies."

My heart might just break if he keeps asking for that. It's impossible and I want it so bad. If this was the first time I was hearing him express that desire, there's no way I'd go to him until we could have a proper lucid talk, but we have both fantasized about sharing a real heat like this with each other. And there is no chance I can knock him up, so that's not a concern we need to have a serious conversation about. I might smell like an alpha lately, but I'm not one in any sense of the word. Certainly not in any way that makes a pregnancy between us remotely viable.

"I know, baby. I'm going to take care of you. You sure that's what you want? Can you take a suppressor so we can discuss it when your brain isn't totally focused on being horny?"

"Took a dose already. Don't like it. What did I tell you yesterday?" Rollie asks.

I rack my brain for the relevant conversation. "That you want to give me your heat?" I guess.

"Yeah. Still want to," Rollie says.

"You didn't, um, take something to uh, induce a heat?" I check, knowing the answer, but needing to be sure.

"You think I'd do that without telling you?" Rollie snaps.

"No." I know he wouldn't, he's the last person who would lie or manipulate me with something like this. "Sorry for even suggesting it."

He sniffles and tries to muffle a sob. Fuck me for making him cry. "You can say no if you don't want me."

"I want you. I want your heat, Rollie. I just don't want you to regret giving it to me," I say.

"Never. Only thing I regret is not asking you to be my mate ages ago," Rollie says.

That's...that has to be his heat talking, but if it will make him happy, I'm open to discussing that kind of roleplay. Once he takes a suppressor to be sure he understands it can't be real. At least, not until we can have a proper talk about it. I'm sure he'll change his mind once the heat pheromones fade.

"Okay, we can talk about that when I get there. Get yourself ready for me? There are a couple of bottles of slick in the hall closet next to the laundry detergent and the towels." I glance over at Ty and he rolls his eyes as taps the Bluetooth earbuds he got from Bram a while back. I mouth an apology.

"Do what you gotta do and don't mind me, I'm just listening to this music really loudly until I can drop you off." Ty waves away my sorry.

"Mhm? You gonna be here soon? Need you so bad, Seb," Rollie pleads over the phone. So I do my best to put Ty out of my mind.

"Soon baby. You want me to stay on the line so you can tell me how you're stretching that tight little hole for me?" I ask.

"Yeah. So tight. Might need my hands free...ungh, oooooh. Mmm. Like that," Rollie grunts. With his phone on speaker I hear all kinds of evocatively filthy sounds.

"What's that, baby?" My mouth is dry listening to his voice breaking in pleasure. My dick reacts to the sounds of his clear enjoyment.

"Knotting plug. Mmm. Hits the spot." He grunts rhythmically, like he's fucking himself with the plug shoved in deep. "Oh, mmm, Seb! Mate, I'm gonna come. Can't...need to so bad. Need you."

"Do it, baby. Come for me," I encourage him. Judging from the incoherent moaning and slick sounds of him fucking himself faster, he obeys. Damn, I want to be there with him right this instant. I glance at the speedometer, and the reminder that music to block it out or not, my brother-in-law totally just sat next to me while I basically had phone sex is awkward.

Ty notices me craning my neck over the console to look, and gives me a knowing smirk. "Driving as fast as I safely can, Seb. Tell Rollie to take a blocker so you can have a talk with him at least semi-lucid before you go barging in, yeah?"

I nod, swallowing hard at the assumption that I'll be sharing Rollie's heat. Because everyone in our family already sees us as mates and of course I'm the one Rollie wants with him for this. I give Ty a thumbs up and talk to Rollie again. "You still there? That was so good, baby. Did it feel good?"

"Mhm." Rollie pants into the phone for a minute then moans. "Want to do it with you inside me."

"I know, baby. Me too. But this is important. Rollie, baby, can you take the blocker Winny left now? So we can talk a bit when I get there?"

"Do I have to? I know it's not real. You aren't my mate for real. But you're the one who wanted to pretend."

"Huh?" I rack my brain until it dawns on me that I did tell him my plan to claim him as my mate for the zoo job benefits.

"For work? So, can't we just pretend to be like any other omega mates and enjoy our heat together?" He sounds so lost and hurt and my knee jerk reaction is to agree to whatever he wants. But Rollie hates lying and I will never knowingly dangle his dreams in front of him just because I want his heat more than I've allowed myself to want anything good for far too long.

Taking advantage of this unexpected heat is not something I can forgive myself for. We need to have a clearer conversation about the things that changed last night. He's said he wants to share another heat with me in the past, but that was before our kiss and my clumsy fake mates idea and just, so many things we need to discuss like rational adults but can't when he's in heat.

A suppressor isn't going to give us enough time to really delve into all of that, but it should at least clear his head enough for him to consider if anything has changed for him. I need to be sure he understands his options. My brain is eager to remind me of a litany of reasons he'll realize I'm not good enough for him if I give him a real chance.

I lick my lips. "Yes, Rollie. You need to take the medicine so we can talk. I need to know you really want to share your heat with me and it's not just the hormones talking, baby."

"Okay. Not gonna change my mind. Hurry home?" Rollie sounds adorably vulnerable and plaintive as he begs me to come home to him, the heat lowering his usual inhibitions. "I'm taking the meds. Want a knot. Will you stay on the line until you get here?"

"Yeah, I'm listening. I'm here. And I'll be there as fast as I can, love." I promise, staring at the traffic and willing the miles to pass faster.

Chapter 9
Rollie

SEB STAYS ON THE line with me for the entire drive home, just talking. At first, I mostly fantasize about what I want him to do to me once he gets here. Seb whispers filthy promises as I fuck myself on a dildo that's a little too small and a little too hard to really satisfy me.

I've already got a knotting plug shoved up my ass, and it's not quite enough. I've gone through most of the modest collection of sex toys that lives in a tote under our bed in an effort to chase an orgasm that's been hovering annoyingly out of reach since I got home.

Seb describing how we're going to enjoy this heat together is the missing piece I need—my mate. I can almost imagine he's the one stuffing me full as I activate the knotting feature on the plug in my ass. That fullness and pressure helps me to focus as the heat suppressor does its thing enough for us to discuss more than how horny I am for him.

I know it's better to talk these things out before a heat, but I've told him I'd give anything to share a true heat with him before this, so surely he realizes it's not just he hormones talking now? I know he's being cautious because he cares, but it's exasperating. My irritation with his emphasis on consent might actually be the hormones talking.

Seb brings up testing concerns and risk assessment and all of that very rational stuff. I tell him how I want to call him my mate and pretend he really can breed me. I know that's treacherous ground with him, but I also know it's something we'd both want in a perfect universe. Not him siring a kit or a clutch, just being able to make one together.

Maybe the suppressor was a good idea, so I don't fuck this up with clumsy wording that makes him think I'd change a thing about who he is. Ugh, now I'm second-guessing why he asked me to ask him about that part again in person. I wish he didn't hang up when he got out of Ty's car.

The front door opening startles me into hitting the quick release button that deflates the bulb on the knotting plug that's still in my ass and I whimper at the emptiness of its sudden lack. I took the suppressor dose he asked me to so we can talk, but I really don't want to discuss sex anymore when we could just be having sex. Foot in mouth concerns aside.

Oh well, he's here now. That's what matters. I guess it's nice that I can think more clearly now that the meds are working, but I was still enjoying the stretch of the knotting toy. I sit up and toss the toy onto a towel that I laid out earlier to collect the other toys I've used for cleaning later. There's no point trying to clean myself up, I'm a disheveled mess from trying to get off on my own in our bed.

Really, the noise of the door opening and Seb's keys and shoes being put away shouldn't be a surprise. Seb told me he was here before we hung up our call. The silly raven had the audacity to ask if I wanted him to come inside or stay with his brother until my heat passes. Ridiculous question.

Obviously I want him here. Forget coming inside the house; I want him coming inside of me as soon as possible, preferably with minimal talking. It's not like he's never fucked me before. Sure, it's different when we're sharing an alpha who can act as a buffer to pretend we aren't really together, but the fact I want to share my heat with him isn't a case of hormonal impulsivity.

I know for a fact Seb can pad through our home with total silence, so he's stomping so noisily toward our door on purpose. Giving me lots of warning of the conversation he wants to have. His footsteps stop just outside our room. I hate that there's a door between us. Even if he is trying to stave off his body's response to my heat pheromones. Consent is great, but he has it. And despite the revelations about his lies of omission pertaining for our HRT, I don't think he'd offer to fuck me if he didn't want to. If for no other reason than that he knows I'd be livid when—not if—I figured it out.

I pause and reach for the door, resting my hand on the smooth wood instead of the knob at the last second. For some reason, nerves swarm in my belly. Why isn't he opening the door? He's just standing there. Not saying anything. Maybe he's having second thoughts?

"Seb?" I ask, my voice shaking on my mate's name.

The lucid part of my brain pipes up with the helpful reminder that we haven't discussed that label properly. He isn't my mate. It's just a game we are considering playing. Even if he agreed to fuck me like one for the duration of my heat.

That stupid, rational bit of me is slipping back under the haze of heat hormones and lust. I'm not sure if I'm imagining his scent wafting to me now, but it has my mouth watering to taste him. I really want Seb to fuck me. I don't need a label to define that this is the shifter I trust beyond all others. The one I've twined into every part of my life and never want to let go.

"Yeah?" Seb asks, he's so close now. I can't help imagining that I can feel the heat of his hand against mine through the door. My scent blocker from earlier is for sure wearing off. Or he's just that horny because I can smell him now.

Lime and vanilla and everything good in the world, I'd never tell him this, but the fluctuating undertones that swing between alpha musk and omega sweetness depending on his hormone levels make no difference to me. It's still him, still the most comforting wonderful scent in the world, even tinged with the enticing musk of an alpha in rut. I know he hates anything alpha about his body, so I don't comment on it. That rut scent is getting stronger along with my own scent the longer we stand here though.

"Need you now. Can we talk more when you're inside me?" I complain, shuffling closer to the door, until my forehead is pressed against it too.

We talked so much on the phone. I know he slept with someone last night. A fellow avian. He'll need to get tested after that, but not for anything he can pass to me. Perks of dating outside my taxonomic class. Seb said he wants to see me before he agrees to letting me call him my mate until the heat breaks. So he can be sure it's really a rational choice and not the hormones talking, whatever makes him comfortable works for me.

"Meds wearing off?" Seb asks.

"Mhm." I bite my lip to choke back a needy moan as I palm my aching dick, I feel so wet and both my holes ache with the need to be filled. I glance over my shoulder at our bed and wince at all the discarded toys I left out when I heard him approaching. None of those dildos holds a candle to the delicious silky flesh over steel sensation of Seb's dick moving inside of me.

"Okay. If you're sure you want me to take care of you during the rest of the heat, open the door. I'll check in with you again during the lulls, but I need you to be sure, baby."

"I'm sure." I nod. Then feel foolish he can't see me through the door. So I fling it open as I repeat the fantasy we explored on the phone while I fucked myself on a toy and each mile brought him closer to me. "I want this. Want to pretend we can just have this. That we can be mates and spend the next few days trying to make a kit."

The sight of Seb standing there makes my mouth go dry and my pussy drip. I'm wetter than ever. Fuck. I stare at him as my brain grinds to a horny halt over the fastest way to get his dick inside me and a knot jammed in my ass.

Seb sucks his teeth loudly, then sighs. "Come here?"

He opens his arms and I go to him, clinging to him and breathing him in. His scent is different now. The heat pheromones are affecting him too. Even if he has more experience controlling it.

I whine and reach for him. "Need you." Need my mate, but I can't say that out loud yet. It's as if Seb hears it anyway and offers me everything he can.

"Hey, look at you. Aren't you just a sopping puddle of need for me? Want my cock omega mine?" Seb croons in a sweetly teasing tone. Encouraging me to enjoy myself.

I rock my hard dick into him and he plunges a hand between my thighs to rub my sensitive shaft, letting me buck into his grip a few times before he works his fingers further back, finding my slick pussy and fingering it open. "I want to fuck you here. This is where an alpha would put his pups in you. That's what you want from me, right, Rollie?"

There's an edge to his tone that warns me to word my answer with as much care as I can manage. What he said isn't quite right, but it's like I'm moving through honey to figure out why. There is a nuance to sharing my heat with him and him alone that's almost impossible to grasp through the burning need of the heat. I know what he just offered is not quite right in a part of me that the instinctual need for my mate wants to bulldoze past.

"Want you," I whimper, draping my naked body bone-lessly over his, grasping his shoulders and humping against his pants. It's true that I want him to breed me. As my mate, not as an alpha. Never that. Yes, that's what was wrong. Not like an alpha. Don't want an alpha, just him.

As hot as Seb breeding me sounds, it's exactly what he doesn't want to hear. It treads directly on layers of trauma. Any hint that I view him as anything other than the omega he is will gut him. Wound him deeper than any violent fuck with a stranger could ever reach inside of him. Maybe part of him wants that—but too damn bad. His fingers fal-ter inside of me and then thrust in harder, almost violently. It's just what I need to crystalize my half-formed thoughts in the heightened arousal of my heat.

"Oh, Seb, yes. There. Like that. Harder. I want my omega mate to breed me. To fill me up with your slick, and make everything feel so good. Mate, *not* alpha."

"Yeah? You saying you don't want me to go into a rut and knot this wet little hole?" Seb twists his fingers as he pumps them in deeper. Still forceful, but the edge of something feral he's never really shown me before is gone from it.

I gasp and thrust to meet him. He knows just how to make my body sing and I don't want to talk more. We had this discussion. Sort of. But I need him to feel good too. Need him to be able to let go and ride the high of pheromones and slick and pleasure with me, uninhibited and without holding back to guard his most tender parts.

He makes me feel so good, I need to get one more coherent thought out, and then I just want to lose myself in enjoying our make believe perfect fantasy. Forget that this shouldn't be possible and it might be a symptom of a serious issue. Forget all the reasons we'd be terrible as mates, and just—live in a moment of perfect bliss.

"I don't want your rut, Seb, I want your heat. I'd welcome making a kit together, but I don't want it to hurt you, mate." I touch his cheek, the smooth skin there is more stubbly than usual from the higher levels of alpha hormones. I swallow down my shame and guilt over taking the meds he gave me without question. I did this to him. Or at least, I didn't pay enough attention to see him using our shared meds as a blade to carve himself into pieces with. No more hurting each other with good intentions. Until my heat passes, I only want to give and take pleasure with him.

"Yeah? You sure, Rollie baby?" Seb leans back to meet my eyes, searching for any doubt. "This is what you want; two omegas sharing a heat with no alpha?"

"Yes." I cup his cheek, using the tenderness of my caress to say everything I can't put into words with my juices dripping down his wrist and the heat pheromones wrapping around us both.

"Mhm, me too. Always want you. You smell so good, Rollie. Like snickerdoodles and solstice." Seb nuzzles into my touch, cocking his head the way he does in his bird form. Inviting me to preen him. Trusting me entirely.

How did I let myself miss out on years of this closeness with him? All because I was afraid. Afraid mating another omega would somehow invalidate my own identity. Afraid he'd lose interest in me the way he does with most of his lovers. Afraid of the gossip and how people will react. None of that matters in the least, a merest spark against the inferno of hope and longing when he turns to kiss my palm, and then my lips.

My family won't understand this. And I could not care less. The animal instincts my heat is bringing to the surface force me to listen to what my raccoon side has been telling me all along. Seb has been the mate of my heart for years. If we never shared so much as a kiss, he would still be my other half. Having him in my life is as necessary as shifting into my second skin.

I whine and try to get him to go back to fingering me, rocking on his fingers and reaching for his wrist. Seb breaks the kiss and gives me a wicked grin.

"Who knew my sweet, polite, little Rollie could be such a needy boy for his mate?" Seb kisses me before I can protest. "You want me so bad, huh? You're desperate to get this tight little pussy fucked?" Seb thrusts into me then pauses until I nod my frantic agreement.

"Yes. Fuck me. Fill me up."

"I will. Soon. You're burning up with this heat, aren't you? Need a knot so bad? But you're too tight for any alpha to have like this, so it's all mine. My own tight little cunt to fuck and breed and fill with our clutch. That's what you want, huh? For me to mate you and make you all mine?"

Yes. That's exactly what I want. Words tangle up in my head and I open my mouth to agree only for Seb to cackle at the raccoon hiss of desperate needy sound that I garble out.

"I know baby, I need inside of you too." He kisses me again, withdrawing his fingers to crowd me toward our bed. "Looks like you tried just about everything to fill up your hole without me, but you still wanted me to take care of you, huh?"

"Yeah." I nod, glancing sheepishly at the array of used and discarded toys. Seb sweeps an assessing gaze over them too and plucks up an old faithful.

"Good boy. Such a desperate little slut, I think you need all of your holes filled, don't you? I'm gonna stuff your ass with a knotting plug." Seb holds up the toy I dropped on our bedding when he got here for my approval and I nod. "Good, present your hole for me?"

I get on all fours on the bed and spread my cheeks, I've seen him do this for alphas often enough to know exactly what he wants. Seb moans and when I glance over my shoulder to see what the hold up is, he rubs his bulge through his pants. "Such a gorgeous boy, so ready for me, aren't you darling? So slick and ready."

I'm not. Not where he's planning to stick that plug, I applied lube for the last round, but it's going to take more for the knot to feel good. By contrast, the hole Seb was fingering earlier has never been wetter in my life and I am more than ready to have him inside me.

Seb snorts, digs through the rucked up mess of blanket for the lube and drizzles a generous amount over the plug and even more between my cheeks before working the toy firmly inside of me. He teases me open, fucking the short firm length in by centimeters until the base is nestled firmly against my ass and the knotting parts are seated inside my rim where I'll get the most pleasure out of it.

"That's it, such a good omega, taking this knot for your mate. You're going to work it the whole time I fuck you, aren't you baby? You can take it until I come inside of you, right?"

I moan my agreement. I can definitely outlast the slow building pleasure that usually transforms into a growing discomfort if I keep the knot in too long. Right now, with the urgent lust of the heat riding me, that hardly seems like a challenge at all. I could take the knot all night. Forever, if it means keeping Seb inside of me. Connected to me. Calling me mate and praising me with his sweet endearments.

Seb makes the prep feel like he's putting on a show for us both. Giving me just enough of the perfunctory stretching it would take to have both of us ready to go if the heat had my slick glands in overdrive, while still taking care not to hurt me or risk the knot toy's bulge from getting too dry when he inflates it.

"You're dripping for me, darling." Seb reaches between my thighs to rub slick over my sensitive inner lips. "Can't wait to come in here." His fingers dip inside of me and I moan as I chase his touch. "I know, you need it so bad, huh? I just need you to roll onto your back so I can get in nice and deep."

I move into position, whimpering at the way the plug moves inside me, setting sensitized nerves tingling with pleasure. I squirm to try to dislodge another dildo from under my back, which has me gasping at the plug jostling around in my ass all over again, pushing forward and making me ache to have Seb breeding me already. I flail around and manage to kick most of the bedding and toys onto the ground with satisfying thumps.

"Seb? Ready? Need you now." I rub against the mattress, trying to get off on the plug inside me, but it's not close to enough.

What's the hold up? I glance over to see Seb finally letting his clothing drop to the floor. My mouth waters and I want to taste him. The last dildo I missed under my hip digs into me. Seb reaches under me to pluck up the last toy. I pull him down on top of me.

"Oof!" Seb's startled expression dissolves into laughter and then trails into a moan as I wriggle under him, lining his erect dick up where I need him, so that it juts into mine when I buck up to try to get his dripping cockhead where we both need it. Inside me. Buried so deep a part of him might never have to leave. I want to melt into one being and as Seb pins my wrists above my head and makes eye contact, he has so much more than just my body under his thrall. "Manners, Rollie. Ask for what you want."

"I want my mate to breed me so deep I can taste your jizz." I pout as I wriggle helplessly under him, still trying to get him where I want him. He wants this too. He said so. I don't know why he's being such a tease about it now.

Seb laughs. "I got that impression, yeah." His smile dims and I can't quite read all the complexity of his expression as he says, "Just need to be sure you're happy without a condom? I've fucked other mammal shifters since my last STI panel, with a condom, but still..."

"I know, you already said that. Don't care. Want to smell you on me. Risk that you're carrying something you can't get is low enough. We'll talk more details when I'm not in heat."

"Okay. Sorry," Seb sounds like he means that on far too many levels. There is so much weight in that one-word apology and I don't want to unpack any of it. Funny how I woke up this morning ready to demand an apology from him and now that he feels compelled to offer one, albeit for all the wrong reasons, it's the last thing I want from him. We still have a lot to talk about. And all of it will keep until after my heat.

"Don't apologize; just fuck me, Seb."

"Such a demanding mate," Seb teases me, trying to re-capture our earlier playfulness. I crunch up to nip at him, going along with it.

"Get your dick inside me, omega." I demand.

"Yes, mate." Seb obeys with only a hint of the feral need to push every one of his own limits that I've seen in him with an alpha between us. I arch up at the first delicious slide of his body slotting inside of mine. Right where he belongs. Where I want him to always come home to when he needs to lose himself. He smells so good. The essence of him that underpins everything else and remains unchanging no matter what his pheromones tell the world about his secondary gender. Seb and home. Mate and mine.

I never want this heat to end. Seb fucks me, the knot toy in my ass fills. I can smell when he's close, our combined slick is a heady perfume I want to bathe in. We slow our pace, dragging out each gentle thrust, flirting along the edges of an orgasm, making this last as long as possible.

The first round rolls into the next and time blends into a cycle of cuddles and fucking and raiding the kitchen for snacks to fuel more fucking. By the end of the first day, I can't tell if I'm dripping with our combined slick, or his seed and I don't care.

For all the dirty talk about breeding, I don't let myself even begin to hope there is any chance of either of us getting pregnant. The odds are so miniscule it would only be inviting in heartache to even entertain the spark of a thought that one in a million things can happen and Seb would be the most amazing parent to share a kit with.

I still like it when he spoons me and rubs warm hands over my belly telling me how full of kits he's going to stuff it after our nap. It's hot to talk about it, and Seb likes it too when we switch roles. He comes so hard I almost worry he'll break my dick when I talk about breeding him. He comes inside me so many times I lose count over the course of my heat.

I lose track of time entirely. The outside world will have to wait. Nothing beyond our bed matters when I get to have my fondest fantasy coming true. I get to share a natural heat with my mate. We can worry about how and why and what it means later. For now, I savor every drop of pleasure with the shifter I love. My inner omega and inner raccoon and every part of me utterly content to be tucked up safe in our den with Seb.

Chapter 10

Seb

ROLLIE'S HEAT IS LIKE living in a dream. Every fantastical moment buried deep inside him is like a taste of forbidden candies. A treasure I don't deserve and could never earn. I want to memorize every moment of this time with him, to carve him indelibly into each of my senses.

No music could ever sound as sweet as Rollie's lust-thick voice begging for my cock and calling me his mate. Mate. Omega. Mine. I call him the same in turn. Let myself babble out the future I'd have offered him if I wasn't so damn broken before we ever met.

Together we paint an impossible picture in hushed pillow talk between rounds of sex. We voice our shared dreams of a typical mating and children that I know can't ever come true for either of us.

I can't give him kits or a clutch. But I can show him how he deserves to be cherished. My perfect omega. Rollie's presence in my life is my greatest treasure, and I do my best to let him see that, just like he somehow still sees me as worthy of his love.

The only marker of time that matters is the ebb and flow of his need as the heat lasts several days. I'm aware that it's fading on the final morning when he wakes me up for another round as he has several times since we started.

I savor every sensation when he wakes me up with needy kisses and clumsy stroking. Urge him to mount my hips and ride my aching cock. I've fucked him so often over the past however many days that I'm sure we'd both be chafed if not for all the slick and the heat pheromones raging between us. His scent isn't as strong with it this morning.

The heat is breaking. This might be my last time to make love to him, without hiding my naked longing for him behind the pretext of a threesome.

I grip his hips to slow him down, the need to draw out this last time almost as urgent and the need to come inside of him again. Rollie bites his lip and whines at me. "One more time, Seb. Mate. One more—just breed me once more."

He stops before he can say the thing we've been dancing around. One more chance to put my kits in his belly. It's pure fantasy. And even then, the idea of my jizz knocking anyone up is stomach churning. It isn't supposed to work like that for any omega.

I squeeze my eyes shut and try to block out the familiar voice reminding me that I'm not a proper omega. That even this fleeting thought is proof I never was. That I deserve to be broken. I thrust harder into Rollie and he moans, rocking to meet me.

"Mm, yes, there. Seb. Oh! Need more. Harder, mate. Please."

I reach up to pull him down into a kiss, rough and devouring. Trying to fall back into my familiar patterns of drowning out the howling voice of all my scars made manifest in a rush of sex and pain and...Rollie cups my cheek in his palm. A gentle caress. He won't hurt me. Not the way I crave. The way that tears open raw, infected scars to let them bleed more.

"Make love to me, Seb? One more time. Just, don't go away in your head like that?" Rollie nips at my lower lip, the twinge of pain focusing my attention and making my dick twitch inside of him.

"Ouch," I whine, but it's not the sting of his teeth that lands hardest. It's the ache of knowing Rollie can see right into my soul. And he'd rather let me focus on a love bite than the well-worn barbs my own brain flings at me, right on cue.

"You're going to stay with me," Rollie promises. His nails score my shoulders where he's resting his hands to balance over me again. Once he's sure he has my attention, he twists the hoop in my left nipple too, giving me the sensations that make my dick twitch without the things that feed the voice of the void calling to me.

"Am I?" I buck up under him, half challenging him and half because I want to make him moan and ride me again and forget all about this little bubble of time where he's focusing fully on me and what I need.

"Mhm. You are. Stop trying to distract me, mate." Rollie grinds down onto me hard and scrapes his nails gently over my pecs, right to my nipples. He pinches and twists both of the silver hoops piercing them. "And we're going to wring every last drop of pleasure out of our heat before it fades, Sebastian. You know why?"

"Why?" I ask him, panting as he soothes away the ache in my abused nipple with gentle strokes of his thumb, then goes back to teasing it. "Ungh, Rollie," I whine, drawing out his name and fucking him a little faster to try to distract him from teasing me.

Rollie's hips rock to meet mine, but he doesn't break his focus at all. In retaliation, he flicks my right piercing, sending jolts of contradictory sensation directly to my crotch. He clenches around me as my dick lights up with sensation and I can't quite still my hips, bucking up into him with more force.

"We're going to make love now, because everyone says that good omega mates spend their heats making their mates come until they can't manage another load." Rollie twists both piercings again, just to the limits of what feels good.

"No. I'm not…" I shake my head, unable to articulate how deep a wound he just jabbed.

Rollie can't know that his words open up an entire chasm of terrible memories. Being told similar things in total earnest by the first alpha I ever loved. My ex meant those things, expected me to live up to every stereotype of what an omega should be. And the minute creep meant I couldn't anymore he threw me out like trash. I believed him. Still do when I'm at my lowest.

My chest is too tight, lungs constricting until I'm certain I can't gasp in another breath, and I soften inside of Rollie. I can't fuck him if that's what he wants. A traditional anything. I can't breathe, because this is so far from anything

I ever believed about him...Rollie stills on top of me, no longer trying to fuck himself on my deflating cock.

"I can't." I don't know if I'm saying that about the sex or my ability to breathe or what. But it's the honest truth. Rollie gets off of me and fusses over me.

"What's wrong? Sebastian? What can't you do? Honey, what can't you do? I...did I say it wrong? You're scaring me. Can you breathe with me, baby?" Rollie asks.

My earnest mate scrambles up to kneel near my head and hovers over me as he tries to figure out what's wrong. He wrings his hands in a gesture so reminiscent of his raccoon side that I'd laugh if I could get any air into my aching lungs. What *isn't* wrong with me?

Rollie reaches for my face, like he wants to check my airway. I breathe in his scent reflexively, soothing and sweet. Even tinged with worry and fear for me. It's still got that extra zing of a heat, but that's fading faster now that I've got his adrenaline pumping. Fuck. Rollie counts out some breathing exercise he must have picked up from Winny or Ty with their therapy bullshit.

I follow along, inhaling him as deep into my lungs as he can get. Savoring this moment, in case this heat is the only time I get to experience what it would be like for him to love me as a mate. A few more stolen moments of bliss. Even a panic attack is better with him next to me.

We breathe together until the fist clenching around my lungs relaxes entirely and the immediacy of my resurfaced memories fades. With a moment to think rationally, it's obvious that Rollie would never expect me to live up to someone else's notions of who we should be. I know that in the hollows of my bird bones. This was dirty talk gone awry.

Normally, echoes of my trauma are exactly the sort of unintended wounds I seek out to flay myself open. Punishments to absolve me of all the ways I can never seem to feel right in my skin. All the ways I asked for every hurt and every invisible scar. Except the only balm that ever truly soothes my soul for more than a moment is right here lying next to me.

I nuzzle into his neck, getting as close as I can to the shifter I love without crawling inside him. I kiss Rollie's throat, mouthing at his skin, tasting days of sex and heat pheromones on him. We are going to need a shower. After. Right now I need one more chance to make love to him. Once more chance to connect. To be his treasure.

"Better?" Rollie asks, squirming when I lick his throat, needing every trace of him I can get. I need to taste every inch of him. Lap up more of the thick sweet ambrosia that is his slick.

"Yeah. Sorry. Bad memory." I shrug it off and he tries to gather me into his arms, cuddling me.

"Want to talk about it?" Rollie offers. He's sweeter than I'll ever be able to believe I deserve.

"After. You're still in heat." It's deflection and we both know it. Rollie doesn't push, but he doesn't let me get away with pretending nothing happened either.

"Mhm. Doesn't mean you're required to service me, Sebastian. I can take the plug into the shower and ride out the last of it alone if that was too intense. You get to say no. And you will still be the very best omega I know either way. That's all I meant. That I have no regrets about sharing my heat with another omega—with you. You are my best treasure, Seb."

"Uh huh," I nuzzle closer, tipping my head toward him so he'll scratch his fingers over my scalp. Preening me as best he can with stubby human fingers instead of a beak. I sigh as he pets me, his love so clear in every touch, it's impossible to deny.

"I'm sorry I made you doubt that for an instant. When I was out of my mind with the heat, before I realized that's what it was, and Harvey had me wait for a ride home in the break room, my raccoon wanted to dig through the walls to find a safe den to hide. You know what he wanted?"

"To go home?" I wave a hand toward our room and all the pretty things we've decorated it with, a perfect nest, or a cozy den. Just what both our animal natures need, despite my insecurities making it hard to claim the space for my own, or really count on anyone to want to be an *us* with me.

"You, Seb." Rollie kisses my temple, a fond counter to the exasperated amusement in his tone. "*You* are all I pictured when I needed to feel safe."

I don't have words for that. Denying him would be spiting myself. Arguing with him over his emotions is pure folly, even if I'll never quite trust that I could possibly inspire feelings like that from any potential mate.

I don't have any words, but neither does the voice in my head that always knows just what failing or deep-seated character flaw to fling in my face. I know that viscous voice of self-hatred isn't gone for good. The reprieve is no less wonderful for being temporary.

Rollie can somehow shut up the vile brute in my head, and if I didn't already adore my omega mate before that, I'd fall for him all over again. If only just for his ability to lance the pressure from old hurts and turn them into—I don't even know. I shake my head, speechless.

"Anyway. I want you to feel safe too, Seb. But I kind of, uh, need to take care of this—we can talk and snuggle more after?" Rollie kisses the tip of my nose, then gently rolls out of my arms to reach for the knotting plug.

"No, let me." I grab his wrist, circling it gently. "I want to make love to you."

"You sure?" Rollie checks warily, but he doesn't try to pull away from me.

"Beyond certain." I nod. The only voice echoing in my mind when he beams at me is his, reminding me that I'm his good omega. His best omega. His mate. "Want to breed my mate one last time for this heat."

I kiss him then, pulling him back on top of me. Rollie and I make out lazily at first, and then more urgently as his slick coats our groins. I'm hard again, aching to pound out my release inside of him.

I ignore the deep tingly ache at the base of my dick that I've read about in books. I'm probably imagining the sensation of a newly formed knot bud to go with my other unwanted alpha traits. That has to be it.

"Mm, need you, Seb, come inside me?" Rollie strokes my length. "Need your pretty little omega cock buried inside me."

"Yeah. Right here, where you're too tight for any alpha, all mine." I nudge between his slick pussy lips, urging him to open and take me.

Rollie spreads his legs, riding me. I grab hold of his meaty thighs and flip us around so I can drive in deeper, the instinctual need to bury myself inside of him urged on by his every needy sound and throaty moan.

"That's it, my treasure. So good. You're so good." Rollie moans the last word as I fuck into him hard enough to have us inching across the mattress.

Damn, he's so good, and his praise rings in my ears impossible to accept, except Rollie doesn't lie. He hates lies, so he has to believe that impossible declaration—he thinks I'm good. He presses his palm over my heart and I'm certain he isn't referring to my sexual prowess. Or at least not entirely, the amount of slick squelching out of him every time I thrust speaks for itself about how turned on he is.

I can't handle the idea of disappointing him when he realizes I can't live up to who he thinks I am, so I give him one thing I really am good at. Sex.

"You love this. Love it when I come inside your hot little hole and leave you a sloppy mess, huh?" I tease as I fuck him harder.

"Mhm. Yes. So messy. Need it. Need more." Rollie is panting and writhing under me and I know he's close.

His heat is telling him he needs more than I can give him without a toy. I was worried that his need for a knot would sting every time, a glaring reminder that we can never work out in the long term. Except we do work and the knotting plug does give him the extra stretch he needs to sate his instincts.

"You're fucking desperate for a fat knot and a belly full of kits, but you're going to make do with this plug and my load dripping out of you for the rest of the day, aren't you my sweet mate?" I tease as I push the plug into his well slicked ass and press the button to make it swell to full size inside of his ass.

"Yes!" Rollie arches under me.

I pin him down and fuck him harder.

"Oh, yes! So good." Rollie keens, nails scoring lines of stinging heat down my back.

Everything about being with him feels so right. I can't help fucking into him faster. For once, I'm fully present with the shifter sharing my bed as he gasps and moves with me, meeting me and taking me to the hilt until his eyes roll up into his head. Rollie's gorgeous face is a portrait of an omega freeze-framed just before he comes. Like he's caught the wave of his own pleasure and wants to ride it forever before letting it crash down over us both.

"Mmm." Rollie shudders against me, his cunt squeezing my cock and making that tingly feeling spread along every inch of my dick. It's like he is milking every drop of pleasure out of me.

"Fuck, you're incredible." I cling to him, fighting back my release to let him take as much as he wants.

With an effort, I slow down to match Rollie's pace; let him control the steady build of this final orgasm. It feels momentous. So much bigger than just busting a nut with him.

"So close. Wanna come together." Rollie can read me like a book, even in the throes of passion and caught up in the last remnants of what might well be his only natural heat.

Whatever this does or doesn't mean for our future, it is special. Important. He's important. We both want to savor every moment. He locks eyes with me as I move inside him, those soulful blue depths beg me for what he truly wants. What I suspect he's wanted for a long time, and been too afraid to ask for.

We agreed to play at being mates for the duration of his heat, but it's obvious he doesn't want it to end now that we're on the precipice. Neither do I, even if it terrifies me to consider tying myself to him like an anchor. He deserves so much better than me. He deserves exactly what he wants. I don't know the right thing to do here, but for now, all I need to do is give him exactly what we already agreed to. A perfect heat with his mate, pretend or not.

I press my forehead to his, nuzzling our noses together. "Not gonna last much longer sweetheart, you feel too amazing." I press gentle kisses to his cheeks.

"Come." Rollie commands, voice gravelly with unspoken emotions.

I don't hold back, thrusting fast and furious as he comes undone around me. Wave after wave of his cunt undulating around my dick. I gasp as lightning flares in the base of my cock and the orgasm feels like nothing I've ever experienced before.

I grip Rollie tight, and he clings to me. We anchor each other as we're set adrift in an endless tide of pleasure. I kiss him, needing to connect to him more, to be inside him in every way possible and let him inside me as his tongue fucks into my mouth and we swallow each other's desperate needy moans.

My entire cock is a rocket exploding into the night sky in a shower of sparks. I cling to Rollie, push my tongue and cock in more insistently, needing to be connected to him. Grounding myself in his presence as pulse after pulse of pleasure bursts out of me to fill my mate. He's squeezing me so tight in his arms, like he needs me to hold him together as much as I need him.

A new sensation joins the symphony of heat-enhanced pleasure. His pussy clenching around me always feels incredible, but this is more than that. It's like a fist wrapping around the base of my dick, fucking a secondary orgasm out of me while I'm still shooting. Like my entire existence is nothing but an expansive pleasure taking root and flowing forth to fill the tight hole around it and without Rollie's body there to cradle me I might just fly apart at the seams.

Whatever that new feeling is, Rollie moans and rides me through the entire thing, his internal muscles still working my length. There's no way it lasts as long as it seems to, the pair of us riding out the aftershocks for what has to be a blink even though it feels like I might just keep fucking my cum deeper inside of him for an eternity.

It's sheer bliss. I'm buried inside of the omega I might finally be able to admit out loud I love as we both revel in the best orgasm of my life. I want to shout our love from the rooftops, no more caveats or pretending he's not the only forever I want. I hope it's the best sex of his life too. I never want to have to separate, so I hold him. And kiss him, and rock our bodies together until I've softened enough that moving makes my dick slip out of him and both of us gasp and wriggle closer together. Rollie gathers me into his arms and kisses my forehead.

"Mm. Best sex ever," he jokes as he nestles his head on my chest.

"Mhm. Ten thousand out of ten, no notes. You're pure perfection," I tease him.

Rollie snorts, like he thinks I'm joking and then he sighs. "I think my heat is over."

"Yeah?" I snuffle at his hair. "Hm, can't tell. Let me see." It really is hard to tell when we both smell thoroughly of sex and the room reeks of his heat pheromones. He's probably right, but I still take the easy excuse to nose into his armpit and inhale, much to his chagrin as he laughingly shoves my face away.

"Hey! I need a shower, you perv."

I chuckle at him and tuck him back against my chest. "Yep, your heat is definitely over. You didn't care how deliciously ripe you smelled while it was still going strong."

"Rude!" Rollie nips at my nipple, then sucks it into his mouth. His wet heat engulfing the sensitive nub would normally have my dick perking up, even just a twitch. But I don't have a drop of libido left after that last round.

"See? No more wild heat pheromones making my dick spring back to life at the drop of a hat either," I tease, gesturing at my very spent dick where it remains limp against my thigh.

"Guess that means we have a lot to discuss?" Rollie bites his lip and glances around the room, avoiding eye contact.

"We do." I want to chicken out. Tell him we can shower first. Eat. Check the time and heck, the date for that matter. Check in with family and work and dive back into all the routines that his unexpected heat forced us to put on pause.

We could easily latch on to finding any and every excuse to never talk. Never put this bond we've built at risk by demanding it hold the entire weight of all my baggage.

I can come up with a million excuses and circumnavigate the globe by moving the goalposts on this. But Rollie deserves to have the mating he just showed me a glimpse of. He deserves everything and not having the conversations we need to is holding us both back from that. Even if we ultimately decide we can't find it together. Whatever my brain tells me about how richly I deserve a lifetime spent in limbo, he doesn't. So I don't make excuses. I card my fingers through his hair.

I'm not ready to talk, and I'm even less ready to relinquish this easy familiarity with his body. "What should we talk about first?"

"I don't even know." Rollie sighs. Then he yawns. I can't stop myself from yawning too, and that has us both giggling. "Um, I think I need a nap first. Would you, um, shift with me? I just know we have a lot to talk about, but I really don't want to think yet. I only want to raccoon. And my raccoon side feels very smug about our den smelling like us."

I survey our room. My inner raven puffs up with pride at the nest we've lined together. I get up and pile our colorful blankets and assorted throw pillows back onto our bed. I smile as I touch them all.

Objectively, we have way too many pillows, but they make a very nice cuddle pile. It's a jewel-bright kaleidoscope with metallic accents. Each of the various throw pillows has its own unique shape and print. Fabrics ranging from shaggy fluff that feels like hugging a cloud to shiny sequins. Silky satin, thick brocade, intricate beading. A sensory feast. Treasures we brought home either together or to show each other.

Our entire room is like that. A hodgepodge collection of things that caught my or Rollie's eyes and that we added to this space to build a cozy little home together. Rollie is my home. And together we've built a nest worthy of bringing a hatchling into.

That thought of futile nesting deflates the swelling emotions in my chest. Yeah. I don't want to think right now either. I want to preen my sweet raccoon mate and pretend things can be as simple as our love letting us create a family together that can overcome any obstacle.

"Yeah. A nap would be good. You need a good preening." I ruffle his hair and Rollie bats my hands away with a pouty scowl. So damn cute. I want to kiss his adorable pouty lip. And that's my cue to shift because we need to talk before I just bulldoze in assuming that things he said in the throes of his heat are what he still wants now that it's over.

Rollie watches as my feathers sprout over my skin. Shifting in front of another person is intimate, but it's far from the most intimate thing I do with my best friend on a regular basis. I squawk at him to shift too, then flap up to our bed so I can get cozy with him.

If I wasn't so focused on him I might have missed the next words that he barely breathes when he thinks I'm too busy fussing with the pillows to notice. Even so, I almost miss it under the sound of him bundling our sex toy collection into a towel to clean them before storing it all back into the plastic tote where it stays most of the time.

"Love you, mate," Rollie shakes his head at me in fond exasperation.

Mhm. Mate, the title settles my nerves and I fluff out my feathers for a lazy preen while I wait for him to tidy up enough to join me. Each toy lands atop the others with an oddly satisfying thud. Rollie mutters about how we need to disinfect them all after our nap. True, but that hardly matters to my raven right now.

I dismiss his continued mumbling as boring human things. I stretch out one wing and idly check my flight feathers. And I might croak a little to remind him it's naptime.

My silly raccoon. They are notorious for getting days and nights crossed. Good thing he has me to remind him. I sidle closer and call again. Rollie glances at me and holds up a finger. That usually means wait a minute. Boo. I'm sleepy now. I clack my beak in irritation. Rollie chuckles.

"Impatient as always, bird."

I preen my shoulder pointedly when he glances my way, showing off my feathers, and reminding him that mates preen each other so he needs to join me in our nest now.

"Yes, I'm stalling, you daft bird." Rollie glances at me with a soppy smile. "Don't know how to get it through your thick feathery head that I love you. I want to be your mate. Only ever yours."

I caw at him. No fair talking when we agreed to nap first. Before I can shift back to scold him properly, or just say what we need to say, Rollie plops down next to me and offers me his hand. I snuggle in under his palm and he smooths my feathers.

I preen his fingers with my beak. Rollie lets me finish the gesture, then he lifts his hand away and shifts. His raccoon is soft and sweet and adorably fluffy. I march right up to his head, preen his pretty facemask, and then settle in to nap next him, tucking him under my wing like a chick that needs to be protected and kept warm and adored. Rollie nuzzles his face into my side and curls his elegant striped brush of a tail around us.

Talking can wait. Sleeping together like this is for family. Mates. I never have the right words with Rollie, but somehow, he always seems to understand. And I am going to tell him. Later. He is everything good that I want and at least in my feathers, I'm finally ready to reach out and ask if I can have this with him.

Rollie is my treasure and I sleep well beside him, no need to hide just how close I want to be to him any longer. I have the most restful sleep I can recall ever having with my mate in our nest.

Chapter 11

Rollie

Mmmm. I wake up in my fur to the familiar dim pre-dawn light of my cozy den, utterly content at being surrounded by the combined scents of mate and home. If I didn't have a full bladder urging me out of bed right this second, I'd snuggle back down next to my mate and put off the need to return to the human world a little while longer.

My inner animal isn't entirely convinced that I *really* need to go all the way to the bathroom for that, but I have enough of my human faculties to know better. Even if we already need to wash all the evidence of my heat from the bedding.

My raccoon huffs about silly human sensibilities while my human side twinges with all the complicated human emotions about what might be my only natural heat being undoubtedly over. My raccoon is more practical. Pee first. Feelings after.

I stretch and Seb chirrups a soft protest at being disturbed. I pause, warm all over at knowing he is still snuggled next to me, then ease myself out from under him. He grinds his beak and resettles his feathers with a sound like rustling leaves.

I glance back at him, regretting leaving the warm, dozy comfort of our cuddle nest. Seb tucks his beak behind one wing and continues to sleep. I watch him for a long moment, wishing I could just stay here with him. Stretch out the dwindling moments before we have to get back to reality and all our outside obligations.

It would be easier to let go if I felt more solid in knowing I'd have more of this shared domesticity. Years of getting to watch my mate sleep or join him in the bed or wake him by preening his soft, glossy feathers to look forward to. That's still up in the air. Still left for us to discuss.

My bladder urges me out of bed though. I shift as I hop out of the bed, landing on my human feet with ease. I dig my phone out of the mess of discarded clothes on the floor, then grab the first clean PJs I find in my drawers to change into. If I get dressed then I have to stay up and deal with what happens next.

There's so much to sort out though, and part of me wants to cling to the fantasy spell Seb and I wove while I was in heat. A shared future. It's so tempting to just get back in bed with him, and pretend for a while longer.

No more putting off the hard conversations that we should have had years ago. Now that I'm more lucid, I desperately need a shower. Not that I don't want to smell like Seb. I do, but my hair being crunchy with cum and slick is a bit much. It will be easier to face the serious conversations looming over us if I don't smell like he fucked me seven ways from Sunday.

Ugh. I fight back the preemptive grief of knowing exactly the kind of intimacy I stand to lose with Seb if our conversation goes poorly. Not focusing on that now. Not until he's awake.

For now, I can focus on more practical matters. A shower is just the beginning of the cleanup I need to do after spending fuck knows how long in bed together—I reach to check the date on my phone, except the battery is completely drained.

I snort and shake my head at my priorities with the heat hormones driving my choices. Yeah, charging it didn't cross my mind once Seb got here. So, phone, shower, and breakfast. Good plan.

I shuffle to the bathroom and plug my cell into the charger by the sink, then adjust the water while I make a mental to do list to keep from dwelling on my growing anxiety over the unknown. Seb's hair products next to mine make me weepy at the thought of their potential absence. *Enough, I am not going there.*

I get out a fresh towel and step into the water. How many times have I taken for granted that I can join Seb in here? How much longer will that last if—nope, I'm not borrowing trouble.

I adjust the pressure setting on the shower head down to narrow jets that sting my skin and distract me from my thoughts. It's only a limited success as I lather up the dregs of the shampoo and make a mental note to pick up more at work. Which reminds me I don't even know when my next shift is.

Once it's a reasonable hour, I need to figure out how much work I missed and call Harvey. Not to mention calling my endocrinologist to figure out what the hell happened. I shouldn't be having a heat. Even with the synthetic inducers Seb and I fooled around with, it took more than the usual dose to get even a fraction of the effects I had with this one.

So something weird and probably not great caused this and I should probably stop taking Seb's HRT, even if it wasn't doing fuck knows what to me. I shiver at the icy dread of just how catastrophic of a warning sign the heat could be. Not going there. Borrowing trouble I can't control is pointless.

So I focus on what I can control. The rough scrape of Seb's mesh bath sponge thing scouring my skin. A million tiny tasks that I can plan. The fridge probably needs a deep clean and I need a meal plan for the week and a plan to get the time off I might need for medical stuff while not further overburdening my coworkers by making them cover for me again so soon after an unplanned heat leave.

None of that really matters right now. We have a few shifters who are more than happy to pick up extra hours. Harvey isn't going to be upset that I needed heat leave, the store has always had a generous policy around that.

My static human doctor will probably scold me for going around him to get omega HRT after he told me it might exacerbate my underlying hormonal imbalances that my human HRT is meant to control, but that's nothing new.

Only now I can't keep going around his human-centric biases when he ignores that I'm not a static human; there is no treating the human parts of me if he's ignoring that *all* of me is a shifter. An omega shifter who feels wrong in my skin without the hormones Seb sacrificed so much to give me.

Fuck. I crank up the heat until the jets of water burn. That's better. Mostly. Can't think when the water is searing away my troubles. Just like how Seb buries his despair in pain he can control.

How many times have I stepped into this shower to hold him together after he breaks himself apart? I've gotten so used to him being part of the fabric of my life that I've accepted a status quo I don't think I can handle going back to now.

For years, the good times when I'm living my best life with my best friend at my side have been worth supporting Seb through the times when he gives in to his worst impulses. But the good times seem to be getting shorter and further apart and now I've had a taste of what it would be like to have him in my bed as a lover rather than the best friend I occasionally share an alpha with.

How many more times can I handle him shoving me away one minute, then coming home to snuggle next to me, smelling of a stranger and hollowed out by the things he does to exorcize his demons?

I don't dare to let myself believe that we can continue this newfound level of intimacy, but I can't handle too much more of this dance of total intimacy and retreat with him. Two steps closer before he launches himself into his usual depression spiral of unhealthy coping mechanisms. Never knowing when he's going to run from what he can't face and leave me behind with my heart on a platter for him all over again. One way or another, I need to break my part of our toxic cycle.

I love him too much to watch him hurt himself any more. Is he going to punish himself for this beautiful interlude by taking bigger risks? Can I handle standing by and watching him self-destruct and knowing I lit the fuse this time? What choice do I even have in that? Other than walking away before I get a front-row seat to him unraveling?

I turn my face into the hot, high-pressure jets, letting it pelt into me until I can pretend it's the shower and not my own tears stinging my eyes. Once I start crying, I can't seem to hold anything back.

Great wracking sobs that flush away all the festering rot of swallowing down my emotions around Seb shake my entire body. I love Seb and watching him hurt himself hurts me. It hurts too much to keep doing it. And I can't keep waiting to see if he'll ask for the help he needs on his own.

As much as I love the friendship we've built our shared life around, I need to know exactly where I stand with him.

With or without the hottest sex marathon of my life that we just shared, I want what we have to be my future. But only if he can commit to it too. Only if he can stop punishing himself for things he couldn't have ever controlled.

I cry until the hot water washing over me turns tepid. It's a catharsis I didn't realize I needed to let go of all the ways that keeping the peace and silencing my own needs has hurt. A release valve on the anger and resentment over him withholding information about the HRT he shared with me.

I needed that. A way to reset my emotions to a place of calm where I can have a conversation with Seb when he's awake. I'm still scared, and anxious that asking for what I need will result in losing the omega I love, but if I'm that scared of losing him, then maybe he's never really been mine to lose.

I dry off, get dressed, and leave my phone on the charger so I can focus on making a nice breakfast. Once I turn it on, I know it will bombard me with an unending barrage of notifications and urgent tasks and things outside my den that need to be dealt with.

I'll get to all of those demands soon, but first I need a hot meal. And I want to have one last taste of the normalcy I've loved about living here with Seb; breakfast together.

We can have our big serious conversation with bellies full of hot food and then...well, I'll worry about how to move forward once I have all the facts. It's really up to Seb whether I'm doing this with my best friend at my side as my mate or if I need to move on from offering my heart to someone who can't accept it.

...

Chapter 12

Seb

THE ENTICING AROMA OF bacon and coffee mingled with the combined scents of home and mate wake me from my post-heat nap. Heat. *It was a heat.* Not the other word that clings to the back of my mind and makes me shudder.

Even in my feathers, I shy away from the words that don't match who I am. Alpha words. Alpha reactions to being with an omega in heat. Knots and rut. I aggressively preen my feathers. The sting of too much pressure on a blood feather clearing away the familiar ticker tape scroll of self-loathing thoughts before it can really get going.

The only thing that stops me from plucking out the thick shaft of my flight feather entirely is the fact Bram will notice. He'll notice and he will not stop hounding me about it. Birds who pluck their feathers are not okay, and nothing will convince my nosy family to drop the issue if I start up with that old habit again. I let myself preen a blood feather a little too aggressively as a compromise, tugging on the shaft until it throbs like a cavity in my human teeth. It hurts and I know better than to do it.

Rollie's scent lingering on my feathers calms the bonedeep ache that urges me to punish myself. I leave the sore spot along and turn to actually preening. Even though picking cum out of my feathers is a pain. Sleeping in our sex nest has my feathers in desperate need of a good cleaning so I hop and flap my way over to the vanity, perch on the back of the chair that's already scored with layers of my talon prints and savor the taste and scent of Rollie all over me.

Preening the evidence of his heat from my feathers requires meticulous care. And every taste of him is a visceral reminder of getting to be with him the past few days. A chance to savor all that mind blowing sex with the omega of my dreams. Time for my raven to make it crystal clear that our nest is perfect with just the two of us in it. No need to bring in an alpha.

Rollie is perfect. My perfect mate. My raven lingers over a sense memory of Rollie begging to make a clutch together. I still can't give him that. My raven croons a broken little cry at the reminder. The thing that always drives me to my worst choices is that I can't give my mate the one thing I'm made for. Marin called me broken, and it still hurts me every time I hear those words on repeat in my brain because he was right.

I can't be what any mate deserves. For most things, my raven might not do static human emotions, but the depths of his grief at not being able to raise a clutch with his mate is such a bone-deep longing that I can't stand being in my feathers just then.

I shift back. I still can't fix what's wrong with me, but I can at least make sure I didn't do lasting harm to Rollie by messing around with our HRT. The shifter specialists at the zoo will make sure Rollie is healthy and get him on the right dose and dosage form. Oh, shit, that reminds me—hopefully I still have the job I left without a word of warning after my first day.

I need to call Bram and Ty. Or Felix? Someone from the zoo. See if I still have the temp contract at all. When it comes to this, my raven is still the broken omega boy who believes to his core every heated word tying my worth to what creep took away from me. Everything I took away from the alpha I thought would be my mate. Except Rollie has known about my diagnosis forever. He knows, and he still wanted to call me his mate.

I was still the only one he wanted in the grips of his heat. Not an alpha. Not the version of me that smells like an alpha, so he can pretend to have the picture-perfect stereotype of what an omega should want. Me. Rollie wants me.

And if the best omega I know can know the depths of my brokenness and love me through it, then maybe I can find a way to believe him instead of the words that have been imprinted on my psyche for far too long. Giving myself over to an alpha who only ever saw me as something to use, carving his words into my heart and flaying myself open in hopes of erasing that mantra has only ever driven the rot deeper.

Maybe it's time I let that hurt go. It's certainly time to face whatever Rollie has to say to me. I'll grovel on my knees for a chance to make things right with him. To prove to him that I can be the mate he deserves. And the first step to being that is taking care of him—no, not just him. Taking care of both of us.

I grab my phone, ready to make the call to straighten out my work situation and find a way to book a more urgent appointment to get us both tested in light of the heat and that...I knotted him at the end. I swallow down the burning lump of pain at having to admit it. We can fix this. I am going to fix it. And that might take an uncomfortable amount of candor, but I can handle it. For the future Rollie deserves, I'll face down all my demons.

My phone is dead. That's annoying. I plug it in to charge, then head to the bathroom for a quick shower. Rollie must have used all the hot water, so I take the world's fastest tepid shower before the water gets too cold to stand another second.

Once I'm clean, I pad naked back into our room and pull on a pair of Rollie's comfy flannel lounge pants, tightening the drawstring so that they hang loosely from my hips. It occurs to me that wearing his clothes like it is second nature hits differently after hearing him call me his mate in the throes of passion.

It's a warmth that blooms in my chest. A sense of rightness and belonging. The weight of that shift in perspective staggers me. I've known our friendship blurs the lines most people draw between friends and lovers for ages.

It's just that until Rollie offered me his heat, I didn't think he wanted more than the mostly platonic intimacy we've shared for years. The familiar routines we share. Meals together. Social niceties that assume inviting one of us means welcoming both of us. The comfort of sharing a bed with another shifter.

As an avian, my instincts scream for me to hide any vulnerability from the flock I rely on for safety. It's ingrained so deep inside my raven's heart I'm not sure if I can get past the certain knowledge that any sign of weakness means certain death. But Rollie has seen so many of my rawest moments over our years together. Moments every part of me trusts him to hold with all the care he shows me in everything.

Rollie makes even the part of me that is all feathers and talons and instinct feel safe. Ever since I moved out of the apartment, I shared with Bram just before he got mated to Ty, Rollie has been my everything. I glance at the top of his dresser at all the little treasures I've given him, proudly displayed.

It's all there. Every shiny bangle and bauble. A pretty picture frame that he refused to use for anything but a nice picture of us together that he badgered me into taking with him, prismatic glass figurines of our animal forms. A big marble with smokey swirls of blue glass that reminds me of his warm eyes. My own little shrine to the shifter I've loved in every way I felt like I could.

Maybe wearing Rollie's clothes will seem like a declaration that I don't want to go back to before his heat. A visual cue that I am all in and I want to be his mate if he still wants me. Come what may. Hatchlings or no, getting my hormones to cooperate so I can smell and feel like an omega again or not.

Unless it's sending too strong of a message? I pluck at the soft fabric, considering. Does wearing this seem like I expect him to keep me now that his heat has passed? I don't want to bulldoze over what he wants in this. I take a deep breath. There's still bacon waiting in the other room. And even more delicious, the shifter I want to make my mate in truth.

First, I check my phone.

Twenty percent. Eh. Enough to turn it on and make a call. I tap my fingers impatiently on the side table while the phone boots up. It takes forever, so I distract myself by bundling our dirty linens into a heap by the door to wash after we talk. We have spare sheets in the bathroom linen closet, so I grab them and by the time I have the bed made up in fresh linens and the windows open a crack to let things air out, my phone is beeping away with all the back-to-back notifications from the past few days.

I can hear Rollie singing to himself as he cooks. I glance at our door, antsy to go to him. To touch him and smell him some more. To reassure myself that I didn't figure out that he somehow wants me too late, just in time for him to change his mind.

Rollie is the most perfect omega I can imagine, so how could he want me for a mate? The signs have always been there. I run through them in my head as I scroll through the notifications that finally seem to have stopped rolling in, one atop the next. I scan each line and dismiss most of them as unimportant.

Signs Rollie has had a crush on me. How he smelled so sad when I stumbled in late and got so protective around my revolving door of alpha lovers. Protective, but not overbearing or trying to control me. He's always been the best friend I could want, but when we shared alphas earlier on, he'd get so shy around my nakedness that he'd only touch me if the alpha told him to, but lately that has changed.

Lately, I've noticed he only gets off during our occasional three-ways when I'm the one making him come. I lick my lips and try on that new understanding. All those little incongruences confused me when I noticed them. So I chalked them up to me misinterpreting everything.

Because the voice in my head that hates me wouldn't ever entertain the idea that Rollie could ever want me as a mate. Even now, I have to bite my cheek until I taste the coppery tang of blood to shut down the voice telling me that I really must be delusional this time if I think he still wants to promise me forever now that the heat hormones aren't addling his rational thoughts.

I shake my head and focus on the notifications that remain after thinning out unimportant messages from alphas who don't matter and all the usual spam. That leaves a handful of messages and missed calls from family and an email from the zoo with my copies of all the paperwork I signed with Pat while I was angsting over how cute their baby was and how I'll never get to have that. I prod the sore spot where I bit myself earlier with my tongue before I can settle into a gloom cloud about that.

I skim the messages. Bram rambled at me. Winny and our folks checked in to see if we needed any supplies dropped off. Ty left a message reassuring me that they took care of the paperwork to get me an official emergency heat leave.

I even have a voicemail from Jolene, the supervisor I met already, assuring me that my only concern should be taking care of my mate and that I can come back for my next shift once Rollie's heat is over.

I shoot off a quick message to Ty that the heat has ended, but Rollie and I need a chance to debrief about how it went. I consider what to say, then tell them that I may or may not need a ride into work later this morning. I get a reply from Bram instead. Telling me Ty already left to get Myra to her gran and surrogate grandmother's place. My brother thinks I should just take the day to rest and recover with Rollie anyway and plan to start back at work tomorrow.

I send back a thumbs up and shove my phone into my pocket. I could easily let Bram goad me into an argument about whether I need to rest after spending days holed up inside my mate. Arguing logistics with Bram is worse than pointless.

I can grab a rideshare into town if I need to. Or use my wings to get to work later. The only reason to stay where I am, sitting on the edge of our bed, is to put off the moment when I have to crack my heart open for Rollie. Let him see that I'm a risk worth taking.

My raven should be ready to burst out of my human skin and flee in terror at the level of vulnerability this conversation is going to take. He's not though. He just wants to go out there and fuss over his mate. Preen feathers—or fur, as the case may be—that have to be caked in the evidence of our passion. Feed Rollie and snuggle with him and dote on the shifter who I want to be my flock for always.

Well fine then. I get up and let myself scurry toward the shiniest treasure in this nest lined in all the pretties that have caught our eyes over the years together. I slink across the soft, colorful rag rug in the hallway that he got at a surplus place. Trail my fingers under the mismatched picture frames that we filled with a hodge-podge of pictures of and from our siblings and niblings and parents.

Myra drew the last one for us. Me and Rollie in our animal forms with her and her two little siblings from last winter, when Rollie and I were watching the three of them during Bram's heat. Blah. Not thinking about how the newest nibling due any time now came to be. Not even a little.

Good thing the sight of Rollie bent over to get something that smells mouthwateringly of fresh cinnamon rolls out of the oven drives any thoughts of my brother right out of my head. His heat might be over, but the omega I want to be my mate is still even more appealing than the smorgasbord of breakfast foods he's already covered our kitchen table in. Bacon, hash browns, coffee with the sweet creamer he knows I love and rarely ask for.

I don't really have it in me to fuck again right now, but I can't tear my eyes off his perfect ass. It's not just that he's hot. Rollie turns with the finished rolls and grins at the sight of me. I saunter closer to him, taking in every inch of his perfection. His smile reaches his eyes, as if I light up his life the same way he does mine.

Rollie's eyes flick over me, lingering on the fit of his pants low on my hips. A possessive heat lights up his gaze at seeing me in his clothing. That tugs on something so much deeper in my heart than lust and desire. It's a reflexive pride that Rollie, gorgeous and kind and oh so sweet in every way, would want to stake his claim on *me*.

I don't entertain the thought that, of course, he has to have come to his senses, and the food is a way to let me down gently. A nudge toward a reset back to our friendly routines. Everything he's said and done screams that he wants the same things he's been saying since that lucid moment at the start of his heat. Rollie wants me.

"Hey, just in time. I was planning to put these on the table and come wake you up to eat." Rollie turns to set the pan on the stove top and reaches for the frosting packet, even though they're too hot and it will all melt. I shake my head, because that is so typically him. He likes it gooey and dripping and doesn't care if anyone else thinks it's wrong.

"Hugs?" I ask, sidling closer.

"Mhm, need my hands to finish these." Rollie nods toward the counter, his focus on the food as he spreads a thick layer of the icing onto the first roll.

"Mm, smells amazing." I fit myself against him, arms low around his middle.

My body is electric with tingles at being pressed up behind him. I rest my chin on his shoulder and even I'm not sure if I'm referring to his sweet cookie scent or the breakfast he stress-baked for us. Some combination of both, probably.

Rollie sighs contentedly and leans into my embrace. I dip my head toward him, inviting him to preen me even though our angles are all wrong for that and he's busy. We have more pressing matters at the moment. It's okay, all I need is the reassurance of touching him.

I want to be close to him for this. If Rollie wants to preen me, then we can work through this. It would mean he wants to figure out where we go from here together. Still best friends—after his heat, I'm sold on the idea that best friends make the best mates. I just hope he can get there too, because in the past when either of us jokingly floated the idea of just agreeing when other shifters assume we're mated, we've nervously agreed that the stakes are too high to risk losing our friendship.

For now, I savor the moment of getting to inhale Rollie's scent up close and match my breathing to the steady rise and fall of his back against my naked chest. I can feel his pulse this close, like our hearts are thudding in each other's chests, the two of us merging until they feel like a single pulse sustaining us both.

That's how much I need him. And it's probably too much to put on him. He can't be the only reason I get up each day and resist the void calling me to its embrace with such seductive silence from everything inside me that's been too loud and wrong for too long. But it's not up to me to decide what he can handle.

"Mm. All done. Come on, we should eat." Rollie gently pats my hands, and I let him go. He turns to loop his arms around my neck. His smile dims and I guess my worry must show on my face, because he sobers too. "And talk."

"Yeah. Talk." I swallow hard, dread making my belly flip and my skin itch with the need to shift and fly away. Rollie reaches for my hand and I clasp onto him, needing the connection more than I can express.

"Hey, it's all good talking, Sebastian." Rollie rubs his hand along my arm soothingly. "Mostly. Once we rip off the bandaid about that stunt you pulled with your omega HRT prescription. But I need you to stay this time. Finish the entire conversation."

Rollie meets my eyes and I nod. Then he turns to take the baking sheet to the table, so he won't have to watch his next words land. Because maybe he's part avian himself for how hard it is for my Rollie to ask for what he needs. "I know it's hard, but if this is going to work, then I need to know that I can have a conversation with you without having to manage both of our issues, okay?"

"Yeah. That's more than fair." I swallow the lump of emotions in my throat. He's right that it will be hard. And he more than deserves even the most Herculean of efforts from me. "I won't leave you hanging like last time. I'm sorry."

"And I can't...I know you don't make a habit of lying to me. But finding out you withheld key parts of the truth about the HRT hurt Seb. On levels I shouldn't have to explain to you. I don't know if I can handle a betrayal like that from you again." He blurts it as he fusses with getting the tray of cinnamon rolls lined up at just the right angle on the table. So he won't have to face me.

I feel like shit for hurting him already, but now that he's putting all the pieces together for me, I feel sick to my stomach. I didn't make the connection between his past with his family and hiding things from him. That's no excuse. He's right that I should have. At best, it was callous not to realize just how deep a wound I was treading clumsily around with my scheming, despite the best of intentions.

It goes without saying that I did it to help him, only ever to help him. If I could, I'd give him every desire of his heart. Rollie deserves everything that I don't. To feel right in his skin and in shifter society. To be the omega he was always born to be. He's the most brilliant bit of shine I've ever found and every day that I get to keep him in my life is a better one than I have any right to experience.

I'd sacrifice everything for Rollie. And instead of help-ing, I made him feel like I was just another in a line of people who took choices about his body and health away from him. Worse, by keeping things so secretive, I withheld his private personal information in the name of knowing what's best for him better than he does. I made decisions for him that, at best, we should have made together, with both of us fully aware of the potential risks.

Shit. I hurt him in ways he confided to me almost broke him in the past. It would be so easy to make that about me. Sink into self-recrimination when I owe him an apology.

"Rollie, I'm so sorry. I didn't realize—I thought I was just hiding what it would do to me. Not what it would mean for you. I didn't..." I shake my head at myself. There is no good way to finish that sentence.

I didn't mean it? My intentions don't matter and this is coming out all wrong, but I can't seem to sort out what to say to capture how deeply I regret everything. Self-med-icating both of us might have done some sort of lasting physical harm—as evidenced by the impossibility of his heat and my body's reaction to it—I fucked up. It's time to own that and fix it the right way.

"I'm sorry. I can't tell you how sorry I am. It's not an excuse, but I hope you know the only reason I didn't tell you everything was so that you wouldn't say no solely for my sake."

"I would have." Rollie shrugs. "I'd have said no, and it should have been my decision. Or at the least, a choice we made together. Maybe if I'd had all the facts, we'd have figured out another way, or not. But what's done is done. Do you get why I was mad?"

I nod, still too nauseated at the parallels to his past that I should have connected to my actions to join him at the table. There's a tiny vicious part of me that accuses me of just acting blithely, willfully ignorant to my own patron-izing behavior. Not *wanting* to see that I was acting the part of a typical alphahole. Like how my ex used to dangle presents in front of me to win me over, except I shudder at the comparison. I wasn't trying to manipulate Rollie.

I wasn't playing the hero with our meds because I want-ed to woo Rollie with gifts no one else could give him. Sure, I wanted to show him the things I could never bring myself to say. Things like love and forever and home that my ex turned into impossible lies. But I did it for him, not to stroke my own ego. I never intended to use anything I did for Rollie as a string to control him.

Rollie deserves a mate who can say the hard things. And one who can treat his tender places with the same care he's always shown mine, protecting me better than I can protect myself from the things that shred my heart.

"Stop that." Rollie nudges my chair out from the table with his feet and waves wiggly fingers at it in a flustered invitation to join him.

"Hm? Stop what?" I play innocent and he sees right through me, rolling his eyes at me and sighing affectionately.

"Stop blaming yourself and sit with me." Rollie points at the chair. I slink closer and sit in it gingerly. I want to touch him, and I feel like I haven't earned that right. Not until I do enough to fix the hurt I caused. I can't help the way my inner raven has me tilting my head toward him, a plaintive begging for my mate's touch. Pathetic featherbrain, but apparently that's just the right move.

"Ah, come here." Rollie clucks over me and drags my chair closer to his, close enough that when he takes the invitation to card his fingers through my hair, the firm touch presses my cheek into his shoulder. I sigh into his sweet skin, believing his gentle touches as he invites me back into his space as much as the sweet words he murmurs to me.

"You're already forgiven, Sebastian. Try as I might, I can't seem to stay mad at you."

"It's my super power," I tease, nuzzling into his neck and inhaling deeply. "I'm far too charming to stay in trouble for long."

Rollie snorts, his nails scraping deliciously over my nape. "No, I think you've got that backwards; it's all your charm that gets you into trouble more often than not."

"Only the best kind of trouble," I joke without thinking, lifting my face off his shoulder just enough to make a faux-seductive face at him. It's the sort of calculatedly care-free banter I throw around with cousins and flockmates who have no stake in the perennial good-natured teasing about my active sex life. Mostly, they are fascinated by stories about other species of shifters and their anatomical alpha quirks. Like Gary and his hemipenes. Except with Rollie, I don't want to pretend.

Rollie nudges me up off his shoulder and fixes me with a serious expression. That makes my heart drop to my toes. What could be more serious than breaking his trust with our meds?

"So, I guess that's as good a segue as any to talk about the mate thing. It wasn't just my heat talking: I want to be mates. Do you?" He watches me, his expression guarded.

"Yes." I nod emphatically, bobbing my head in a way that feels right to my inner raven for swearing myself to my mate.

I can't help the sudden visceral memory of the night we met. How pretty he was with his clumsy, guileless flirting, even after splattering my shoes in puke. My raven knew from that first moment Rollie was something special. A soothing balm to all my broken bits, too precious to treat like the interchangeable shifters I fuck and discard.

"Yeah? It's going to mean changing things, Seb. I can't keep biting my tongue and watching you spiral. I can't keep answering the phone with my heart in my throat, praying that this isn't the time you're calling to say good-bye again." He holds my gaze and we're both haunted by the night I almost drove into the ocean. "If we're doing this, then I need to be the one you come to when you need to lose yourself in sensation." He drops his gaze to the impeccably set table and won't meet my eyes. He turns away to pour coffee from the carafe on its pretty tile mosaic trivet into both of our mugs.

I don't miss the fact that he hasn't specified which sensations he's offering me. I can't imagine him dishing out the rough, uncaring sex that makes me feel like a worthless object for him to use. He won't let me goad him into tearing open old traumas the way I've made a habit of doing with the string of pliable alphas I play with.

Rollie is leagues above the alphas I use before they can use me, so I've rationed the barest tastes of his sweetness.

A night here and there, with a third as a buffer to guard his heart from me. And keep me from greedily gorging myself on as much of him as he'll let me have.

He gulps down the first steaming sip of his coffee, looking like he'd rather swallow his next words along with the brew. "I've done an abysmal job of setting boundaries, and that needs to change."

"Absolutely." I'd promise him anything, but better to listen to what he needs instead of bulldozing in and assuming I already know what that is all over again. "What are you thinking?"

"First, you can't withhold information that impacts me and my health. Lies, even lies of omission, can't become a habit."

"Yeah. Okay. Um. I guess part of that might include you knowing more about the risks I'm taking?"

Rollie looks queasy. "What kinds of risks? Seb, you promised..." Rollie can't finish the sentence, but I know what he's referring to. I promised I wouldn't try to kill myself again. I promised no more drinking and driving. I promised so many things. So I mostly restrict my self-flagellation to sleeping with alphas who hit all my trauma triggers.

"Nothing that bad," I assure him. "I don't fuck bare with other avian shifters. Um, or I usually don't. I already told you I messed up after the party, but I'll take care of that. And I don't fuck bare with static humans. I just, you know, find alphas who sound like my ex when they fuck me." I can't watch his reaction to this. "Mostly over the top alpha bullshit about how I exist to milk their knots and breed their pups. Most of them don't actually mean it the way he did, but they also don't ask too many questions when I ask them to pin me down and rough me up. Most alphas don't ask too many questions when a hot hookup begs them to pop their knot, even if I'm not really slick enough for it."

"Seb..."

"I know." I flash him my most winning smile, but bravado isn't going to get me through this conversation when he just spelled out why he values honesty above all else. "I know it's not okay. *I'm* not okay a lot of the time. I get that it's fucked up, but it makes me feel more omega. The way I felt before creep. If I'm focused on physical pain and being helpless under an alpha, then the parts of me that creep is taking away and changing don't hurt as much. I don't feel as broken."

Rollie sighs. "It doesn't last though, dearheart. You come home and you're still a wreck. It's just that you give yourself permission to feel the hurt when it's a hurt you asked for."

"Yeah."

"Okay. I can work with that. From now on, you are going to ask your mate for what you need. And if you need an alpha's knot, then we can make plans with one of the ones you actually trust, but if what you need is permission to grieve the things you lost, you've got it. Or if you need your mate to remind you that you are as much of an omega as I am, I'll do that too. What you can't do is put yourself in harm's way. You do not deserve to be punished, you are not broken. Got it, omega mine?"

I bite my lip. *You're as much of an omega as I am.* Those are the same words I offered him as a lifeline when he was floundering around in endless rhetorical circles over how to tell if he was really a trans omega, or just rejecting his existence as a beta.

It had seemed so obvious when we were talking about him. The way he lit up when I got him a special body spray meant to help him pass as an omega with other shifters. The way he seemed so much more confident when alphas I flirted with at the bar referred to us both as pretty omegas.

We discussed so many nuances of gender sitting on his old place's creaky porch swing, heads tipped together in the dark while it seemed like the rest of the world slept and the stars were our only witnesses. It almost knocks the wind out of me to have the same trick turned on me.

It's true that he's an omega. So I can't argue that I'm not in the face of him linking the validity of our identities together without tearing him down. Heats and babies aren't a guarantee for any omega. Bodies aren't meant to fit in boxes. Just because creep threw my hormones out of whack doesn't change that I've always been and will always be an omega.

Maybe it's time to stop resenting the only body I get and cope with how all the changes creep and years of neglecting my health have caused. No more making room to carve out an exception for how my body and dysphoria have to define me. Rollie deals with the same dysphoria, but instead of wallowing in how his body doesn't fit, he's been working to embrace the parts that do and accept that the parts he can't change don't have to define his worth.

Rollie nudges our knees together. "Seb? Are you okay?"

"Yeah?" I meet his eyes again, the word bitter on my tongue. I promised him the truth. "I mean, no. But I think I want to figure out how to be?"

"That sounds really good."

"If we're mates, we'll have to figure out what needs to change about our sex lives. What we've been doing during your heat works for me. And as far as sharing alphas, I'm still a fan of the occasional threesome. But uh, how I sometimes make risky choices around sex on purpose might not be the best? So we can negotiate some guidelines that work for us both until we figure out the best ways for us both to get what we need, if you want?"

"That works. You know how I feel about you using sex to hurt yourself, but we can reassess the details as we go. Sex isn't the most important part of what we have, Seb, but yeah. It's something to discuss. The part I hate about our current arrangement is worrying when you go out that it's going to be the time you don't come home. If we stick to the safety rules we agree to, then I'm content with still having some degree of openness with your trusted fuck buddies. So, what do you say? Mates?" Rollie asks.

"Mates, I agree. I lean in to kiss him. Rollie meets my lips in a chaste peck.

I'm just considering deepening the kiss when Rollie's stomach gurgles loudly and I can't hold in a snort of startled laughter. Rollie presses his fingers to his mouth to stifle a giggle of his own and that breaks some of the seriousness of the conversation.

"We can keep talking, but it sounds like my mate needs to eat." I tease him. He glows at the shiny new title now that it's more than a sexy temporary role. Or at least, well on the way to becoming our reality.

"Mhm, my diva of a mate slept in while breakfast got cold." Rollie ruffles my hair. "Who knew heats are more fun with two omegas to share them, huh? Tuckered you right out. Can I fix you a plate?" He reaches for the bacon, hovering his hand over the tongs. I nod and he loads up both our plates with all the delicious food that's gone cold while we talked but still smells amazing. The fact I'm eating food my mate made for me makes it that much better.

We still have to work out some details, especially about my bad habits. By mutual accord, we keep things light while we eat, exchanging jokes about what our friends and family must think of the two of us holing up together for an unexpected heat.

We agree to handle their questions honestly once we leave our private little nest here. We're mates, so of course we shared Rollie's heat. No need to delve into private details beyond that. I work my way through everything on my plate and watch in pleased admiration as Rollie peels apart his second cinnamon roll. Once it's a long strip of dough, he tears off bite-sized chunks.

Rollie licks the glaze from his fingers delicately between bites. I can't tear my eyes off him. It's probably the pheromones or honeymooner infatuation. Yet I can't believe I'm the lucky shifter who my sweet omega plans on spending the rest of his life loving.

I rest my toes on the rung under his chair, where he's got his crossed ankles propped. The need to ground myself with his touch is impossible to ignore. I rub my toes along his arch. Rollie nudges closer.

There's one more thing I need to apologize for before I share the big news about my new job and admit to one more way I didn't fully consult him on a major life choice. In my defense, that insurance paperwork where I listed him as my mate isn't a lie anymore, and I did mention it in passing. The hiring process just went way faster than I could have anticipated, so I don't think it will change anything, but this wound clearly still hasn't healed for either of us.

We've never really cleared the air properly about the night I almost died. How we both know nothing about it was an accident. He saved my life, and I didn't want him to.

"Rollie?"

"Hmm?" Rollie hums as he savors the last of the icing.

"I don't think I ever told you that I'm sorry I called you that night. On the cliff when I got my DUI."

"I'm not." Rollie snaps.

He scowls and swats the air near my knee so he can get up and plop himself in my lap. I grunt at his weight settling over me, and cling on tight. Rollie makes me feel like he can keep me from going back to the crumbling edges of places in my mind that I know I shouldn't venture, but can't seem to resist testing.

Rollie has shown me in his every word and deed toward me that he doesn't wish I'd been more successful that night. Another way we aren't the same, because all too often I think everyone might have been better off if I'd resisted that need to hear his voice once more, heeding that desperate tiny part of me that wanted him to save me from myself.

Rollie tangles his fingers in my hair and tugs sharply. It's just enough of a sting to focus my thoughts. He presses our foreheads together and gazes into my eyes as if he can see through to all the filth in my soul.

"I'm only sorry you got anywhere close to actually doing it. Never for a second think I'd have preferred any outcome that didn't have you still sitting here with me, Seb. Maybe that's selfish, but I want you here with me. I want to grow old and cranky with you right here next to me. I want your raven to preen my raccoon's fur when it's all speckled with more white than gray, like my gran's." Rollie teases me about how much I like his uniquely raccoon shifter agouti hair color. "So you tell me before the void's call is too loud to ignore from now on, and we'll figure out how to make sure you're being my sweet omega diva for a lifetime, okay?"

"I promise."

"Good. I think that's the big stuff? Like I said, I can accept sharing you if the occasional alpha hookup is something you need, but only if it's not going to take you back to the brink of that precipice and thinking the drop is worth silencing your demons."

"Um. Yeah. Maybe the occasional threesome for fun, with us both. Because I like sex. But it's better with you." I shake my head sheepishly. "This not lying by omission part is hard, Rollie."

Rollie nips at my nose. "You don't have to tell me absolutely everything about everything. Just things that directly impact me. General guidance, if it's something that you think 'oh no, I don't want to upset Rollie with this information, I better not tell him' then that's the sort of thing that might be good to mention. You don't have to share every time you pop a boner at the sight of a sexy alpha at a club and decide to flirt. I know you're an incorrigible flirt."

"Yeah, charming the pants off everyone is my superpower," I wink at him playfully. "But yeah. Okay. So this is relevant. Most of the time when I'm hooking up, it's so I can drown out lies that my brain won't stop telling me. So, I don't think I want a free pass to fuck around with other people. I want it to just be something we do for fun together. Unless you want to keep that part of our dynamic the same? Knowing we come home to the same bed and I can make you come in that bed whenever we both want now is the part that matters to me."

"Sticking with some degree of open relationship works for me, but so does fine-tuning our rules to make sure both our needs are met. No judgment, but you seem to have a much higher sex drive than me, so we'll see what works for us both."

"Yeah. That's, uh, a thing. Some people get depressed and sleep all the time and have no libido. I get kind of hypersexual. And the alpha hormones haven't helped. Like, with the heightened sex drive or making me hate everything about myself and how wrong my body feels."

"Ty and Winny have that online shifter therapy service through the flock account, right? Maybe you could talk to them about trying it?"

"Yeah. I'll ask. Or I can see what the zoo offers." I grin and squirm, excited to tell him all about how I can finally provide for him without taking away his choices.

"Oh? Did you talk to Bram about the temp job?" Rollie grins, reflecting my enthusiasm back at me.

I nod, bursting with pride. My inner raven positively preens as I offer him the best part of it. "Yeah. The day you went into heat, that's where I was. Ty took me to the zoo office and vouched for me. So Pat, the boss's assistant, had me sign a contract and work my first shift right there. And I even called the zoo's shifter health clinic to make appointments for hormone testing for us both. You know, cause of all the side effects from our HRT."

"Us?"

"Fuck, that's the other thing I need to tell you. I might've told them you were my mate so I could put you on my insurance. I figured enough people in Four Corners assume we're mates since we're roommates and there's only the one usable bedroom. We don't exactly hide the fact we share a bed and smell like it. So, yeah. Figured it was close enough to true to count. If not in the traditional sense, I've considered you my life partner for a long time, Rollie," I say. There's technically a second bedroom in the attic, but the angled roof is too low for me to reach most of it without stooping down or smacking my head, so it's mostly a dusty storage space.

"Like we're in a QPR?" Rollie asks. "The queer platonic relationship in that comic Myra is into lately?"

"Yeah. Like that." I nod, breathing a sigh of relief that he gets it and he isn't mad. "I swear, I was going to tell you that night and make sure it was alright with you, but then you were in heat and there wasn't a good chance to have a discussion. Are you mad?"

"No. You told me as soon as it was practical, and I'm not going to quibble over whether it was fair to put a conventional label on what we are to each other before we got up the guts to have a real conversation with our hearts on the line and define things properly. Besides, static society setting the norms that define us by how they view relationships and family to deny us access to shifter specialists isn't really something I'm inclined to get too tied up in moral knots over. Thank you, Seb. I know you've been worried about the zoo making your dysphoria worse."

My mouth is dry at how easily he sees through all my pretenses. That's not the reason I've told Bram I can't work with him. It's not the entire reason I've said no for so long, just a part of it. It's true though, and I didn't need to say it aloud for Rollie to understand me. I can't be the weird broken omega they plaster on inspiring posters about the good work the zoo does to fix defective shifters.

I eat obediently as I mull over the whole situation with my new job. It isn't what I expected so far. Bram makes everything seem so intense and even if I told him how I feel about being some disability poster child, I know he'd insist that's not how it is. And maybe it's not the intent, but the fundraising push he spearheaded to get Winny's shoulder reconstruction funded felt that way.

His Pollyanna ability to always see the best in everyone is part of what makes him wonderful, but it's also a huge reason Winny and I were both so frustrated with his pushiness about helping her fund her surgery.

The worst part is, neither of us can even stay mad at our clutchmate because the reason Bram doesn't get why it bothers us is that it would never in a million years occur to him to view disability as something to judge and look down on us for. I've defined myself by my lacking for so long, it was impossible to see what value I had to offer anyone.

Bram isn't an objective voice on that. Ty might be. And Felix, their boss, giving me a chance to prove myself carries more weight. The zoo didn't sign me up as a charity case. They gave me a job because the zoo's mission is to improve the lives of shifters both through gainful employment and by winning over the zoo's visitors with cute animals and facts about how for all our myriad differences, we shifters and our static neighbors have more in common than not.

"You can quit if it's not good for your mental health, you know that, right?" Rollie presses.

"Yeah, thanks." I smile and push food around my plate. I carefully don't make any promises about that, and then I wonder if that counts as a lie under our new rules and scowl at him. "I'll tell you if it's too much?" I offer.

"Mhm." Rollie sees right through my squirming efforts to be honest without over-promising and gives me a bemused smile. "I'll check in about the work next week, once you've had a chance to get a better feel for it, but for now eat your breakfast, mate. Got to get up our strength after the heat." Rollie gestures toward my plate with his fork and shoots me a flirty wink.

I nod and lean closer to him, grateful for his understanding as I consider whether the job might actually be as good a fit as Bram has tried to tell me for years. His entire "we're ambassadors to the statics" schtick feels like Bram's pie in the sky thinking, but jobs and research into shifter health are reason enough to support the cause for me.

Hell, getting Rollie the testing and hormones he needs to feel right in his skin and get to the bottom of his impossible heat are more than enough to win me over for life at this point. It's good work, and I didn't hate the shift I did with Ty. Rollie and I devour more of the feast he prepared for us than I'd have guessed we would. Days of being holed up in our room apparently built up quite the appetite.

Just when I can't imagine taking another bite my phone rings when I glance at the screen, I recognize the number from the zoo health clinic.

"Hello?" I ask, waiting with bated breath.

"Hello, this is the shifter health clinic at Willowdale Zoo, Terry speaking. I am calling for Sebastian Korbin." The same scheduling person I spoke to before is calling. My heart races. Is he about to tell me there was a mistake and I can't see the doctor? Did taking leave on such short notice screw up everything after all?

"That's me, Seb," I say, even as I'm leaping to the worst possible reasons for the call.

"Hi, Seb, I'm calling because we had a cancelation today and Dr. Martinez noticed your file on our list. I see the system has you listed as taking heat leave until tomorrow, but he asked me to call and see if you are able to make it in today, he wants to see you and your mate as soon as possible."

"Oh, um, yeah. My mate's heat is over. That would be, um, yeah, that would be amazing."

"Perfect," Trent says, then he gives me the details of where to go, what to bring, and what to do when we arrive.

I gather the information while Rollie gazes at me looking like he's ready to burst with all his questions. Terry has a lengthy spiel about Dr. Martinez and why our case caught his eye. I'm all but speechless by the time I hang up. Bram has been going to this specialist since he found out he was expecting Kyrie and Leighton. I've lost track of how often my brother has tried to entice me into working with him by dangling the promise of the doctor's expertise in managing creep.

I just didn't realize that the same doctor Bram has talked my ear off about because he's been so supportive of Bram's mixed species pregnancies has also co-authored dozens of groundbreaking papers about fertility restoration in avian shifters with creep and interspecies genetics saw my information on the schedule and flagged the fact that I'm mated to a fellow omega as a promising case for his research.

I grin at Rollie as I put my phone away. "We have an appointment to test our hormones and get our medication situation fixed." I'm already standing to gather up our plates and put away leftovers as I relay the details to my mate. He smiles at me and I savor every touch as we work in tandem to tidy away our breakfast and get ready to leave.

Rollie is going to have the help he needs, and maybe I don't have to be quite so broken. For the first time in ages, I have hope that I can be the mate he deserves.

Chapter 13
Rollie

My head is spinning as I try to process the emotional tilt-a-whirl I've been on all morning. My heart is soaring as I drive toward the zoo with Seb's hand rubbing my thigh, squeezing my shoulder. My mate is sitting beside me, touching me like he can't believe we're mates either. Like it's as much his dream come to life as mine.

Seb is my mate now. A giddy gleeful part of me just wants to shout it to the world. The best shifter I know chose me as his mate! I wish we could spend the day curled up together exploring the newly drawn boundaries of our relationship.Now I can pull him in and kiss him when he looks at me all starving to be touched and afraid to ask for more than a friendly nudge or quick pat on the head. Both of us holding back and hiding the depth of our connection for fear of crossing lines that might bring our careful status quo crashing down around us.

It's hard to believe it was really just a few hours ago that I was sobbing in the shower and girding myself up to lose Seb once I finally found the courage to speak up and set firm boundaries. Except, by some miracle, Seb found a way to overcome the double whammy of both his avian instincts and trauma that have always held him back from showing any vulnerability, even to me.

Not that one conversation and amazing sex can solve everything that's wrong with us, but if Seb sticks to his promises, and I stay firm in no longer enabling his cycle of self-harm, then I think we can make this mating work. If love can be enough, then we'll be fine.

And as if Seb opening up to me and making a plan together to make our mating work wasn't enough of a miracle, somehow, impossibly we have an appointment that might actually address the root of his depression. That's one of a handful of reasons important enough to pry me out of our cozy den when I'm still letting the thrill of getting my dearest desire sink in enough to believe it's real.

The creep he hasn't ever fully gotten under control with doctors who aren't well versed in shifter health still fuels his dysphoria. Not getting that under control and minimizing his alpha traits is what drives his need to escape from his own body and mind. It's the biggest trigger for his trauma.

His well being is my priority here, even as Seb grins nervously over at me and repeats his spiel about the specialist who made room in his schedule to see us today. He looks so proud to be able to give us this.

Confidence looks good on my mate. It's like having something he believes is worthy to offer the people he loves shields him from the lies he believes about himself. Someday, I want to help him believe that he's a worthy enough offering all on his own. More than enough to make me thankful for every moment that I get to claim him as my mate. Too bad most of our loved ones already think we're mated in every way that matters. Seb's cousins are going to give us so much shit for finally making our mating official.

My emotions about the appointment are more complicated, clouded with bad memories of static clinics that never made room for the most important parts of me, but I don't want him to think I don't appreciate the sentiment behind him doing this for us. He wants to take care of me—all of me—on a deeper level than anyone else ever has.

"I can't believe Dr. Martinez is actually seeing us! It's so much faster than I expected. I was afraid it would be a problem that I took heat leave on my second day, you know?"

"I know." I pat his hand, the traffic is getting heavier on 295 as we skirt around Saco and toward the zoo. Still, talking about the doctor is easier than delving into all the reasons that the meds we were on for so long suddenly had weird side effects for us both. How the heat could be a bad sign of something very wrong. How it probably touches on his medical trauma from when he first developed creep. "Thanks for taking care of me during my heat, Seb."

Seb snorts. "As if it wasn't entirely my pleasure. You don't have to thank me for that. And now that we're mates, dropping everything to take care of you during a heat is the bare minimum you should expect."

"We both know it was a big thing to even be asked. You aren't an alpha, asking for you during my heat doesn't mean I see you as one. You know that, right?"

"Yeah, you made that clear." Seb leans in to peck a kiss on my cheek. "One of the many reasons I love you, mate of mine."

"And, when you need or want to plan your own heats, you can expect me to take care of you too, okay?"

"Yeah." He swallows hard. I don't make him promise, heats aren't a guarantee for either of us and asking for anything is hard for Seb. We'll get there.

"Exactly. So we're on the same page. And now we've got a specialist who can work with us to figure out any future heats." I pivot back to where we are headed with enough optimism for us both despite my own misgivings about what the doctor might say. The denials of huge parts of who I am and fighting for the bare minimum compromise that I've come to expect. "I'm glad they got us in so fast."

Seb's hand slides from my shoulder to massage the side of my neck, getting my scent on him. Bird wants to preen me. My silly mate can't keep his hands to himself and it feels oh so good not to have to hide my responses from him on any level. For him, where a touch happens indicates intent more than the type of touch.

My brain knows that my head and neck indicate affection. But my body still reacts to him making it feel good no matter where he touches me. Instead of squirming away to hide it, I lean into his hands. Let myself indulge in the flush of warmth coursing over my skin. It isn't quite arousal, but it doesn't really scream friends either. He always does this to mc, keeps me teetering on the line between affectionate and amorous when he gets handsy like this. He leans in closer to scent me without being too distracting.

"Ooh. When cuddles and preening turn you on, I don't have to stop and pretend not to notice how much you like it anymore, huh?" Seb sounds delighted at that. "It might be fun to still play coy sometimes." I laugh. It wasn't exactly a secret, and he's checked in about it before. I enjoy flirting with our blurry lines as much as he does, even when the implications and potential risk to our unspoken boundaries clouded things.

"Yeah. Anyway. Like you were saying, I'm kind of shocked it happened so fast too. The health plan for us both is why I took the job. But it feels a little like everything is lining up too perfectly to trust it right now. Between the appointment and landing the most amazing mate I can imagine. But yeah, I am hoping we can get the hormone thing figured out properly. You deserve that."

"You do too," I reach over to bump his knee, indulging my newfound freedom to touch without overthinking where and how and what message it sends—friend or mate, that distinction no longer matters between us, if it ever did.

Seb squeezes my shoulder just this side of painfully. I pat his hand to warn him off and he switches to playing with my scruffy hair. "Sorry, I'm trying to believe that. And I'm nervous about the testing and what it might say. But if anyone can get us sorted out, it's this guy."

"I'm sure he will have answers for us." I match Seb's vagueness for now. I am certainly not bringing up how I felt him knotting me at the end of my heat when it would only make him feel more alienated from his body. Seb has to know it happened and we both know it can happen with avian omegas who have long-standing untreated creep. Better to retread comfortable ground here. We might have to share all the uncomfortable details at the appointment, but we don't have to hash them out in the car too. "He's the doctor Bram and Ty see for their kits, right?"

"Yep. Bram adores him, brags about all the extra pre-birth baby pictures he gets." Seb says, his tone of fond exasperation with his clutchmate almost covers the underlying sadness that goes hand-in-hand with talking about his brother's pregnancies. "Because of the whole interspecies thing."

"Then I'm confident he can help us." I flash Seb a smile, and then I have to focus on the road as we take the exit for the zoo and navigate past the employee parking to an access road marked for authorized personnel only.

Seb directs me to an employee lot next to the zoo's health clinic. He tells me where the receptionist directed us to park and he looks proud as a peacock as he pulls out his employee ID, takes my hand and strides into the building with supreme confidence.

He glances over his shoulder at me and flashes his most gorgeous grin as he gestures gallantly for me to walk inside first. His sweetness and naked desire to take care of me makes my heart skip a beat at getting to be the one he smiles like that for, I want to make him feel as cared for and adored as he is doing for me.

"Ready?" Seb squeezes my hand smiling reassuringly at me as we approach the receptionist's desk.

"Yeah, it's going to be good." I force a tight smile, wishing I could let myself get caught up in his enthusiasm. Hoping for this to work out the way he envisions is a bridge too far, but I can still at least give this plan a chance. It's better than going back to my usual endo and giving up on getting omega HRT.

"Liar." Seb leans down to murmur into my ear, then he kisses my cheek and loops his arm around my waist. "I can answer most of his questions if that's easier for you."

Oh, shit. For a wild moment it's tempting, it's on the tip of my tongue to agree to letting Seb shoulder the burden for me. I swallow hard and start to nod, except my stomach swoops in a wild panic at even the thought of handing over control of my medical decisions to anyone. No matter how much I love and trust Seb. I shake my head.

"I'll tell him my medical history. But you can do the other talking as long as we make any treatment decisions together?"

"That works. Let me know any other ways I can support you. And soon we'll both have everything sorted out so that everyone will know we're mated omegas." Seb flashes me a lopsided grin. I force a tight smile too, trying to trust my mate with impossible things.

"Yeah." I take a deep breath of his scent to bolster myself. I wish I could shrug off a lifetime of experience telling me that he's being naïve to trust doctors and just share in his eagerness that this doctor will have good answers for us, but baby steps. It's easier to handle my nerves with Seb holding my hand. And the promise that we are going to be there for each other no matter how it goes. Seb searches my face, to be sure I don't have anything to add before he steps up to the counter to get us registered for the appointment.

Seb bounces on his toes as he hands over his employee ID, his proud smile impossibly even more dazzling with his full charm at full wattage as he introduces me as his mate for the first time. Warmth suffuses me at how good that sounds, the fist of anxiety squeezing my heart loosens the slightest bit.

I squeeze Seb's hand, exchanging grins over publicly declaring each other family. The politely smiling shifter at the desk hands us clipboards to fill out our medical history for our files once we are checked into their system for the appointment.

We sit, but I can't get my nerves to settle. I keep shooting Seb anxious glances over the paperwork, and he does the same. It's a lot to cover. Surgeries, every diagnosis, medications. All the complicated history around my genetics and experimental therapies my parents foisted on me before I even understood the concept of consent.

I'm offering up all my old hurts to this stranger in a lab coat yet again, and for what? In the hopes that this doctor will actually listen?

I have so many doubts about whether any doctor can really help us at this point. Some of Seb's alpha symptoms might not be reversible and that will crush him, but Seb's hopeful smiles bolster me. I want to hope, for both our sakes, but the questions already have my mind racing through a reel of my worst experiences in similar clinics. I rush through the first few sheets, trying not to overthink it.

Beside me, Seb's toes tap out a metronome beat. The shimmer of his pink glittery boots keeps catching my eyes when he fidgets until I hook my foot behind his ankle to nudge my toe against his instep. Seb shoots me a sheepish glance, but I just smile and run my toe along his shin.

Even in a place that makes my stomach churn with dread, there's still something euphoric about having everything between us out in the open.

I flip to the final page. I skim my eyes over the entire page and groan internally. What should be the easiest part of this feels like the worst minefield. The form wants my demographics and next of kin. I fill that bottom bit out first. Seb—always Seb. Even if he wasn't my mate, he's the first one I want contacted in an emergency. He's the family who lives up to the title at every chance.

Out of the corner of my eye I watch him twirl the cheap pen between his fingers to admire the way the fluorescent lights glitter against the clear plastic facets. Seb notices me watching and sheepishly goes back to filling out his form. He tips his page toward me, proudly showing off my name as his first contact too. Bram is the next line and I snort.

Seb rolls his eyes. "Pretty sure he still hasn't fully forgiven me for calling you instead of him that night," he grumbles.

Yeah, that was years ago, and it is still way too soon to even obliquely joke about that. And even if Bram was hurt by the fact that I was the one who messaged him about the attempt, he was infinitely more concerned about his brother than his own hurt feelings. But Seb does have a point about the second contact.

If my gran and gramps were still alive I'd put them down on that line. I toy with listing my alpha sister, except both of my siblings would tell my folks if they caught wind of anything happening to me and my worst nightmares involve waking up in a hospital with them looming over my medical care.

I consider listing Bram, or one of Seb's other relatives, but Bram would be hurt if I don't pick him. Much as I love both of Seb's clutchmates and his folks, just considering Bram getting an emergency call makes my heart race and my throat feel like it might close. He has the best intentions, and he's been working on his tendency to act first and ask second, assuming he knows best. His history around nosing into his siblings' healthcare just has too many parallels to the ways my parents made my choices for me. I can't handle that.

So I write in Harvey's information to obviate the issue. He's been more of a mentor and surrogate parental figure to me than a boss for years. I trust him. And I know he looks out for displaced young wolf shifters who find their way to the Four Corners pack for various reasons. He even takes them to medical appointments, so he's done the emergency medical thing for several of them over the years.

I know Harvey counts me among their number. One of his strays, as some of the pack elders call us when they look down their noses at new arrivals to the town. We all came to Four Corners looking for a sense of community I never had growing up. Harvey and Seb gave me exactly what I was looking for when I moved here and more.

It's like a warm hug to put Harvey's name down and know that I have not just two people I can trust implicitly, but that narrowing down the second one actually took an effort. I've come so far. That gives me the courage to fill in my own demographics at the top of the page.

Full legal name. I tap my pen, hating that I have to fill in the name my parents pressured me into when I transitioned. They insisted that I needed new identity documents to reflect my new primary gender. A good strong name that a static man might wear with pride, so I'd be able to pass.

Fuck. I scrawl the name I almost never need to use then painstakingly print the more obviously shifter middle name I go by in all caps and circle it for good measure before I see the clinic has a line for filling in a preferred name next to the legal name line. Oh—that hits right in the center of my chest in a good way.

Cautious hope takes root in my heart. I'm trying to trust Seb's judgment that this place will actually help us despite a lifetime of dashed hopes that doctors will listen to me. It seems like no matter where I go, some things never change from the weird dots stippling the ceiling to the shiny linoleum and the sterile antiseptic odor that tickles my sensitive shifter nose.

All of my static human doctors seemed interchangeable too, at least in the parts that matter. They have never acknowledged all of me or asked what my priorities are for treatment. This place at least has layers of different shifter scents as an undertone to unscented cleaning chemicals.

The clinic has enough natural ambiance to make it clear that both sides of our shifter natures are welcome without being overpowering. Is it really possible that who I am as an entire being will matter more than rigidly sticking to guidelines and research that wasn't done on or about shifters? It seems far-fetched. Let alone shifters like me and Seb with added layers of complexity on top of the ways all shifters' primary and secondary genders intersect.

Most static humans view shifters through their own biases. They want us to fit neatly into their static gender categories; no challenging the social order. So most static humans fit us shifters into their familiar categories based on our primary gender presentation with a bit of hand waving to jam pregnant omega into a sort of woman lite box.

Sometimes that part gets messier, or outright hostile. Hence the need for shifter communities like the raccoon gaze my parents raised me in and Four Corners. And for aspirational places like this zoo to build bridges between shifters and statics.

Bram and Ty truly seem to believe their jobs help normalize our differences and all the things we have in common with statics so that their kids will grow up in a more accepting world. I want them to be right, even if I privately agree with Seb that it's still safer to build our own communities while we work on those kinds of dreams.

Four Corners is the first place where I haven't felt a paralytic pressure to conform to norms that don't leave room for me. Whether as a beta with no set role to fill within my family and our wider raccoon shifter gaze, or later as an omega who lacks certain key traits most potential mates expect in a prospective omega mate.

Seb breaks me out of thinking about that when he rests his head on my shoulder. "You need help finishing the form, omega mine?"

I card my fingers through his hair, automatically giving him the preening attention he craves. "No, just bad memories. I finished the forms." I show it to him after he sits back up.

"Cool, I'll give these back then?" Seb takes my clipboard up to the counter after I nod.

I distract myself from the way my mind is racing ahead to how to distill my entire past into as few words as possible by savoring the way Seb looks when he's bursting with pride. It's justified, I know he took the zoo job entirely to help me access hormones, despite his anxieties around being seen as an alpha outside the familiarity of Four Corners and his usual hook up spots. The way he throws his shoulders back and struts up to the desk to get us checked in reminds me of the adorable raven shifter kids I've met and grown to love over the years.

There's a particular phase between gap-toothed grinning school kids and angsty teens that they all seem to go through once their elders trust them to start pushing the boundaries of how far they can venture from home in their feathers. Most of the not-quite-fledglings love any chance to show off their newest bits of shiny treasure-- more often than not their prizes consist of tinsel, broken bits of jewelry, coins, or food wrapper scraps. Anything pretty that catches their eyes on the wing is fair game to puff up the feathered little rogues' pride.

I like seeing this sweeter, self-confident side of Seb, so I grin and give him a thumbs up when he glances back at me. Seb chats with the shifter sitting there for a moment, then returns to sit beside me, head propped on my shoulder and fingers twinning with mine to calm my nerves.

I stare at Seb's shiny pink glitter combat boots as he stretches long legs in front of himself and taps his toes.

We don't have to talk for him to comfort me with gentle touches as we wait. The doctor calls us back before I can get restless from sitting here.

Seb is still beaming and puffed up with pride when he turns to take my hand and lead me after the doctor to his office. Panic claws at my insides at the inevitable course this appointment will follow. Like every intake appointment before this. It's always felt like my family and the doctors they took me to only saw what I lack. Missing genes that left me missing pieces and needing hormones I should be able to make on my own. I try to hide how intensely uncomfortable I am with being here.

If Seb and I can both get the right dose of HRT in the end, the appointment will be worth it. I can live as an omega without hurting Seb anymore. That's the reason I don't run for the door.

We sit in an exam room with a desk in it. The doctor introduces himself and pulls up our files and makes small talk, most of which Seb handles while I quietly panic beside him. I catalog the room for escape routes, it's a subconscious reflex for my inner raccoon to mark out good hiding spots. Medical offices haven't ever felt safe, and this is going to be hard.

I'm going to have to recite all the ways I'm broken in front of my mate. I'm not sure I have the strength to handle that. Even considering it reduces me to the scared kit who couldn't stand up for himself when they talked about seeing if they could get my ovaries to develop enough to bank eggs in case I wanted children when I was older. That was when I had a period for a few cycles, but my parents opted out of egg preservation for me. Seb notices me freezing up and slides his chair closer so he can rub my back soothingly.

Dr. Martinez seems to notice too. He's gentle with me as he pulls my entire sordid past out of me. I tell him about years of testing and endless injections with cocktails of hormones that were supposed to fix me but only made me feel more broken. barely gathering up the courage to ask if I can please have the boy hormones instead of the girl ones.

I can't convey just how much it hurt to see the frozen look in my parents eyes, weighing having to tell everyone their daughter is a son now. In the end they shrugged. My primary gender didn't matter to them. Regardless of boy or girl, to them I was a broken beta with no future in shifter society. They figured when I grew up and had to make my way among static society, it might be easier if the world saw me as a man.

The first part of the appointment is an overwhelming exercise in explaining my entire medical history to a stranger. It's the sort of thing that throws me right back into that headspace of being a pre-teen. The appointment that shattered my trust in the adults I relied on to take care of me. I thought I was on the verge of puberty for years, watching my peers outgrow me. My parents knew all along that would only happen if and when my doctor approved started growth hormone injections. They told me I needed blood work to be sure, but I might just need vitamin injections to help things along.

I only learned the truth about any of it because a last minute emergency meant my pediatrician handed my appointment off to a colleague who didn't know that no one had told me that the static doctor who attended my birth told them I was intersex and suggested genotyping to see if my secondary sex might help them decide whether to raise me as a boy or a girl.

I get through the entire history, up to getting omega HRT through Seb and whatever might have triggered my heat. Dr. Martinez listens, only interrupting to ask clarifying questions. And then he asks me something no one else in his position has.

"So, what are you looking for from me today?"

"I don't know? I want to be on omega hormones. And I don't want to stop taking testosterone. But I don't know how I could have had a heat, so I'm scared that maybe my doctor was right to refuse to prescribe both at once?"

"That's a good place to start." He nods. "If you agree to it, we can order some blood tests today. I also want to order some scans to rule out some rare but serious reasons for the unexpected heat, but if you've been taking avian omega hormones, we don't have good data on how those impact other types of omega shifter, so I suspect that's the reason for the heat. In that case, getting you on the correct dose and formulation for your body should resolve the issue. How does that sound?"

"Um. Good? I think?"

"Good. We have a nurse on staff who can take blood and vital signs for you both once I'm done speaking with your mate. In the meantime, if you'd be more comfortable shifting until I'm done talking with your mate, I can step out and let you do that."

I consider the tempting offer. If I take my fur I can curl up in Seb's lap and nap until it's time to go. But if Seb wants me to listen in, I want to be here for him. I glance at him and bite my lip, not sure what I even want to ask.

"It's fine if you want to shift, baby, I've got the rest of this covered. No final decisions without you, like we agreed."

"Okay. Yeah. I want to shift." I nod.

The doctor shows me to the curtained off exam bed and steps out to give me privacy and I spend the rest of the appointment cozy and warm in my mate's arms with him stroking my fur.

I have to shift back for the blood tests, but I get to take my fur for the ride home since Seb insists that he's driving. He lets me perch on his shoulder, my tail curled around his neck to help me balance as he handles scheduling the scans for another time.

We leave with prescriptions and a plan. I've never left a medical clinic with this much optimism before. I'm actually beginning to trust that we might just get to the bottom of whatever fluke happened to trigger my heat and Seb's knotting. On the off chance that it wasn't just because Seb was giving me too much of his own prescription. It all seems a little too good to be true, but maybe we both deserve a little more good in our lives.

Chapter 14

Seb

WITH MY NEW JOB and my new mating, it's strange how easily I fall into my new routines. Not that much really changes with Rollie and I making our mating a reality. The shifters who teased us for sharing a bed and a home and most of our social circles weren't far off the mark.

Except that now I get to kiss him on the couch when we snuggle before bed, or slip my hand into his pants to tease him during the boring bits. And I get to bury my nose in the soft skin at his throat even as I bury my cock inside of him. We make lazy love in our colorful blankets most nights. That level of frequency might just be the novelty of getting to fuck each other whenever we want, but I'm enjoying it and Rollie seems content with the increased intimacy too.

Rollie smells so good lately. I can't get enough of his sweetness. It's like being on the correct hormones has his spicy cookie aroma in overdrive or something. He tastes as good as he smells, so his increased sex drive might have something to do with how often I've been asking to go down on him. I love alternating sucking his cute little omega dick with lapping up his juices like they're the sweetest nectar.

Work is good too. Better than I'd have expected. Ty and I have been carpooling. Since we drive right past the market on the way, Rollie usually joins us when he has a morning shift. It might be less peaceful once my brother isn't on his clutch leave with the new baby. Once he's joining us for the drive, I'm sure his constant chatter will fill the silences Ty doesn't seem to mind. It's been nice to spend time with my sibling-in-law, even if we spend much of it listening to the radio and talking about our mates and my niblings.

It's been almost three weeks of sharing the daily drive when things get weird. Our follow-up with Dr. Martinez is in a few more days, so I know Rollie is feeling antsy about that. I chalk up the weird little shift in his sweet scent to nerves. Not that it really smells like the acrid anxiety stink, but what else could it be? For some reason, Ty keeps surreptitiously trying to scent my mate. It's weird. Rollie gets out at the market, then opens my door to kiss me goodbye and, mhm, yeah, he's definitely...spicier? Maybe something like warm vanilla? Weird.

"Um, kinda feeling queasy about tomorrow, so I might order in for dinner, if that's cool?" Rollie says.

"Yeah, that sounds great. If you call something in near the zoo, we can pick it up on the way home," I offer, glancing at Ty to be sure she doesn't object. It's a femme day for her, the swishy floral skirt a clear sign of which pronouns to use.

Ty nods. "Bram has been asking for spicy food to try to evict the chick, so he'll be pleased for an excuse for takeout."

"Nice, I'll give him a call later to coordinate our cravings," Rollie jokes.

Ty, who was taking a sip of their coffee, snorts so hard I shoot them a worried glance even as a bit of their coffee sprays my arm. Ew.

Rollie and I both fix the bear with concerned glances. "You alright?" Rollie asks.

"Yes. Swallowed wrong. You give Bram a call, I'm sure he'd love to hear from you, Rollie. We should get going so we aren't late though."

"Yeah." Rollie hesitates, glancing between us, then shrugs, leans in for one more lingering kiss, and saunters away. It's just as well that Ty is driving because I can't tear my eyes off my mate's delectable round ass as he saunters into his workplace.

"Wow," Ty says. She shakes her head as she pulls away from the curb and heads toward the highway. "So, um, you mentioned you are seeing Dr. Martinez. Any news you two want to share?"

"Hm? Just that we are getting the HRT we both need," I say. And even if I don't really buy that I deserve to get the things I need, Rollie does. Rollie deserves a healthy mate, so I'm taking my full dose the way I'm supposed to. But that doesn't seem to be what Ty is asking with the probing edge to their questions.

"Seb, I know you birds like to play into the whole featherhead stereotype, but we both know you aren't an idiot. If you have something exciting that you want to control sharing, it might be good to make any announcements before people scent the obvious on your mate. We're all going to be so happy for you."

"What are you talking about?" I demand, because obviously I wasn't imagining her scenting my mate, and Rollie is fucking delicious, but he's all mine to smell and mark!

"You really don't know?" Ty shoots me a puzzled glance.

"Know what?" I demand, suddenly on edge because I have no idea what she is implying about Rollie and I don't like feeling out of the loop when it comes to my mate.

"Well, shit." Ty clenches their hands on the steering wheel, then pulls over again, a block away from the market.

"What are you doing? We're going to be late."

"Yeah, not the biggest issue here." Ty shrugs. "We are going to discuss this first, and then we can get to work. So, the doc didn't, uh, I don't know, give you something to trigger that heat of his?"

"How?" I snap at her, exasperated with her heavy-handed insistence that she knows best when she's asking such ridiculously clueless questions. "I didn't even take the job until he was already in the prodrome, you were with me all day before the heat, and we only saw the doctor after it was over. What does that have to do with—Oh." My stomach feels like it might drop right through my toes. Ty thinks Rollie is pregnant. Rollie can't be pregnant. I'm the only one he's been with and—well, it's impossible on so many levels. "Shit. Ty, he can't be pregnant."

"Well, your mate smells pregnant Seb. I've had enough cubs to recognize the signs, so you might have longer before most people would notice, but it's not something you can hide forever or ignore."

"No. It's not possible." I might be sick even thinking about what else could mimic that change in his scent though.

The litany of scary diagnoses we are supposed to be ruling out with the imaging Dr. Martinez ordered. Next week is supposed to tell us everything is fine and Rollie is healthy and the heat was a silly mistake because I gave him too high a dose of avian omega hormones. If he's really sick—there's a part of me that already knows what I'll do if I lose Rollie. Not that I can tell anyone that particular truth. Especially not my mate.

If we learn the worst, he'll have enough worries of his own to shoulder. I wish Ty could be right and Rollie smells so good because he's pregnant. That something so miraculously wonderful could be real for us, but Rollie and I don't get to have the perfect life my brother and his mate created with such seeming ease. "He can't be pregnant."

"Normally, I'd remind you that you are not, in fact, one of those cubs who I owe sex ed talks to, but I can see you're freaking out, so let's skip that part. When do you see Dr. Martinez again?" Ty asks, voice so gentle that their kindness might break me.

"Next week. But Rollie can't get pregnant, Ty. You don't understand."

"Not to contradict you, but I have an inkling. Let's try not to jump to conclusions though. Rollie did have a natural heat, right?"

"Yes."

"And you were, uh, unmedicated at the time, right?" They ask as delicately as possible.

"Yes. I fucked up my HRT and basically let the creep turn me into an alpha." I huff, because that shouldn't matter.

"Yes, that. I'm not here to make you feel worse about it, but when I was driving you home you were responding to his phone call like, um—like any mate would react to their omega's heat. So given that, maybe don't panic yet and see if the doc can squeeze you both in for a checkup today? Just to be sure?"

"Do you think he would do that?"

"He's come in after hours for Bram and I when Bram had some contractions that wouldn't stop after he shifted early in this pregnancy, so yes, I suspect he will make time for something like this. Call him to ask. And then you can go ask Rollie if he can skip his work shift today to come to the clinic with us. Alright?"

"Yeah. Okay." I pat my phone and then come to my senses. No choices about Rollie's health without him.

"Actually, I think I'll talk to him first and then we can call the clinic together."

Ty nods and settles in to wait for me. "Either way, I'll be here to drive when you have a plan. Go talk to your mate."

I'm not sure how I'm going to convince Rollie to clock out for a trip to the zoo when he just took so much time off for his heat.

Rollie's entire face lights up when he sees me enter the store with a sheepish wave. "Hey, um, can we talk about something real quick?" I ask, feeling self-conscious in a wolf-run store. Marin hated Harvey, so Rollie's boss can't be all bad for a wolf alpha, but still. It's hard to trust anyone who smells like my ex, even a little. I'm trying with Harvey, for Rollie's sake.

"Hey, what are you doing here? Don't you and Ty need to get to work?" Rollie is already walking around his register to greet me with a kiss though, so I don't think he's upset that I'm here, just confused.

"Yeah. We do." I nod, but it feels like my throat might just close up when I try to say more. Rollie looks as amazing as he's been smelling lately, so vibrant and alive and I can't reconcile that with the terrifying worries Ty's questions unlocked in my head. I don't want to scare Rollie or give him false hope about the impossible explanation Ty offered to me.

No knowing what to say anyway, I don't speak. I meet Rollie halfway across the store. He crashes into my arms in front of an end-cap displaying gum. I bend to kiss him like we're the only ones in the world. His arms loop around my neck and I gather him into my arms, wishing I could shield him from every bad thing under my wings.

I can't, but when he pulls back to search my face, I inhale his reassuring scent and I know I have to tell him why I'm here. Even if I wasn't planning to bring him to work with me for extra testing. This is exactly the sort of thing I promised not to keep from him when we discussed our mating. I cup his face in my hands, trying to memorize the happy glow of his bemused smile.

"What is it?" Rollie asks. "Not that I don't enjoy getting an extra goodbye kiss."

"You smell different."

"Yeah, hormones are wild like that, my scent changed when you were sharing your meds with me too, remember?" Rollie doesn't make it an accusation, but I still feel the sting of how much that choice hurt him.

How much is my arrogant attempt at playing doctor still messing with his body if that's why he smells like he's carrying a clutch. My clutch. Fuck. I might be sick at the irony of my broken body working in the exact wrong way, except if Rollie could actually get pregnant finding out we're having a baby would be among the best days of my life instead of vying for the worst news ever if it means his weird heat was the first sign of something terribly wrong with him.

I shake my head. Worry about the worst once it happens, for now we just need answers.

"This is more than that. This is..." I swallow thickly, I need to force the words out, but it's hard with Rollie's brow furrowing at me. "Ty says you smell pregnant."

Rollie's face falls. He shakes his head and steps back out of my arms. "That's not funny, Seb."

"I'm not laughing."

"Seb—I can't...I would give you a clutch if I could, but it's not possible." Rollie steps back again, his arms wrapped around his middle protectively.

"Exactly how not possible is it though?" I ask, not because I really have much hope in the sort of happy ending neither of us believes can be ours, but I'd grasp at any straw if it means Rollie isn't sick.

My mate huffs in irritation. "I've told you I can't; you know I wouldn't lie about that."

"I know. I'm sorry, I'm just grasping at straws, Rollie. If there is any chance would you humor me and come to the zoo clinic to see Dr. Martinez for our follow-up a little early? We can call together and see if the doc is willing to squeeze us in? I'm kind of freaking out here because you really do smell like Ty might be right and..."

"And that's scary. I know." Rollie fills in when I can't finish my sentense. He reaches toward me, and I take his hands, drawing him back into my arms where I can inhale his sweetness again. It's soothing, even if it's impossible to ignore the heady new layers to it that I can't dismiss now that Ty confronted us with the potential implications. I nuzzle into his pulse point, wishing we could retreat into fur and feathers and I could just preen him, or fight away any bad things with beak and talons.

"Don't get your hopes up, Seb." Rollie nudges my face away from his throat. "The endo who saw me as a teen said my ovaries were basically menopausal before I went on T. Oh, shit. I forgot I need to reschedule my next shot with my endo. I missed the last appointment because of the heat. Maybe that's why I smell weird?" Rollie offers the alternative explanation hopefully. I want to latch onto any alternative possibility, so I nod along.

"Yeah. That could be it," I agree. "But I'd breathe easier if we see the doc as soon as possible."

Rollie bites his lip and glances around the store. "I guess, but I've already taken time off for the scans next week and the heat and Harvey has been wonderful about it, but I—"

"Sorry, not to eavesdrop, but I've been debating whether to slip one of these into your locker for the past few days, son." We both startle when his boss breaks into our conversation and hands Rollie a pregnancy test off the shelf. "And for the record, Harvey would happily drive you to the appointment himself." Harvey winks, and much as I'm normally wary of the pack after Marin, I might have to grudgingly admit I like my mate's boss. "Start with taking that, so you have a better idea of what you're working with and whatever it says, let your mate take you to get checked out."

Rollie bites his lip, gaze darting from me to his boss to the test and the back employee only area. He shakes his head, but it's an uncertain gesture, not a no. "I don't know what to do."

Harvey pats Rollie's shoulder. "One step at a time. Do you want your mate with you?"

Rollie nods. "Seb?"

"Yeah, I know all about pee tests," I try to make it a joke, but it's not. I took so many of those damn tests when creep turned my scent into queasy tilt-a-whirl that had Marin swinging from doting mate to taking swings at me at the drop of a hat. I might throw up if I ever have to take another of those things. But Rollie needs me to be strong, so I put my around his shoulders and steer him toward the bathroom near the registers.

"Use the employee restroom, and whatever that says, take the rest of the day off, Rollie. I'll clock you out." Harvey says

Rollie looks ready to protest, but then he swallows it down and nods. "Thanks."

"Of course, keep me posted when you have anything to share," Harvey says.

"I will," Rollie agrees, clutching the test to his chest as we walk down the cereal aisle. Rollie pushes open the door to the back and leads the way to the restroom there. His hands are shaking as he fumbles with the box so I end up having to unwrap it for him, the packaging hasn't changed from when I was using them years ago. I skim the instructions, but those are the same too.

Cap off, pee on the thing and...apparently hyperventilate because my entire future hangs in the balance between the lines that may or may not appear.

"Hey, breathe. This is going to be okay." Rollie plucks the plastic dipstick from my hand. "Seb, breathe with me, you're safe. This stupid thing doesn't get to tell us whether we're worthy to be omegas or mates or anything else."

"Yeah. Okay." I still can't control the panic, but objectively he's right.

"Breathe with me?" Rollie takes a few exaggeratedly slow breaths, until the black spots dancing at the edges of my vision recede and I can actually handle this. Shame flushes through me, replacing the panic. I'm supposed to be here to support Rollie, not the other way around.

"Sorry, I'm good. I didn't realize that would be a trigger."

"Want to talk about it?" Rollie offers, and I'm tempted to take any excuse to put off bad news, but there isn't much to say that he doesn't already know.

I shrug. "Marin wanted pups, so when I couldn't give them to him it was bad. But that's not what this is about. I'm scared that I really fucked up with giving you avian HRT and that it might have done something to you that we can't fix."

Rollie nods and swallows hard. "If it's positive, are you going to lose it again?"

I shake my head, and then nod. "Maybe?"

"Because you don't want a kit with me? Or not one that you sired?" Rollie sounds so scared, I reach for his hand, he lets me take it.

"No." I don't even have to think to give him the honest answer to that. "Never because of that."

"No?"

I sigh. "I mean, in a world where you were super fertile and we could plan a heat where I had the option to take alpha HRT on purpose to give us kids, I'm not sure I could handle it, but if it happened already then I'd be thrilled."

"Yeah?" The naked hope in Rollie's voice on that single word echoes my own.

"Yeah." I nod, more sure of it for having said it. "I'm not scared that you might be pregnant, Rollie, I'm terrified that you might be sick."

"Okay. I still don't think it will be positive, but I guess there is a tiny chance? Before my primary gender transition I did have a few cycles. I guess, in theory, the requisite organs exist? Even if they're not quite right."

"Is that your way of telling me not to spiral if it's positive?" My attempt at humor falls flat.

"Yes. No spiraling. Even if it isn't good news. I need you to be okay, Seb. You sure about this, or should we wait until we get to the clinic?"

"That's up to you." I sigh, because if it was up to me, I'd put off any confirmation of my fears until we get to the clinic, but this is Rollie's health and it's his choice.

"I want to know. Call and see if we can get in today?" Rollie urges me. He clings to my hand as I make the call, putting it on speaker so Rollie can hear.

Terry answers the phone at the zoo clinic and tells me that getting Dr. Martinez to squeeze in a quick checkup shouldn't be a problem, given the circumstances. I thank him and hang up.

Rollie takes a deep breath and forces a smile. He holds up the test. "So that leaves this, do I just pee on it?"

"Yeah." I nod stiffly. "Pee, then wait for the results."

I turn away to give him some privacy, and to hide how much the entire thing is getting to me. This isn't the same as those other tests. And I don't even know what result to hope for this time. Negative might mean it really is just all the hormonal fluctuations from adjusting his medications making his scent change. A positive might mean a miracle or a nightmare and I can't decide which way the odds are leaning on that. It's far from the first time my mate has peed in front of me. We've been sharing a bathroom for years, but it's still a little awkward to just stand there in his work bathroom while he does his thing.

Rollie caps the test, shoves it into the box without looking at it. He washes his hand, then reaches for my hand.

"Aren't you going to wait for the results?" I wave at the box instead of taking his hand, Rollie just keeps reaching for me until I place my palm in his.

"I'll check it in the car. You don't want to know yet, right?" Rollie gives me a quick squeeze, then he tugs me toward the door.

"It's your call," I insist, even as relief washes over me at not having to face my fears quite so soon or so viscerally.

Rollie shakes his head. "Finding out for myself is my call, but I can respect that either answer is only going to make you worry more until we see the doc, so this way we both get what we need."

"I need you." I pull him into my arms and hug him tight.

"Need you too, Seb. Come on, we shouldn't keep Ty waiting and the sooner we get there, the sooner we'll know what we're facing."

"Whatever it is, we'll face it together," I say, and then I follow him out to Ty's sedan, hoping for the impossible, afterall, it wasn't so long ago that I was certain he could never be my mate. Sometimes impossible dreams do come true. I ignore the treacherous voice telling me that my dreams always inevitably turn into nightmares.

Chapter 15

Rollie

THE DRIVE TO THE ZOO seems interminable. Ty makes a few awkward attempts at reassuring small talk before Seb cranks up the music. I stare at the box that holds a potential answer. A part of me is hopeful that if the avian hormones gave me a heat, then maybe they also did the thing that human hormones couldn't and I might actually be able to give us the family we both want.

If I peek inside the box and the test is negative, then that tiny kernel of hope will be gone. Which isn't honestly any worse than where we both thought we stood on the possibility of children when we promised to build our lives together. But if it's positive...

I want to watch Seb fall in love with our kit. I want it with an intensity that reaches right into my chest and squeezes tight. If I can give us that future, then it would be the most amazing gift. But if it's positive because I'm sick, I know my mate too well to believe he'll find a way to that future without me to remind him he deserves it.

I glance at the dashboard clock and then at the huge text on the front of the box bragging that it gives accurate results in two minutes. So, time to find out. I slip the test stick out of the box and stare at the two pink lines that stand in stark relief against the white field. Pregnant. Right? The key printed on the stick confirms it.

I bite my knuckle to keep in the gleeful little squeal I want to voice. I want to celebrate. I want to believe the best for as long as I can. I know it's foolish and the odds are against us and even assuming that the test is accurate, a million things could go wrong and bring my miracle to a crashing halt.

I don't care. For this moment, I am going to let my heart soar on raven's wings with the hope that I can have it all. The mate I love and a child to raise together. All the things everyone growing up told me I would never be able to have might just be mine. Even if I can only believe it for as long as it takes to drive to yet another doctor who is waiting to unravel my dreams.

Seb is staring out the window. I want to tell him. I want to celebrate. I want to joke about testing whether it's too late to sneak another kit in there, or at least make a valiant effort at it. But he'll only worry more if he knows so I calmly snap a picture of the test and slip it back into the box. Then I tuck the box into my work bag and shove it under my seat.

It's much harder to shove the news out of my mind though. I keep bouncing between imagining what my little raven might look like and the risks of a mixed species pregnancy. Bram always has the risk of carrying a mixed clutch of eggs and babies without the requisite genes to take an avian form, but I think that's because he's an avian shifter. I'm tempted to text him to ask, but if I tell Bram then the entire flock will know by supper time. And I can't tell Bram before I tell his brother.

Alan. My little brother has mixed species babies too. We aren't close, but maybe this is the sort of thing he'd actually have an interest in bonding over? I hesitate, this will get back to my folks. I know that. It might be worth it to have a closer relationship with my brother though. If anything can finally bridge the gap between us, it would be having a bonding over having similarly medically complex pregnancies.

I text my photo to my little brother before I can chicken out of asking him for this one last chance at a connection.

Rollie: Hey, so my mate and I have been seeing a shifter specialist about having kits.

I get a response shockingly fast. Alan usually doesn't reply to me right away, which is fair, he's busy with his kits. The speed of this reply has me questioning just how much of that delay in his replies is on purpose though. Because he's not usually interested in what I have to say.

Alan: OMG! Is that *your* test? How?! I didn't know you finally nabbed a mate! Who's the alpha father? I thought our folks said your ovaries are junk? Is the test really yours? What's going on, did they secretly bank your eggs and not say anything until you got mated or something?

Alan: It is a father, right? You were always more into guys. But an alpha sister-in-law would be cool too. I'm sure the kits will enjoy a new auntie or uncle equally. Unless you're with a static?

Rollie: Um, it's Seb. We're mated now. Officially.

At first I don't even notice the slew of little digs. That's just how Alan always talks to me. Then the palpable enthusiasm of his responses hitting my phone in a rush dims. The next message seems to take ages to arrive and I skim back over all his barbs.

I try to convince myself it's not personal. My newest nephew is a colicky baby, he probably woke up fussy. Nothing to do with me and Seb at all. Except it's right that on my screen that Alan doesn't see me as his equal. His next words confirm just how little we still have in common. He's the same petty boy who broke our toys rather than share them, just to see me cry.

Alan: Um. Right. Your omega roommate?

Rollie: Yes. I love him.

I don't owe him even that much of an explanation. Heck, maybe I don't owe him anything anymore.

Alan: So, is he carrying then? Did you meet the alpha who knocked him up? You really think you're going to be in the picture as a parent with them?

I'm tempted to correct him, but after a moment to swallow down my outrage I realize there isn't a point. He might not even believe me at this point, since my folks made it clear to the entire gaze I'd never be a parent. Fuck. He's going to tell the entire family and I don't want them knowing Seb's personal information. They don't get to know something so vulnerable and intimate between my mate and me.

Rollie: I was there for the conception. It's not really relevant how it happened, is it? I thought maybe you'd have some tips about carrying a mixed species kit for us, but I'm sorry to bother you.

It's sinking in that Alan isn't going to give me what I need. Not at all. He isn't ever going to understand anything about me or Seb or our mating. And he doesn't want to. Maybe it's time to accept that Alan will never be interested in the kind of brotherly bond Seb has with his siblings. Heck, the bond I have with his family and even Ty is closer than my bond with Alan or my sister. Contacting him was definitely a mistake.

Alan: Sure, Thomas. Whatever you say.

Rollie: Could you just do me a favor and not tell our parents about this?

Alan: Do you really think they're going to care that your roommate is having a baby, Thomas? Maybe when he and his mate ask you to move along that will be what it finally takes for you to realize you'd be better off among the statics where you belong.

Right. Angry replies twitch at the tips of my fingers, but in the end, Alan is only making it easier for me to let go of those last shreds of hope for a connection that's only ever been one-sided.

Rollie: Sure, have a nice life Alan.

I hit send and then I block him from my contacts, my parents have been blocked for ages already. I consider doing the same for my sister, but she's the best of the lot and I like her mate. She can tell me if there's anything I need to know. Like if she and her mate change their minds about remaining childless. Or maybe if one of Alan's kids need a kidney, short of that, I'm not really interested in further contact.

Scrubbing Alan from my social media takes most of the rest of the drive, so if nothing else, it's a good distraction. His betrayal makes it easier not to worry about the test or give away just how excited I am for the possibilities it represents.

Ty is late for work, but she still drops us off right at the doors to the clinic before going to park and clock in for the day. She wishes us luck and I wink and give her a thumbs up as I guide Seb inside the clinic. He's moving woodenly. Dreading what we might hear.

"Rollie and Sebastian Korbin, right?" Terry greets us as we walk in.

"Yeah," I don't correct his assumption that we share a last name. Seb made the appointment, so Terry is probably looking at his file, not mine. Names are something we need to discuss, but I definitely want to take his name before our kit arrives. Assuming I really am carrying our baby. I rub at my belly for courage.

Seb gives me a startled look, but he just smiles and squeezes my hand instead of correcting me. Judging from the sappy warmth of his smile, I suspect he'll be cool with sharing his surname with me.

"Perfect, Dr. Martinez is in with another patient at the moment but one of his nurses is going to take your vitals and get you set up with some preliminary testing first and he'll stop in to see you when he has a second, sound good?"

"Yeah." I nod, of course an important specialist can't just drop everything to see us right this instant. But the testing is good. It will mean real answers sooner.

"Great, Tammy will be waiting for you in room 6." Terry gestures down the hallway.

I head to where he indicates. Seb crowds after me, walking too close, like he is afraid to be parted from me. I'm used to being tested and poked and prodded and not knowing what's going on. I hate it, but I'm used to it. So I go to the room and confirm my identity and Tammy does her thing.

I only squirm a little when she has to try twice to get an IV in for the bloodwork. She tapes it in place, implying they might want more access fast. Great. I try to calm my anxiety about that. One of the scans scheduled for next week requires contrast dye, so maybe it's for that. Seb looks like he might pass out at the sight of my blood.

"Do you need to do a pregnancy test too?" Seb frets, his grip on my hand just this side of too tight once the neatly labeled tubes of blood are delivered.

"No need, we're going to check that with the blood we already took, but for now, your file indicates you had a spontaneous heat under three weeks ago?"

"Yes," I confirm.

She checks her notes and then has me change into a hospital gown thing while she goes to find an ultrasound machine on wheels. Seb spends the time pacing the room. I sit on the edge of the exam table. I've had internal scans before. To assess just how messed up my insides are and whether the hormones the static endocrinologists were giving me were actually working. The results always left me feeling more broken, but this time—this time they're going to be able to tell us whether the picture on my phone is the best news possible or the worst.

"Seb?" I reach for him and he whirls to face me, when he sees the fear on my face he comes right up to me and hugs me.

"What is it?"

"Do you want to know what the test said? Before she uh, shows us whatever is or isn't going on?"

Seb hesitates searching my face. "You want to tell me?"

I nod.

"Okay. I want to hear it from you."

"It said I'm pregnant." I rest a hand low on my belly, hoping that's all this is. Seb's hand covers mine and he nuzzles his face against mine.

"Then until she shows us otherwise, that's what I want to believe this is."

I kiss him then, wishing it could be as simple as celebrating our good fortune. That I really get to be the luckiest shifter alive.

Seb startles back away from me when Tammy taps peremptorily at the door upon her return. He doesn't go far though, staying by my side as she gets her machine ready.

Seb holds my hand and my gaze, and I cling to him and our hopes with all my courage as I follow instructions Tammy gives me with an impassive tone.

The longer she takes, the more I'm braced for the worst. If she can't find anything, then that test means something else is pumping out pregnancy hormones and that isn't going to be good news any way I slice it.

"Sorry," Tammy says and my heart plunges to my toes. Seb crushes my hand. "It took me a minute to find the heartbeat because you're so early, but would you want to hear your baby?"

"Hear a heartbeat? There's a baby?" Seb lights up so much he's incandescent. That more than anything drives it home. This is real. Our baby is real.

"Yep, like I said, you're early still, but measuring exactly where we'd expect given the dates of your last heat. Am I correct in guessing that congratulations are in order?"

"Yes." I nod.

"Then congratulations. Here, sometimes it's easier to believe with more proof, right?" Tammy turns the screen toward us and hits a button that plays a flickering gray and white static I can't decipher, but Seb's free hand goes to his mouth and he swallows a surprised little sound.

"That's our baby?"

"Yep, you see? Here's a live view," Tammy switches the view on the screen to a view of a wiggly greyscale gummy bear in a dark circle of clear space. I've seen early images like that before and it starts to sink in that this is real. Joy bubbles up inside me that this is truly good news.

"We're having a baby." Seb sounds so dazed I'm half afraid he might pass out.

"Seems that way," I agree. "Do you need to sit down?"

"Rollie, we're going to be parents," Seb bounces as he turns to kiss me, his gleeful smile is so beautiful and I can finally start to feel safe hoping that our baby will have that same sweet smile.

"Technically, Dr. Martinez will need to confirm with you, but there's a healthy gestational sac with a good sized yolk and a baby measuring as expected for the dates. He'll have better information on what to expect given the baby's mixed shifter heritage, and I'm not supposed to share too much, but I do a lot of these scans and from what I can see here, your baby is snuggled in right where they belong in your uterus. I've got what I need, do you want me to print the pictures?" Tammy slides the probe out of my body. That's a relief since it was getting uncomfortable.

"Yes to the pictures, please," I say.

"So, this means Rollie doesn't have some weird tumor making him smell pregnant?" Seb asks, back to wary in a heartbeat. I don't blame him. It's so hard to trust good news coming from anyone in a place like this.

"I can't make any official diagnosis for you, and we are running a full blood panel to be certain. But let me check in with Dr. Martinez to come see if he wants any other images before I let you get cleaned up and back into your clothes, sound good?"

"Yeah." I nod, I'm all for anything that hurries this part along and gets us home where we can celebrate properly faster. Tammy steps out of the room, giving us a moment of privacy with our news.

"So, we're really going to have a clutch."

"Yeah. Looks like it. How do you feel about it?"

"Honestly?"

"Always."

"Terrified, but so excited. I'm not sure it's going to really sink in until the hatchling is here. There's so much to do to prepare. We're going to need a nursery. I guess we'll have to finally clean out the attic bedroom for the baby once you're far enough along to start nesting." Seb looks startled. "And I guess maybe we won't need an actual nest for the egg, huh? It will be a birthday and not a hatchday?"

"I think so? Maybe if you were carrying the kit it could be born as an egg?"

"Oh, yeah, Bram mentioned something about that. Doesn't matter. I want to see them in their fur with their cute little bitty eye mask."

"I want to watch you preening their downy baby feathers."

Tears glint in his eyes as Seb leans in to kiss me. "I want everything with you, Rollie. I was so scared when Ty said you might be...I was so scared I was going to find out I'd have to figure out how to say goodbye to you and I don't think I can."

"You don't have to. No goodbyes, just hello to this new little one."

"Yeah." Seb kisses my forehead. "I'll love you forever."

"Right back at you." I lean up for a kiss, and Seb gives it to me, lips meeting sweetly. If we were anywhere else other than a doctor's office, I'd be tempted to deepen the kiss, pull him down next to me. But no way I am taking this any further here. Not even the best news ever can counter just how uncomfortable medical offices have always been. "Um, so, I guess now when we tell everyone we're mated we might actually have news that won't be completely obvious to share too?"

Seb laughs. "Yeah, maybe, except Ty already noticed the change in your scent, so we might not be very good at surprises, mate of mine."

I join in his laughter, the two of us giving in to hysterics beyond what his quip merits more to let out all the tension and worry that lead up to this moment than because anything is actually funny. "Well, we'll just have to tell them all after Cory's fledging ceremony this weekend. Cause I have a feeling even if it's not obvious from my scent, it will be once I refuse to have a drink."

"I won't be drinking either. Maybe not at all anymore. I think maybe I shouldn't risk making bad choices when I've got a mate and kit depending on me to be okay."

"You think that's what you need?"

"Yeah. Maybe?"

"Then we can both stop. I don't need it either and we can just bring whatever's in the house to the party to get rid of it."

"The cousins will love that," Seb teases.

"Yeah. That's a nice added bonus. Your health is the part I care about. I want to support you, however I can."

"You do. All the time, in all the ways."

Before we can get any sappier or start kissing again, Tammy comes back and tells us the doc wants us to stick around until they have the lab results that they can run in house back so he can assess the need for supplemental hormones or anything else I might need.

All my history with doctors tells me that 'waiting on test results' means cooling our heels in the uncomfortable waiting room all day. So I'm honestly surprised when Seb asks if we can go for a walk and Terry tells us that as long as we don't wander too far, we can grab a snack at the themed butterfly cafe just inside the public areas of the zoo closest to the clinic while we wait. He'll call when Dr. Martinez is ready for us.

I'm not even a little hungry, but Seb insists that I should at least have a drink and the cafe has floral iced teas in a rainbow of bright colors. We each get one and sip them at an outdoor table, just watching the crowds go past. I'm startled to still have more than half of my tea left when Terry calls us back to the clinic.

We're waved right into Dr. Martinez's office when we arrive and he greets us with a warm smile.

"First of all, Tammy tells me our little surprise is good news?"

"The best." Seb wraps his arm protectively around my waist and I beam at him.

Dr. Martinez nods and smiles. "Congratulations. I also understand there is still some question of how this happened?"

"Yes," Seb and I say in tandem, our eyes meet and I can't help smiling.

"Well, the more established answer first, you both stated that Seb was the only possible second parent?"

"Yes," I say, flushing because it's on the tip of my tongue to tell the doctor that Seb's the only one who has ever come in that hole. The only one who ever will.

"In that case, I am confident in saying that low levels of exogenous hormone caused a paradoxical boost in his endogenous sex hormone production resulting in an accelerated alpha reversion secondary to creep."

"What?" Seb asks, head cocked in avian interest.

"It's rare, but one of the ways we've seen families like yours grow is that sometimes too low or too high a dose of hormones for creep in avian shifters can cause significant alpha traits up to and including sperm production in the non-dominant ovotestes and knot formation."

"Good to know." Seb sounds dazed, but he's still holding me so I don't think he's upset at the news that he for sure knocked me up and there is a reasonable medical explanation for it.

"As to how Rollie was able to ovulate, based on the hormone levels we took immediately following Rollie's heat, his omegestrol levels were unusually elevated along with luteinizing hormone, progesterone, and a lower than expected free testosterone, given that you take supplemental doses of that," The doctor references his file notes as he recites the data.

"Um, what does that mean?" Seb asks. We both stare at the doctor and he looks slightly sheepish as he scrolls through the open health record on his computer.

"Sorry, I'm fascinated by these results and the implications for our research, but that's no excuse. And I'm sure not what anyone wants to hear from me in this office." He gives a rueful chuckle. "I assure you that I am well versed in mixed species pregnancies and no matter how your kit was conceived, I do have the expertise to help you through this pregnancy. As to how it happened? In plain language, the tests we ran at your first visit seem to show that you had a natural, fertile heat secondary to hormonal ovarian stimulation induction and triggered by a hormone surge."

"Huh?" I hug my belly protectively, not sure what a lot of those words mean when they're all strung together like that.

"It appears that by taking a high dose of avian omegestrol you stimulated your ovaries in much the same way that we would use medication to help any infertile omega to get pregnant. Then your coworker's heat pheromones triggered a heat response and your body responded as we would expect in any healthy young omega, which in turn amplified your mate's fertility." For all his frenetic excitement over the news, the doctor avoids calling Seb's response to my heat a rut, and for that I'll be eternally grateful.

"So, there isn't something terrible going on with him? Seb demands.

"Nothing that appeared on our scans," the doctor confirms. "As to what happens next, since we changed your medication to the mammalian formulation after your last visit, I put a rush on today's progesterone levels and you do appear to be producing enough to sustain the pregnancy, but if you are worried then we can still supplement with a topical cream that you'll need to apply daily for the first few months of gestation, how does that sound?"

"I want the cream." I say, it requires no thought at all. If this is my only chance to have a baby with my mate, I'll follow the doctor's advice like it's the word of god to do everything in my power to deliver our baby safely.

"Great. Topical progestins should have minimal side effects on your body other than helping to maintain the pregnancy. I'll write you a prescription and see if I have a sample tube for you to use until you can get it filled at your pharmacy. Speaking of which, when was your last dose of testosterone?"

"Just before my heat started. I'm due for another shot, actually," I say, groaning internally at needing to deal with the logistics of that.

"No, you can't take—" Dr. Martinez cuts himself off when he sees the way I flinch from the command in his tone as he threatens my access to a necessary piece of who I am—"Sorry, let me rephrase. If you plan to carry the pregnancy to term, it would be best to stop taking your injections and wait until after you deliver to resume. Does that sound reasonable?"

I hesitate, considering. I knew that T while pregnant was a big no-no, but it still hurts to hear I have to cut off a part of myself, however temporarily. The kit I'm growing is worth any sacrifice, it's just a sore spot for any doctor to take away pieces of my identity like that. Seb hugs me and whispers that he's there for me and if I can't do it, he'll still love me just the same. And the fact it's presented as a choice slowly sinks in. I have a choice and it's an easy one. I can stop my meds for a few months until my kit is born.

The rest of the visit is quick, mostly notes on the top dos and don'ts of a mixed species pregnancy. I leave the appointment with my head spinning. I've got our baby's first pictures, a topical hormone supplement and a plan for regular follow-ups with Dr. Martinez. The mixed genetics of my kit make the pregnancy risky in the sense that there isn't a clearcut template for what exactly to expect.

Seb and I have so much to discuss and plan and only a few months to prepare for our kit to arrive. But as we leave the clinic I'm buoyant with hope for our future. Seb can't contain his happiness either. Smiling over at me every time I pat his thigh or rub his neck.

Even though my prenatal care means I have to keep coming back to the clinic for frequent follow-up care until our kit arrives, I'm overwhelmed with joy. It helps that, for once, I've got a doctor I am coming to trust despite my fears and all the times medical care ignored my needs. It's only been two appointments, but Dr. Martinez seems different.

So far, he listens and gives me options. If that continues, then I'll have the support I need to get through the next few months of constant medical appointments unscathed. So while I don't love the idea of so many clinic visits, it's worth it so that Seb and I can soon welcome our child home.

Seb has already texted to arrange borrowing Ty's keys to take me back me to rest and let the news sink in and then return to finish out his shift at the zoo. That way he can get some hours in to give us a financial cushion for our kit's arrival and Seb going back to work will mean Ty still has a ride home. Much as I'm excited to celebrate with my mate, having the afternoon to myself will mean I can process everything this pregnancy will entail before we celebrate the news together after his shift. Mostly I'm excited to tell our family.

Ty has already agreed not to mention anything about the kit I'm growing until after Cory's upcoming fledging ceremony. We're planning to attend, but I might need to slip in late so I don't steal the spotlight with my news until he's been celebrated, given my scent is already changing.

The entire drive back to Four Corners, I can't stop touching Seb, just needing to connect with my mate. It seems like I don't need to temper my giddy glee anymore, we're going to have it all. It's so wild to think that a month ago I was certain I'd never have any of this. I keep smiling at the little black and white printout that is going in our most glittery, gaudy picture frame as soon as we get home from work tonight, a promise of our happiness continuing for a lifetime.

Chapter 16

Rollie

WE SHOW UP BARELY in time for Cory's fledging ceremony as planned. Scent blockers are supposed to be safe for me to take early in the pregnancy, but I don't want to take any risks. I cover my scent change with the deodorant I got when I didn't realize I was in heat though, just to take the edge off it.

Cory is the youngest fledgling of the bunch this time and he looks so proud standing in front of the entire rave to declare his chosen name and pronouns to his loved ones. I get all choked up at the acceptance he's so certain is his. I can't help rubbing the spot where my little kit is growing.

One of the reasons my parents used to justify not pursuing egg preservation was that I might pass along whatever it is that makes me a beta. When I whispered that fear to Seb in the safe confines of our den he hugged me tight and made me look at his face as he promised me that even if they're a beta or a latent with no animal form at all, our baby will always be loved and accepted for exactly who they are.

My kit might be part raven, but even if they never sprout feathers, this flock will claim and love them and make them feel a part of it. I believe that, surrounded by Seb's loving extended family, I've never felt more at home. My little miracle won't ever have to prove they belong here. Never have to cut away parts of themself to feel worthy of love and acceptance. The thought has me tearing up as the official portion of the party comes to a close and the new fledglings file inside to shift for their first flight with their recognized adult names.

I'm not the only shifter in the crowd getting emotional. Seb's alpha mom is openly teary, her omega mate handing her tissues. Cory is their youngest, so I guess it's extra emotional for him to be growing up and hitting a major milestone. I wipe surreptitiously at my own teary eyes, already imagining our baby standing up in front of the flock to tell us who they are.

Seb shoots me a worried glance, "You good?"

"Yeah, hormones," I wink at him, and we both grin at the reminder that I get to blame pregnancy hormones for being emotional for the next several months.

"You sure? Everything is okay?" Seb leans in, his words so soft the noise of the crowd should ensure that I'm the only one to hear them.

"Yeah," I answer just as softly, only for his ears. "Just emotional. This kit is going to be so loved, Sebastian."

He grins at me. "Obviously. You ready to tell everyone or shall we give Cory time to land from his first flight before we steal his thunder?"

"Thunder?" Bram asks, scanning the sky. "Is it supposed to storm? They shouldn't be flying in a storm."

Seb snorts. "Wow, someone is getting broody as hell, you ready to pop yet Bram?"

"He is," Ty answers. Bram scowls.

"Being safety conscious doesn't mean I'm broody." Bram pouts, arms crossed defiantly over his comically round belly. The cub he's carrying is probably going to be huge from how he's carrying. I stare a little too hard, wondering what it will be like to be that big closer to my own delivery. I can't wait to meet my kit, but Bram winces as his belly rolls. Oh, shit, it looks like something out of a chest-burster alien video and he grumbles as he rubs the spot where the cub moved.

"Uh huh, keep telling yourself that," Seb teases.

"Ow. I'll remind you of that when you're nesting when Rollie's ready to pop. You know that's a thing with mated omegas, right? Just because he's the one carrying doesn't mean you get out of all the weird hormone fluctuations and nesting urges. I'm going to laugh my ass off when you're trying to drag his furry ass into a literal nest like I did to poor Ty—oh, shit." Bram freezes and I gape at him, expecting that he's going to apologize for outing my pregnancy, but no.

Seb hauls me back a step just in time not to have the water that gushes down his brother's legs splatter up at me. Bram is already yelling for his mate before I've processed that his water just broke.

"Ty!" Bram squawks loudly. "Where are you? Go tell my moms they can't get all weepy about their impending empty nest because our kiddos are spending the night, you're taking me home to have this cub."

"What?" I stare after my brother-in-law's retreating back as he bulldozes through his family to collect his mate, kiss his three older kids and depart.

"Wow, talk about stealing the fledgling's thunder," Seb jokes, loud enough to break the tension hanging over the courtyard. Raven shifters start heckling Bram for creating drama, and congratulating the fledglings, calling it lucky that their fledging coincides with the birth of a new flock member.

In the midst of all that, Seb twines our fingers and gives me a questioning glance, in an undertone he asks. "Well, want me to just say it?"

"Yeah, go for it." I nod. I want him to be the one to share the news. I get to carry our baby, so it only seems fair to give him what special moments I can. I know he's dreamed of being able to announce a clutch to his family. So it feels right.

"While we're on the topic of new flock members, Rollie and I have news too." Seb's voice cuts through the cacophony, and into the lull he says. "Rollie is carrying our clutch."

That sets off even more celebratory noise from the flock. I lose track of all the people who congratulate us. The shifters ruffle our hair and pat our shoulders, all the friendly preening affectionate touches I'm used to from years with Seb. I knew they included me in their number, but it feels good to have my kit accepted and celebrated so enthusiastically. It heals something inside me that I wasn't really aware was shattered.

Eventually their focus dissipates back to the youngsters the night is meant to be about. Cory is the center of a knot of attention given that his siblings are the ones at the heart of the drama. He rolls his eyes at us when we congratulate him on his fledging and apologize for taking the attention for a moment.

"Eh, everyone just want's to see the cub, so Bram's really the one who should be sorry. Maybe they'll name the little one Diva after this," Cory jokes. He really doesn't seem upset surrounded by his friends and cousins. Myra brings over two slices of cake and plops down next to him at the edge of a cuddle pile of fledgling raven shifters. They both dig into their sweets.

"You good with being an uncle again Cory?" Seb asks tentatively.

"Sure, why not? Bet Myra will like a cousin she can send home instead of dealing with crying babies all the time, huh cuz?"

"Yeah, they're a lot, but mostly I like having siblings." Myra licks her fork. "Congratulations Uncle Seb and Uncle Rollie. Once the kid is big enough to need a babysitter I'll let you have my family rate."

"Is that so?" Seb asks.

"Yep." Myra nods solemnly. "I charge extra for bedtime and I don't do diapers, so it'll be a while. Anyway, do you guys think I can have a fledging ceremony too? I know I'm not a raven, but it would be cool, I dunno. Just the babies will get to have a ceremony, so I've been thinking it might be nice to be included too?"

My heart clenches at the vulnerability of her question. I don't know whether to be glad she trusts us enough to ask or to ache for the fact that she feels like she needs to check if she gets to be included. If she counts as enough of a raven.

"Absolutely!" Seb grins at her. "You tell your mapa and dad when you're ready to announce and they'll get it arranged."

"Yeah?" Myra glances at Cory who gives her a thumbs up.

"Told you so, you don't have to fly to have the ceremony. That's just for funsies. If you want to you could take your fur and climb a tree or something instead though."

"Yep, You're part of this flock, Myra." Seb ruffles her hair affectionately.

"Cool." Myra goes back to eating cake, asking Cory a question about a show they both like. My stomach grumbles and Seb drags me over to the refreshments to fill up a plate for me. Before long we're both ensconced in soft pillows along with the same cousins we usually spend these gatherings with. Lydia makes sure Seb and I my beverages stay full of soda and free of booze, and otherwise nothing really changes.

We're still part of their little sub flock, still subject to teasing and jokes about our mating.

"So, are you two going to have to move once the little one arrives? Your place only has the one bedroom, right?"

"Um, sort of? There might be a second bedroom upstairs. Just, the ceiling is low cause of the gabled roof." Seb hunches his shoulders sheepishly. He's told everyone that we're not mates and we just share the bedroom since we don't have a second one for years so that admission is met with an uncharacteristic silence before Lydia socks him in the bicep.

"Oh. My. Gosh. You know I half-believed you that you two really weren't mates all along because of the bedroom thing?" Lydia chuckles and shakes her head in disbelief. "So dare I ask, is going public because of the clutch or because the mating really is new?"

Seb takes my hand and we exchange a speaking glance, I can tell he wants to tease her, and considering how much they've teased us over the years, I've got no issues with that. It's not the sort of lie that's going to hurt anyone or obfuscate anything that matters.

"I dunno, Lydia, what seems more likely?" Seb taunts.

Lydia throws her hands up in exasperation, then looks shrewdly between us. "You really want me to guess?"

Seb glances at me again and I shrug. Lydia is insightful enough that I wouldn't want to poke her about something sensitive, but this isn't really a surprise. "Go for it."

"Rollie?"

"Yeah. What do you think?"

"I think you two are idiots who didn't admit you're both madly in love until Rollie's heat. I think we all knew you were it for each other before you had the slightest inkling. And I think none of that matters as long as you two are happy. Congrats on the clutch."

"Ah, thanks, Lydia. We're really excited."

"You're going to be amazing dads. Just remember all the times you came over and riled up my hatchlings with candy when I finally get to meet my new little cousin in a few months." Lydia cackles at Seb's 'oh shit' face in response. She knows him too well to point out the obvious fact that he thought he'd never have to face that kind of payback, avoiding the sore spot while still teasing him relentlessly.

Lydia gives Seb an absolutely gleeful wink. Even if only a fraction of the mischief he's told me those two got into together as children is true, we're going to have our hands full if our kit is anything like their raven side. I wouldn't have it any other way, I can't imagine a better place to raise my family with Seb.

Epilogue

Seb (Several Months Later)

I SCAN OUR LIVING room again once more to be sure everything is ready for our immediate family to descend and meet Amari. It's a minor miracle they've mostly respected our wishes to keep the visitors to a minimum while Rollie is recovering from his scheduled c-section. My moms and Harvey have come over to help us keep up with laundry and feed us both so we can focus on our baby.

Bram is salty about not being the first to meet his first nibling, but Ty's been good about keeping him distracted. And they're both plenty occupied with their newest cub, Cole. It's a relief to realize how much less complicated I've felt about holding Cole compared to the first times I met my older niblings. I know why, but I'm working on not beating myself up for having emotions. That's one of my many homework goals with my shiny new therapist.

I'm not jealous of Bram anymore, and as hard as it is to admit just how much my unresolved trauma impacted how much we've grown apart since he met Ty; I'm glad I can address it now. I'm glad that with Cole, I've known from the first time Bram passed his chonky newborn bundled up cub into my arms that I was holding Amari's cousin. Not borrowing a moment of my brother's bliss that I'll never have for myself, but sharing it. And today I'll get to be on the other side of that, handing my most precious treasure into my brother's arms and knowing that they're as safe with him as they would be with me and Rollie.

The entire flock wants to meet my kit, obviously. Amari is the picture of perfection in their fur and human forms alike. Rollie says they have my smile, but they've got his wide innocent eyes in both forms and they smell like him, cookies and spice. We're being extra protective, so for now it's just our immediate family coming over to meet my baby.

Harvey and a few of Rollie's favorites from the market and my parents, siblings, and their households. I tried to get my mate to stay in bed resting, but he insisted on supervising me while I put together his favorite recipes for our guests. Harvey brought over platters of fruits and veggies and charcuterie from the market to supplement Rollie's cookies and quick breads and a tasty array of hot dips. And a birthday cake. He was insistent about that. Amari gets a birthday cake of their own even though they can't have any for at least a year. I get it though. He wants our kit to be celebrated.

Rollie and Amari are both napping in our room. At just over a week old, they've shown a slight preference for their raccoon form, so Rollie has been handling a lot of the feeding overnight with that, but during the day I handle most of their bottle feeds.

I'm not even a little surprised when my phone buzzes with a text from my brother letting me know that he's here a little early and didn't want to wake the baby by ringing the doorbell, but he isn't waiting a moment longer for newborn snuggles.

I roll my eyes at his typical pushiness, but I'm grinning as I go to let him in. It's really fucking nice that he cares this much. That he's still the same supportive sweet brother he's always been, even though I've put distance between us.

I expect to see his entire rowdy family at the door, but it's just Bram, holding a gift bag up between us.

"Hi, I just wanted a minute to chat with you before everyone gets here and I figured now that Amari is here, we're both going to be attached to babies for the foreseeable future, so I had Ty take the kids out to pick presents for their new cousin with their bear grandmas."

"Yeah?"

"Yeah. I know things have been weird between us, so I just wanted to make sure we're good. Are we?" Bram shoves the gift bag toward my chest and I take it, looping my fingers through the string handler to free up one hand.

I pull Bram into a hug, inhaling his sweet comforting scent. He's been a steady supportive presence for my entire life and it feels good to clear the air between us officially. "Yeah, Bram. We're good, you didn't do anything wrong."

Bram hugs the life out of me. "Good. I love you, Seb. I hated knowing you were hurting and I couldn't fix it."

"Yeah, I know. I'm good though, turns out I mostly needed to stop believing I was broken." I shrug out of his arms when he squeezes me even tighter. Now it's getting too sappy, I need to reset the tone. I flash him the grin that I know he associates with most of the exploits that got us grounded as fledglings and wag a finger at my clutchmate. "But, no stealing the show this time, or else!"

Bram laughs. "Sheesh, ruin one fledging ceremony with a dramatic labor and they never let you live it down, huh?

Don't worry, Seb, I don't have any surprise pregnancy announcements or anything else in store. Myra is very excited about her fledging ceremony in the fall, but everyone already knows that. I just want to meet Amari. Can I see them?"

"Yeah. They're napping with Rollie now. They're both in their fur, but I was going to roll the bassinet into the living room before people arrive. Rollie is being stubborn and trying to overdo it even though the doc said he needs to rest while his stitches heal, but I got him to agree to letting me wheel the baby out before the party earlier. Make yourself comfortable and I'll get them." I show Bram into our house. It feels so good to be able to claim this space as both of ours. No more trying to tell myself I'm temporary.

My heart melts at the sight of my entire world curled up in the bassinet. Amari is curled up next to my mate like a little cinnamon roll, smelling just as sweet. It's wild how much deeper in love I fall every time I see the two of them together. I can't help preening the fur along Rollie's back and patting Amari's head. They're both so soft and sweet.

I could stare at them all day, but Bram is being noisy in the living room to remind me he's impatient to meet my hatchling. I sigh but the irritation that's been so close to the surface with him lately is gone. I'm just fondly exasperated. And maybe a little smugly proud that I've got something he wants now. I shake my head at myself, that's not how I want things to be between us.

I wheel the bed carefully down the hall, taking care not to rouse either of the shifters napping within. Bram ignores all my care and lets out a delighted squawk when he sees my family and I mime clacking my beak at him in warning when he makes grabby hands at my sleeping kit.

"Sorry." Bram backs off, looking chagrined. "Ohmygosh, Seb, kits are so little! Cole is going to look like a giant next to them."

"Yeah," I chuckle, our baby is petite and perfect. And Cole would have looked huge next to Amari even if the cub wasn't months older. I gently lift my kit from the cozy bed and hand them to Bram. He snuggles Amari under his chest, cupping both hands protectively under them and cooing sweet nothings. Rollie whimpers in his sleep, moving toward the warm spot where our kit was and I rest a hand on his flank to reassure him that the baby is safe and he can go back to sleep. He yawns, and settles at my touch. Trusting me to care for our treasure.

"Hi, little Amari," Bram coos. "I'm going to be your favorite uncle, fair's fair, my hatchlings all adore your daddy, so you basically have to like me best. You're going to have so much fun playing with your cousins."

"Sure you are, Bram," I tease, but my heart is overflowing at getting to have this moment with him, not quite what we daydreamed as fledglings. When we dreamed aloud about having mates and kids and who we would grow up to become, I could never have imagined this. My dream sounded a lot more like what Bram has. An alpha mate, a huge family, and a big house.

Turns out, I didn't know what I wanted when I was a teenager. Rollie and Amari are so much more than the half-formed shadows of them that were all I was capable of dreaming. Bram snuggles Amari while I finish getting the last few party things in order, but shortly before everyone is supposed to get here, they startle awake with a dirty diaper and shift into their human form at the shock of it. Bram grins at me.

"Guess the tables have turned, and that's my cue to hand the baby over now, huh?" Bram holds Amari out to me. "Oh, they've got his curls, I wondered if that was his natural hair color or premature graying."

I snort. "Rude. They're very distinguished. Rollie says it's agouti, and it's very common with raccoon shifters."

"Uh huh, squirrels have fur like that too and they don't have the same hair in their human form," Bram teases me.

"Squirrels clearly aren't as perfect as my mate and our baby then. Um. Just so you know, we're using avian naming and pronouns, like with your cubs, but Rollie slips sometimes, so try to ignore it?" I say.

"Sure, not a problem. I can remind the kids too." Bram smiles at me as he watches me soothe my baby and carry them down the hall for a fresh diaper. I try not to read into it.

But when I get back with Amari in a fresh diaper and a cute little raccoon print romper, Bram is staring at me again. It's a little weird just how intently he is watching me.

"What? Did their diaper leak on me?" I glance down at myself to check. I'm pretty sure it didn't. This is not my first time taking care of babies, even if it's my first time as a parent. He knows I can change a diaper; I've babysat his kids.

"Nothing. Happy looks good on you, Seb. You're a natural with Amari. I—I'm glad you and Rollie got your miracle." Bram smiles so warmly, I know he wanted this for me almost as much as I did. Even when I was being a jealous shit to him and avoiding him.

"Me too." I beam at Amari and they drool at me, not quite a smile, but it's early for that. I wipe away the mess and cuddle them close, only to watch Rollie stirring in the bassinet. My mate is also watching me from his gorgeous furry mask. He raises tiny adorable raccoon hands toward me and I lift him to his favorite perch on my shoulder so we can both admire Amari while I snuggle them. Rollie's dextrous raccoon fingers card through my hair and I duck toward him, offering myself up to his attentions. Bram snorts.

"Ugh, give my nibling here and go let your mate shift before the party. I think he agrees that parenthood looks good on you." I glance at Rollie, reluctant to hand Amari over before I have to. My other siblings and our folks and Harvey will be here soon and it's going to be awhile before I get to snuggle my sweet little darling again.

Bram rolls his eyes at me. "Go steal a minute alone with your mate before everyone gets here. I swear, you're so oblivious sometimes, Seb. I still can't believe you actually figured out Rollie wanted a mating from you before he installed actual neon lighting asking you to be his mate. Good thing for Amari, their daddies figured it out in time for them to exist, huh?"

"Lucky for all of us," I agree, then I glance at my mate. "Should I let Bram hold Amari for a minute?" I ask.

Rollie nuzzles my cheek, tongue darting out in a teasing raccoon kiss that makes me shiver. I hand Amari to my brother and carry my mate to our bedroom, shutting the door on Bram's amused laughter. I know there isn't anything more than kissing on offer for a few more weeks while Rollie heals. Even if he did offer, I'm not into the idea of doing anything that wouldn't make him feel good.

I bring Rollie to the bed. Normally he'd jump down from here with no trouble, but he lets me lift him down so I think he might be more sore and tired than he's been admitting to. Once he's on the bed, Rollie shifts back to human and grins up at me, all sappy smiles.

"You really do look good holding our baby."

"Yeah?"

"Yeah. I love seeing you happy Seb. Now, everyone's going to be here soon, so no more talking about the baby, shut up and kiss me like you mean it."

I carefully crawl onto the bed next to him and kiss him slow and lazy and with a promise of forever in mind. Rollie kisses me back until we're both breathless and I almost forget we don't have long for him to get dressed. The doorbell ringing startles me to my senses and Rollie groans. I laugh at his disgruntled expression.

"It's just as well we got interrupted. You aren't cleared to come yet, Rollie."

"I could go down on you," he offers.

"Nope, give yourself time to heal, darling. We've got a lifetime to make love." I kiss the tip of his nose and wink at him as I get up and offer him a hand to stand. "Ask me again when you're cleared for sex, my love."

"I'm going to hold you to that," Rollie insists as he gets up and rummages for clean comfy clothes.

"Darling, when you get the go ahead, I'll arrange for someone to watch Amari for a few hours so you can hold me to that promise all night long." I wink at my mate. I watch him get ready and listen to Bram as he lets our moms into the house.

Rollie lets me loop an arm around his waist to help him out to the living room and get him ensconced on the couch. Winny volunteers to make sure he doesn't have to get up for anything other than bathroom breaks as we celebrate with the people who love us the most. And for once, I don't care if I deserve this perfect life, I'm going to cling to it with every fiber of my being because Rollie and Amari are worth loving with everything I am and if they can love me, then maybe I'm worth it too. I'm the luckiest shifter alive. I get to spend the rest of my life loving the mate who took an alpha's trash and saw a treasure worth keeping.

Thank you for reading Seb and Rollie's story! If you enjoyed this book, I'd appreciate if you leave a review. If you haven't read the rest of the series yet, be sure to grab Bram and Ty's book Papa Bear and Felix's book, Squirrel Trouble.

If you are looking for non-omegaverse books that deal with fertility and trans characters, check out my contemporary trans romance duology Party of Three and Balanced Party (both books follow a queer polyamorous family made up of a nonbinary woman, a trans man, and a cis man, both books are part of a longer series, but the duology can stand alone). I also have a few other books with pregnant trans characters (Puppy Love and Saving Throw).

Since this book deals with some heavy mental health themes, I just want to mention that if you are struggling with your mental health, know that you are not alone and there is help, please reach out to local resources or contact the national suicide prevention hotline or other crisis support lines in your region.

Acknowledgements

I cannot thank my beta readers enough for their attention to detail and quick turnaround on this book. Seb and Rollie's story would not be as strong as it is without their unwavering encouragement and support. It's a stronger book for their involvement. So thank you Leslie and Isaiah, I appreciate you. You both make me a better writer.

And thank you, dear reader, for letting me share my words with you. Getting to be on your bookshelves (digital or otherwise) is my dream come true <3

Appendix
Notes on Omegaverse Terminology

Hey there! I'm a bit of a biology nerd, so one of the fun parts of writing shifter omegaverse romance for me is getting to play around with a combination of real world biology trivia and omegaverse lore. For instance, avian shifters with creep reverting to an alpha gender presentation is based on actual bird biology where among chickens, hens who lose function in their dominant ovary sometimes undergo virilization and develop the secondary sex traits of a rooster. Here are a few more quick notes on omegaverse terminology/biology if you're new to the genre or my take on the omegaverse:

In this version of the omegaverse, all shifters have a primary and secondary gender. Primary gender refers to a shifter's gender as it exists in modern western human culture (man/woman/nonbinary). Primary sex assigned at birth is based on genital appearance and can be male, female, or intersex regardless of secondary gender.

Secondary gender designations refer to a shifter's gonads, shifters may be born with any combination of gonads and external genitalia. Without genetic testing, secondary gender at birth is generally only revealed when a shifter reaches puberty and either develops a knot (or species specific variation), a heat cycle, or neither. Alphas produce sperm, omegas produce eggs. Betas are those shifters who do not fit neatly into either of the previous categories and/or who do not identify as being either alpha or omega.

Omega males do not experience as much genital growth around puberty as their non-shifter peers. They develop with what is technically a cloaca with a shared terminus to their reproductive and digestive tracts. Male pregnancies are common and accepted among shifters.

Alpha females have a blind vaginal canal and no womb, and they develop a pseudo-penis during puberty. Exact details vary among shifter species and some individuals display variant biology. But alpha females are capable of insemination across shifter species.

Betas are often infertile but otherwise develop largely as expected for a static human of their primary gender at puberty.

Not all shifters identify with one or both of the primary and secondary genders assigned to them based on their anatomy at birth. Shifters can be any combination of trans and cis primary and secondary genders and even for cis shifters, their presentation might not always align with who they are, as with Seb in this book when his medical condition impacts his health.

Also by Alex Silver

Drew's Haunted Hangout (*A Hauntastic Haunts Short Story 1*)
Rafael's Haunted Halloween (*A Hauntastic Haunts Short Story 2*)
Lee's Haunted Holiday (*A Hauntastic Haunts Short Story 3*)

Merry Exmas
Contemporary Holiday Romance
Christmas Carl (M/M) #1
Christmas Angel (M/X) #2

Table Topped
Contemporary Romance
Roll for Initiative (M/M) #1 Gui & Paz
Charisma Check (M/M) #2 Theo & Jude
Saving Throw (M/X) #3 Errol & Rene
Plus One Bonus (M/X) #4 Max & Si
Dump Stat (F/F) #5 Laura & Alice
Party of Three (M/M/X) #6 Pia, Emil, & Gregor
Balanced Party (M/M/X) #7 Pia, Emil, & Gregor

Summer of Adventures
Kinky Contemporary Romance
Dungeon Master (M/M)

Knotty Boy (M/M)
Service Call (M/M)
Picture Perfect (M/M)
Puppy Love (F/X)
Stud Muffin (M/M/M)

Psions of SPIRE
Urban Fantasy
Shelter (M/M) Novella 0.5
Bright Spark (MMMM)Book 1
Bold Move (MMMM) Novella 1.5
Keen Sense (M/M) Book 2
Weak Link (M/M) Novella 2.5
Quick Fire (M/X) Book 3
Clear Sight (M/M) Book 4
New Look (M/M) Novella 4.5
A SPIREverse daddy kink standalone
New Ground (M/M/X)

Shared Universe Series
Diner Days - Low-Angst Trans Romance
Cramming at Randy's (X/X)
Super U - Superhero Romance
Super U: Rising Storm (M/X)
Final Days - Zombie Romance

The Willows (M/M GNC)

Anthologies
Playing With a Full Deck: Stories of Hope in Hard Times
All Amped Up (F/X hope punk)
Listen: The Sound of Fear
Haunt (M/M trans gothic horror)
Fix the World
Upgrade (gay trans cyberpunk)

About the author

Alex Silver (he/them) grew up mostly in Northern Maine and is now living in Canada with one spouse, two kids, and a lovebird. Alex is a trans guy who started writing fiction as a child and never stopped. Although there were detours through assisting on a farm and being a pharmacist along the way.

Visit me online at:

http://alexsilverauthor.wordpress.com/

Browse my entire book catalog at:

https://www.amazon.com/Alex-Silver/e/B07NPBW615

Join my Facebook group at:

https://www.facebook.com/groups/alexsalcove

Follow me on BookBub at:

https://www.bookbub.com/profile/alex-silver

Follow me on Twitter:

https://twitter.com/asilverauthor

Sign up for my <u>newsletter</u> for a free short story at: <u>http s://landing.mailerlite.com/webforms/landing/i2w6l7</u>

And as always, consider leaving a review on Amazon or Goodreads if you enjoyed this book, reviews are of vital importance to independent authors, thanks!

www.ingramcontent.com/pod-product-compliance
Lightning Source LLC
Chambersburg PA
CBHW031305280626